THE BOYS
OF FIRE
AND ASH

MEAGHAN McISAAC

DELACORTE PRESS

Text copyright © 2013 by Meaghan McIsaac
Jacket art copyright © 2015 by Philip Straub

All rights reserved. Published in the United States by Delacorte Press,
an imprint of Random House Children's Books, a division of Random House LLC,
a Penguin Random House Company, New York. Originally published
in hardcover as *Urgle* by Anderson Press Limited, London, in 2013.

Delacorte Press is a registered trademark and
the colophon is a trademark of Random House LLC.

randomhousekids.com

Educators and librarians, for a variety of teaching tools,
visit us at RHTeachersLibrarians.com

Library of Congress Cataloging-in-Publication Data
McIsaac, Meaghan.
The Boys of fire and ash / Meaghan McIsaac.
pages cm
Summary: Urgle and two other Brothers of the Ikkuma Pit, where boys are abandoned
at birth and learn to fend for themselves and rear their younger brothers, embark on a
quest to rescue Urgle's brother, Cubby, who has been carried off by monsters into the
forest from which no one has ever returned.
ISBN 978-0-385-74445-4 (hc) — ISBN 978-0-375-99167-7 (glb) —
ISBN 978-0-385-39013-2 (ebook)
[1. Fantasy. 2. Brothers—Fiction. 3. Adventure and adventurers—Fiction.
4. Kidnapping—Fiction. 5. Monsters—Fiction.] I. Title.
PZ7.M4786562Boy 2015
[Fic]—dc23
2014006600

The text of this book is set in 10.5-point Village.
Book design by Heather Kelly

Printed in the United States of America
10 9 8 7 6 5 4 3 2 1
First Edition

THE BOYS
OF FIRE
AND ASH

FOR MOM AND DAD

PART ONE

ONE

"Damn it, Cubby! I said go back!" My voice cut right through the rumbling thunder of the Ikkuma Fire Mountains.

The brat just stared at me, his blond scraggly hair covered with ash, his cheeks streaked black from the sweat mixed with soot. His little face was wearing that annoying scowl he saved just for me.

He'd been following us since the A-Frame, all the way to the Hotpots. I looked back towards our triangular dwelling, now just a brown-colored dot in the distance against the charred black earth.

The Ikkuma Pit, our home, is just a giant hole filled with black rock. Black rock and the discarded junk of people living on the outside: metal scraps, soiled clothes, and us, the Ikkuma Brothers. Normally, the blanket of ash that covers the place cushions your foot, but as I stomped away from Cubby, shards of black crystal and stone hiding beneath the soft, squishy layer stabbed at my bare feet.

I knew my job, knew I was supposed to love my Little Brother no matter what, but right then I wanted to punch his stupid scowling face.

"I want to go hunting!" Cubby screeched for the eightieth time that day.

The mountains groaned, just as sick of hearing his incessant whining as I was. Hunting for Slag Cavies with Av was supposed to be my time, my break, a chance to get away from him and just practice. And Cubby knew it.

"Forget it, Urgle. Just let him come," said Av. Av was my best friend, a great hunter, and the best shot in the whole Ikkuma Pit. He'd never had much patience for arguing, though I guess he never had to worry about it—*his* Little Brother was a breeze.

"Av, no way!" I said. "He can't navigate the Hotpots!"

"I can so!" screeched Cubby.

"You can't!"

"Relax!" Av yelled, gripping fistfuls of his dark, matted hair. "I'll help him across, all right? Everyone stop the yelling."

Furious, I wiped away the sweat dripping down my cheeks and took in a deep breath through my nose, the hot, dry air singeing my nose hairs and rushing a warm calm into my lungs—for the moment, anyway.

Cubby's scowl disappeared, replaced by a big fat grin. *Thanks, Av, big help.*

Cubby always got his way. Not because he should, but because he wouldn't stop pushing. Ever. Not until he'd made me as mad as he could.

I glared at the field of Hotpots stretched out before us, pools of molten lava glowing an ember red. I fought the urge to toss the kid in and be done with him.

From somewhere, a voice sniggered, "Goin' to hunt them big bad Slag Cavies, Urgs?"

Two grubby Brothers were squatted over a small Hotpot not far off—Fiver and Wasted. Fiver was sneering, pleased with what he considered a good joke, his thin lips spread across his fat face, while his Little Brother, Wasted, stifled his laughter while heating up some pebbles for a game of Whip It. My cheeks burned. It *had* to be Fiver who watched me lose an argument to my Little Brother. All my life, I've got on OK with everyone. I'm certainly nobody's favorite person, not like Av—everybody loves Av—I'm just sort of there. But for Fiver, I was *too* there . . . and it bothered him.

"Those junk rodents aren't bad practice," he went on. "You just keep at it. Maybe this'll be the year you finally make the Hunting Party."

At that, Wasted could contain himself no longer, and he exploded with wheezy laughter.

"Yeah, keep it up, you two," warned Av. "Urgs has come a long way with a spear. You'll see."

I hadn't. I had terrible aim, bad eyesight, and poor hearing, and I was slow. The exact opposite of the Brothers in the Hunting Party. No matter how much Av practiced with me in the Landfill, I never got any better at hunting.

"Oh, I bet," laughed Fiver. "From what I've seen, Urgs, you're gonna need a lot more help than even Av can give you."

I clenched my jaw and spat. Fiver was right. At the rate I was going, I'd never make the Hunting Party before my Leaving Day.

"Remember," said Fiver, "you keep the sharp part of the spear pointed *away* from you."

Wasted's laughter turned into a fit of hysterics, and I couldn't tell if the rumble vibrating my chest was the rumble of the Fire Mountains or my own wild fury bubbling up inside.

Cubby stepped out in front of me and Av, his filthy face wearing a new scowl, this one for Fiver. "He knows how to hunt!"

Just what I needed. My Little Brother fighting my battle for me. I swallowed the groan rising in my throat.

Fiver's beady, dark eyes narrowed on little Cubby, his mouth oozing into a fatter grin. "Never even had a chance. Poor little scroungee."

"Hey!" barked Av.

I watched Cubby. His voice had caught in his throat; his mouth hung open, trembling.

One word, and it was like Fiver had punched us both in the face. Scroungees were Brothers who could only scavenge the junk piles in the Landfill for food, Brothers who couldn't hunt because their Big Brother was a useless lump who couldn't teach them how.

I grabbed Cubby's boney shoulder and pulled him in behind me. "What did you just call him?"

"I know a scroungee when I see one. That one's a scroungee."

"What's your problem, Fiver?" said Av.

Cubby was close to tears, but Fiver had meant the insult for me more than him, and he'd got the rise he wanted.

"That's it!" I growled, throwing my pack to the ground and advancing on Fiver.

Av leaped out in front of me, trying to calm me down, but Fiver was on his feet, waiting for the brawl, his amused sneer begging me to let him have it.

"Relax," said Av. "He wants this, Urgs. Come on, it's getting late."

"It won't take me long," I said through gritted teeth. In fact, I was ready to let Av talk me out of it; Fiver was easily

6

a foot taller than me, weighed about as much as two of me, was stronger and faster. I didn't stand a chance.

I felt a tugging at my arm—Cubby. "Did you hear that?" he whispered, his wide eyes staring up at the tree line of Nikpartok Forest, the dense wood that surrounded the Ikkuma Pit.

"What?" asked Av.

"I heard something."

Everyone's eyes followed Cub's, up the steep black walls of the Pit to where the withered trees peeked out. I listened. Nothing but thunder and the quiet bubbling of the Hotpots.

"It's a forest, Cub," I told him. "It's filled with creatures."

"Like you would know," giggled Wasted.

My cheeks burned for the second time. I'd never been into the forest, never hunted anything but Slag Cavies, and everyone knew it.

"All right, all right," said Av. "Let's just get to the Landfill. Give me your pack." He snatched it up from the ground by my feet and fastened it securely onto his own pack. "You take the kid."

"What? I specifically remember you saying you'd help him across the Hotpots."

Av ignored me. He faced the first row of smoldering Hotpots, took a few big steps back. Then, with that speed no Brother could match, Av ran full tilt, hands open, always open, slicing through the air, and leaped, landing with a thud on the other side.

"Come on, Cub." I crouched so he could get up onto my back.

"No way!" he shouted.

"I don't blame you, kid!" laughed Fiver, sitting back down beside Wasted.

"You can't make that jump," I told him.

"Can so."

"You can't!" I snapped.

"I can!"

I turned away from him. *What an idiot.* The Hotpots were no joke. Brothers died in them all the time and he knew that.

"Cub!" called Av. "Listen to Urgle."

"Fine," he groaned. Fiver and Wasted sniggered some more. I was humiliated.

Cubby shimmied onto my back, his sweaty arms wrapping around my neck. I was suddenly nervous; I'd never made the jump with this much weight. Didn't help that I had an audience in Fiver and Wasted.

"You're holding on tight, right?" I said. "I mean like really tight."

"Yes!" he snapped. "Let's go."

I backed up farther than usual. I charged ahead, leaving my hands open like Av. It had worked for him. I came to the edge of the first pot and jumped.

"Scroungee!" yelled Fiver, but he was too late, I was airborne. I came down with a thud, Cubby's chin slamming into my shoulder, and my left foot slid back, nearly dipping into the boiling lava.

Fiver. He'd wanted me to fall. Wanted me to burn. If he'd yelled a second sooner . . . I would have.

When we reached the Landfill, the three of us stood and scanned the giant trash mounds, our eyes peeled for movement. Rusted metal branched from the mounds, reaching out, refusing to stay buried—smooth, rough, twisty, flat—all of it busy and messy, a lot of noise for my eyes. Not a Slag Cavy in sight. No problem, though; there'd probably be

8

hundreds beneath the trash, scavenging for food. I didn't really care. I was still seething about Fiver.

I viciously unhooked my pack from Av's back and began fishing out my spear and thrower.

"Just forget him, Urgs," said Av.

Easy for him to say.

Cubby was chewing on his dirt-crusted fingers, no scowl anymore, just wide, wet eyes.

"I'm—I'm no scroungee," he murmured.

"That's right, Cub," said Av. "You're not."

My blood was boiling. "It wasn't about you, Cubby. It was about me."

"But he said it to *me!*"

"You don't even know what it means."

"I know it's really bad!"

I ground my teeth and clenched my fists to keep from slugging the kid. It wasn't him I was mad at, it was Fiver, but Cubby had a way of annoying me like no one else. I turned my back on him to stop the argument and hunkered down on the rusty shards to fish out my hunting gear.

"There it is again," Cubby whispered. "Can you hear it?"

"It's nothing. Stop scaring yourself!" He had been a paranoid mess about Nikpartok Forest creatures all his life. The kid had nightmares every time the Hunting Party brought back a big animal he didn't recognize.

Cubby came over to me and sat down cross-legged with his head in his hands, watching eagerly.

"I think the Cavies are gone. I haven't even seen one," he said.

Showed what the kid knew. He didn't take in anything I told him.

"Slag Cavies live under the trash, Cub," Av explained as

9

he inspected his sling. "Dens and tunnels all through the mounds."

"Why?"

"Jeez, Urgs, don't you teach the kid anything?" laughed Av, smacking the back of my head. Great. First Fiver, now Av.

"I teach him plenty!" I snapped. "He just forgets!"

"You're right, I'm sorry."

I shot Cubby an angry look for making me look like a bad Big Brother. He didn't notice. He was staring at my daggers.

"Don't even think about it," I warned.

"This one's new." His grimy little finger grazed the handle of my newest piece and I slapped it away.

"It's not finished."

"I like it." He grinned, his fingers fidgeting in his lap. I tried not to smile. I liked it too. It was one of the best daggers I'd made in a while. The blade was a polished black fire glass; all my blades were made of fire glass. It was all over our mountains—smooth, shiny black rock that flaked into the sharpest edge, if you worked it right. When this one caught the light, it showed a red stripe pattern that I'd seen only a few times in fire glass. Sort of a shame I'd have to give it up.

"Don't get too attached," I said, "because it's leaving with Digger." Digger was the oldest out of all of us, sixteen, and considered himself some kind of leader. Which was stupid. In the Ikkuma Pit there are no leaders. Big Brothers take care of their Little Brothers, hunters hunt, healers heal, fixers fix. No one needs to tell you to do your part, you just do it. I hated when the tall, gangly jerk gave me orders. Good thing his Leaving Day wasn't far off.

Av bent down to take a look, rubbing his thumb over the

end of the handle. The handle was made of bully wood; Av had brought it back for me after a day in Nikpartok with the Hunting Party. The wood was dark, nearly black, and very hard. It had taken me a long time to get used to the way it ground under my tools when I tried to carve it. It took a long time, but I got the hang of it eventually.

"I get it," he laughed, tracing the image creeping up its side, five perfect notches splayed out from the butt to the blade. "They're fingers! That's great!"

I nodded. Digger's Little Brother, Fingers, came to me after Digger made his Leaving Day announcement. When a Big Brother decides his Little Brother is ready to handle life on his own, he makes an announcement. Always the same announcement: *"When the next baby is dropped, I will leave to make room for him. He will take my place."* It's a big deal. The boy who leaves and his Little Brother usually exchange gifts. Fingers wanted to give Digger a dagger and asked me to make it. I'm not a big fan of Digger, but I usually get asked to make a dagger for Leaving Days, so I told Fingers I'd do it. The Brothers seem to like the ones I make best. It's the one thing I do really well. This one I was particularly proud of. I had Fingers grip the handle and I traced his fingers with a bit of charcoal and carved away.

"What's this for?" asked Cubby, pointing to a circle impression where the blade met the handle.

"A-Frame," I said. That's the one thing I put on all my daggers—a small piece of wood from the A-Frame. A little piece of home.

"When you make mine," he said, sitting on his hands, "can you make it with *your* fingers?"

I shook my head. "You said you wanted a curl, like the one I made for Asher." The list of demands for Cubby's dagger was endless. I'd promised I'd make him one on my Leaving Day, and every time I made a new dagger he liked, he asked for his to be the same.

"Yeah, but I like this better."

I chewed the inside of my cheek to keep from laughing. He'd like the next one more, and the one after that even more.

He pointed to the glinting red stripes in the glass. "And that too. Make mine with that."

I wouldn't. What Cubby didn't know was I'd started his the day he became my Little Brother. So far, I had the blade complete. It was made of fire glass, like the rest, but this was special. I'd found the stone years ago, back when I was a Little Brother. There was a thick line of blue at its center. I'd never seen that color in fire glass. Reds, purples, oranges, maybe some yellow from time to time, but never blue. When I finished working on it, Cubby's blade had this long, thick blue swoosh flowing at its center. I'd been so busy getting the blade just the way I wanted, I hadn't had time to think about the rest of it.

"Cubby," said Av, "you know making it look good doesn't make it work good. It's how you use it that matters."

Cubby shrugged. Something in the mound must have caught his eye, because he got up and left us to rummage through the junk. He loved collecting worthless trash from the Landfill, stashing it away in his little hiding place he liked to pretend I didn't know about.

"Don't do any of that fancy stuff for me when I go, Urgs," Av went on. "I just want three real good blades. Light and easy to throw."

I looked up at him. "What? What do you mean?" Av and I were the same age; everything we did, we did together.

He was dropped at the wall only a few days after me, and he got Goobs not long after I'd got Cubby. We'd never discussed leaving before.

Av didn't say anything, just focused on picking out his wooden darts.

"Av, are you thinking of leaving?"

He shrugged. "Digger's going. He's only two years older than me."

"Two years is a lot, Av." It was. Digger's voice had already bubbled—it had turned deep and scratchy, and his neck had that bubble that only the oldest boys get. He had hair too, right on his chin. Av's voice was still the same, his skin still smooth and bare. He was too young. We were too young.

"Maybe, but Goobs is already the same age I was when I got him."

I wiped the sweat off my forehead. The thought of Av's Little Brother, Goobs, all alone and with a baby made me uneasy. Goobs was the same age as Cubby. What would he do without Av? What would I do without Av?

"But you bring down the most game," I said. "The Hunting Party needs you."

"Fiver'll be with them."

I frowned.

"I know Fiver's not your favorite person, Urgs. But he's an amazing tracker, really. I may bring 'em down, but I wouldn't find them if Fiver weren't out there with us."

I didn't say anything. I hated when Av said anything good about that Cavy fart.

"He's still your Brother, Urgs," said Av. "He's one of us."

Maybe. But I didn't have to like him.

We sat in silence for a minute, both of us watching Cubby tugging on some shiny stick he couldn't budge.

Without Av, Cub would be all that was left for me. And he wasn't ready for me to go, wasn't ready to take care of himself, let alone a new Little Brother. I hadn't taught him enough yet. Maybe Fiver was right. Maybe I was turning Cubby into a scroungee.

Av squinted as he watched my Little Brother, and for a second I worried he was thinking it too. "I had it again last night."

No, his mind was on something else. "The dream?"

He nodded.

Av had always had vivid dreams, ever since we were small. But they never bothered him before, not like this. Lately he'd been having the same one, over and over, and it was one that would upset any Brother.

"About your Mother?" I asked.

He kicked me on instinct, to shut me up. He didn't want anyone to know, and I didn't blame him. It was a secret between us. But there was no one around to hear besides Cubby, and he wasn't paying any attention.

"Sorry," said Av.

I nodded, rubbing my thigh where his foot had slammed into it. "So it was the same one?"

He jabbed lightly at the ground with his spear, staring at his feet. "When they get out there—the Brothers, I mean—outside the Pit. Think it's true about some of them?"

I waited, not sure what he was getting at.

"You know, going to find her?"

No. Without question, no. Not the good ones, anyway. No self-respecting Brother who left the Pit went to find those monsters. No self-respecting Brother would ever go looking for his Mother.

Av was one of the good ones.

When I didn't say anything he hurried by me with his spear thrower. "Anyway, I was just talking. We better get going, here. Don't want to waste the day."

He was just talking. I knew that. Av hated the Mothers just as much as any of us; he'd said it plenty of times. But if anyone heard him talking like that . . .

"I still hear it!" Cubby had freed his shiny stick and was pointing back at the tree line with it. "There's something out there, I swear." One thing was for sure. If Av was thinking of leaving, I was going to have to get better at hunting real fast. If I didn't, I'd let Cubby down.

TWO

I sat on a big scrap of metal, inspecting the black, furry rodents I'd brought down. I'd only managed to catch three Slag Cavies over the course of the afternoon, which was in itself embarrassing. But on top of it, they were awfully skinny for Cavies, probably why I'd managed to hit them—they were slow and unhealthy.

I blamed my poor performance on Av and Cubby. They'd been chattering the whole time about hunting tips and everything I was doing wrong. And I was doing everything wrong, according to Av. But I couldn't concentrate. My mind was on Av, on his Leaving Day. I tried to tell myself it was just talk, like he'd said, but I couldn't help being worried.

"Well?" called Av from the top of a neighboring trash mound. "Head back to the A-Frame? I'm getting hungry."

I'd lost track of time, which wasn't hard to do in the Ik-kuma Pit. The billowing black smoke and ash from the Fire Mountains blocked out the sun and sky; the only light was the orange glow of fire and lava. Time was kept by hunger.

I felt a faint grumble in my stomach and realized Av was right: nearly mealtime.

"Bringing those back with you?" Av said, smirking as he nodded to the Slag Cavies lying beside me. Cubby covered his mouth, trying to stop his giggles.

I scowled at Av, who was holding at least twelve fat, juicy Cavies.

My jaw locked and I got up and looked out across the junk heaps, scanning for another Cavy, a fat Cavy, a trophy Cavy. Then I heard a rustling by my feet.

Poking his head out from under my rusted metal scrap was the little black head of a chubby one. Slowly and quietly, I unhooked my spear from the throwing cradle and held it over the unsuspecting creature. Then, too soon, I slammed the spear down, missing the Cavy and hitting the ground with a crunch. The Slag Cavy squeaked in terror, and in a wild, determined fit I slammed my spear down again and again, trying to nail him. The confused and frightened rodent managed to dart out of the way every time until finally taking off and disappearing down a hole and into the garbage.

I was trophy-less.

Frustrated, I threw down my spear. Then, taking a deep breath that burned away what was left of my nose hairs, I began my walk of shame to join Av and Cubby on top of their mound, waiting to hear them laughing.

But when I joined them, they weren't even looking at me. Av, still and alert, was facing the East Wall of the Pit, his neck cranked up towards the dark tree line, Cubby copying his stance exactly.

"Hear that?" Av asked.

He knew I didn't. I didn't have the kind of ears Av did; no one had the kind of ears Av did.

"No," I grumbled.

"It's getting closer," he said.

I halfheartedly scanned the tree line at the top of the East Wall as I stuffed my gear into my pack. I didn't see or hear anything.

"See?" Cubby whispered. "I *told* you I heard something."

I couldn't help it, I had to laugh. "Av! Cubby's just a big baby. Don't listen to him!"

"I'm not a baby!"

Then I heard it for the first time: a hideous, deep, guttural call from somewhere in the distance.

I stiffened; Cubby looked at me nervously. He was right. There was something out there. The noise was sick, twisted, unlike anything I'd ever heard before. No wonder Cubby was so worried.

"Some kind of bird?" I asked hopefully.

"Nah," said Av. "Bigger than that."

"Outsiders, then? Making a dump?" For centuries, people from beyond Nikpartok would come to the Pit and toss in their junk. I'd never seen it happen, but the Landfill was proof enough, and I'd heard stories from other Brothers who'd seen it.

Av just shook his head.

The call sounded again, closer than before.

Cubby jumped and moved in nearer to Av. Another call, loud and angry.

I jumped and winced when I found myself doing the same.

We watched the tree line, waiting to catch a glimpse of whatever was making that noise. The dead trees, bent and broken, twisted into each other. All was still and silent, not a sign of life. The three of us stood frozen for what seemed like forever. I noticed how ridiculous Av and Cubby looked: Av's brow furrowed in concentration, Cubby's mouth agape in terror.

"By Rawley!" I said finally. "Doesn't matter what it is, it's a forest animal!"

"But—but what if it's coming down here?" asked Cubby.

I rolled my eyes. "Cub, have you ever seen anything but us and Cavies in the Pit?"

"No."

"There you go, then. Nothing can survive down here but us," I said, heading back to my pack. "That's how it's always been!"

Always. The Pit was ours. We were alive here. We belonged to the Pit. Anything outside that and the Pit would make it dead in no time.

Cubby followed me back to my pack and began gathering up my Cavies, but Av stayed rooted to the spot, listening and watching.

The call rang out again, louder, echoing off the walls of the Pit and slopes of the Fire Mountains a hundred times over.

Cubby and I yelped at the sound and turned back to the East Wall.

"There." Av pointed.

I saw movement in the undergrowth, then movement in the treetops.

A two-legged figure burst out of the brush and flung itself over the edge, tumbling down the East Wall—tumbling into the Pit.

Our Pit.

"They're coming in!" shrieked Cubby, the pitch forcing my stomach up into my throat.

"They can't!" I said. "They'll die!"

The figure's limp form bashed helplessly into boulders and outcrops until it managed to grab hold of a rocky ledge.

A shrill wail echoed out from the trees, so hideous and loud I thought my ears would bleed.

Scrambling out of the trees at the top of the East Wall came three pasty, bald creatures. They looked like Brothers, naked, but crouched and disfigured. No, not Brothers. Their sickly yellow color gave them away as something else entirely. The way they moved, jerky and sharp, looked clumsy, but they weren't. Even from where we stood, I could see they were fast, faster than any Brother. They stalked back and forth along the wall, watching the figure, their lost prey, unwilling to climb down after it.

The figure had managed to stop its fall, and was now carefully inching its way down the East Wall. The East Wall had never been an easy climb for the Brothers up or down, and I decided the figure probably wouldn't be able to make it with an injury. But it was doing well, taking the same route the Brothers would take. Its movements seemed familiar, precise.

"It's a man," I said.

"He's Ikkuma," Av corrected me.

By the time the three of us reached the man, we could hardly breathe. We'd run as fast as we could from the Land-fill to the base of the East Wall, Av tirelessly leading the charge, Cubby lagging behind, wheezing and begging me to slow down. When we arrived, a group of Little Brothers who must have witnessed the man's daring escape as well had gathered around him. They were all tentatively sucking their thumbs or holding up whatever rocks they'd found, ready to protect themselves. They didn't need the makeshift weapons; the man had collapsed, motionless in the dirt and rocks on the floor of the Ikkuma Pit.

Cubby stayed back with the other little ones as Av and I moved our way to the front of the group.

We stood over the man, looking down at him. He was covered in layers of hides, types I'd never seen before. Furs with black stripes slithered on white, gray spots circled brown on gold, covering his shoulders and boots. I'd never seen so many skins on one person. The Pit is so hot that the Brothers mostly just wear one skin from their waist down, made from Larmy pig or Arid mule from Nikpartok. This man could have covered ten Brothers and still have skins left for himself. Beneath all that he was wrapped in something, not made out of any hide, the color of an angry bruise. The layers were so thick I couldn't tell if he was breathing. I could see the blood, though. His shoulder must have been wounded by those things still pacing back and forth along the East Wall. They had hurt him good, made him bleed so much that the blood soaked through all those layers.

His belt, the same bruise color, secured his fabrics at the waist, and attached to it was a tube, kind of. It wasn't round, not really; it was as if long flat pieces of animal skin were molded together as round as they could be to form a pouch. The ends were pointed and made of a polished green stone, bright as Cubby's eyes.

One of the creatures let out a call, and one or two of the little ones started crying.

I looked up the black rock face, a wave of nausea washing over me as I realized just how high it was. Somewhere up there, the creatures were pacing.

I could feel Av staring at me. His eyes mirrored what I was wondering. *Is he dead?*

"Hey, fella!" I said. Nothing. The man just lay there. I shoved him with the butt of my spear. "Hey, fella!" I was a bit surprised; I hadn't been particularly gentle with the spear and I half expected him to leap up and grab me by the throat. But he didn't. The man didn't move.

It didn't take long for a big crowd to form around us. The East Wall was visible from nearly every point in the Pit, and before I knew it the entire clan had shown up to inspect the stranger.

"Is he dead, Urgs?" someone in the crowd asked.

I shrugged.

"Urgle!" It was Digger. "Figure out if he's dead or alive."

"What does it look like I'm doing?" I snapped.

"Not a whole lot," he shot back.

Having no better ideas, I wound back my leg and kicked the man right hard in the side. That did it; he let out a groan.

"Alive," I announced.

"By Rawley!" a little voice in the crowd gasped. "Look at his ankle!"

The plain fabrics that covered the man's legs were old, frayed, and too short for him. There, on the inside of his left ankle, was a white, bubbly scar. A circle. Without thinking I scratched my own identical scar with my right foot.

"Urgle?" said Digger. "The scar?"

"It's there," I confirmed.

"Someone run back to the A-Frame!" Digger ordered.

Cubby's hand shot up. "Cubby, tell Crow to bring water and something to carry the man on."

For a second I didn't think I'd heard him right, but the sound of multiple feet tearing off towards the A-Frame told me I did.

"You're gonna bring him back to the A-Frame?" I said.

"Urgle," warned Av quietly, "he's one of us."

"But we don't know anything about him! You can't just—"

"He's Ikkuma!" Digger yelled. "The A-Frame's as much his home as yours."

THREE

I sat alone on my cot, gnawing on the bones of my scrawny Slag Cavy. The orange glow from the A-Frame's hearth fire was making what little greasy meat I had glisten. Cubby had opted to eat with Av and Goobs, leaving me silent in thought amid the evening chatter.

"Looks like your little scroungee's got the right idea," sneered Fiver as he thundered by my cot, with Wasted bouncing along behind him. "Av might be his only hope."

I didn't look at him, I'd barely heard him. I was too focused on the A-Frame's new guest.

The Platform, a big wooden stage at the head of the hearth, was used for making important announcements, playing games, and storytelling. Now it was the intruder's place to rest. Digger had him laid there for everyone to see. Brothers had grabbed their furs and blankets, ready to give this unconscious stranger the skins off their backs just to make him comfortable. Not me. I just chewed on my Cavy bone as I watched Crow, our healer, clean the man's gnarled shoulder. I didn't like it, not one bit. No Brother, once they left, ever came back to the Ikkuma Pit. Ever. So what was this guy showing up for, bringing these creatures with him?

A pot dangling above me hit the left side of my face, then another hit the right, jingling as Cubby scurried up the ladder to his hammock that hung over my cot. Brothers slept in random spots through the A-Frame. Bunks lined the walls; some hung from the rafters, others just lay in scattered places on the floor. Cubby and I had a sleeping place that was pretty secluded from the rest of them—a little nook in the wall just big enough for our beds.

Without warning, Cubby's dinner bowl was shoved into my face, his bony little arm attached to it. I snatched it from him and hung it from its usual hook. At least he'd cleaned it this time.

Cubby hung upside down. "Think he's gonna make it?"

"No," I said. With any luck, he wouldn't.

"You don't like him?"

"I don't know him. So, no."

Cubby disappeared back over his hammock.

A sudden cry echoed through the A-Frame. I saw Crow leap back from the man, who was writhing in pain. He twisted and jerked, then fell quiet and lay limp again.

"He dead now?" someone called out.

Crow shook his head.

Cubby peeked back over his hammock. "Think I'll have a beard like his one day?"

I shot him a look. He was annoying me again. But he just grinned his cheery grin and disappeared back on his hammock.

He was still talking to me. I could hear him mumbling

something about beards and Adam's apples, and then, "Wonder who his Little Brother is?"

"What?" The question caught me by surprise.

"His Little Brother," said Cubby. "He's gotta have one, right?"

I leaped off my cot and headed straight for the Platform.

The A-Frame was a pretty crowded place; I had to jump over little ones wrestling, Brothers sitting on the floor laughing and eating. I knocked over a cup of water, and someone cursed and whipped a greasy bone at me, nailing the back of my neck.

"Urgle!" I heard Digger bark. "Stay away from there. Let Crow work."

I ignored him and quickened my steps. The man had to be pretty old. He looked old. He had as much hair on his face as he had on his head, and his throat bubble was more pronounced than any I'd ever seen. How old would that make his Little Brother?

Crow's hands and forehead were stained with the man's blood as he dabbed at the wound. He hadn't noticed me.

"Crow," I said.

"Hand me that." Without taking the time to look at me, he pointed to a clean rag at the edge of the Platform.

I did, then continued. "Crow, anyone recognize this guy?"

That made him look at me. "What? No. Why? You know him?"

"No. Does anyone?"

Crow just stared at me blankly.

"Urgle!" Digger was on his feet, making a beeline for me and Crow. "I said let him work!"

"Work this," I growled, and showed him my bare arse.

Crow threw his arms out over the unconscious man. "Cover that up, Urgs. I've got a sick Brother here!"

Before I could, Digger made it to the Platform and put me in a headlock. "Wanna show off your backside, eh, Urgle? Well, then get on up here."

He may have been lanky but he was still pretty strong, and as his bony arm crushed my windpipe, he hauled me up onto the Platform to show off my naked cheeks to the whole A-Frame. Everyone broke into laughter at the sight of me and all I could think about was chucking Digger's stinkin' Leaving Day present into a Hotpot.

Crow wasn't laughing.

"He had a good point," Crow said, his attention ever on the patient, even though Digger and I were putting on a pretty amusing show.

"Oh yeah? What's that?" said Digger, ignoring my desperate clawing at his arm.

"Brother," I gasped.

"Speak up, Urgs!"

I pushed my voice past the force on my neck. "His Little Brother!"

Digger released me and the whole A-Frame went silent. The eyes of all the Ikkuma Brothers were on me . . . and my bare arse.

"Keep it down, Useless!" yelled Fiver, followed by a few scattered snickers.

I felt my cheeks burning. I was blushing in front of everyone and I scrambled to yank up my Larmy skin.

It was at this point that Digger decided my question was worth asking, and then, like it was his idea all along, he addressed the Brothers.

"Does anyone," he yelled in his best leader voice, "know the Little Brother of this man?"

Silence.

"Does anyone," he tried again, "know this man?"

"It's hard to know what he looks like," said a little voice, "with that beard."

Cubby was right. The man had a full-blown bushy red beard that covered half his face. Not to mention how filthy and bloody he was. It would be hard for anyone to recognize him.

"Shave it off?" Digger whispered.

"What?" I said. "You mean should we shave it off? Or are you asking *me* to shave it off?"

"You know how to shave?" asked Digger, raising an eyebrow.

"You're the one with the face fluff on his chin!"

"I don't shave it!"

"I'll shave him," said Crow. "Get me a knife. And round up all the Big Brothers. If anyone is going to recognize him, it'll be them."

It had taken Crow a ridiculously long time to hack off all that facial hair; the Little Brothers had fallen asleep by the time he'd finished. Crow had left a number of new cuts for the guy to add to his already impressive collection of wounds, but at least now we could see him.

All the Big Brothers, there were about thirty of us, huddled around the comatose stranger. We stared. I racked my brain, trying to remember all the faces of Brothers that had left.

"I know him," said Shroomers.

We all turned and stared at the chubby fifteen-year-old.
He had his head down, shifting his feet.

"Well?" Digger was impatient. "Is he your Big Brother?"

Shroomers shook his head. "Cole's."

Everyone froze at the name. Cole was dead.

No one spoke. I didn't know if they were all taking a
moment to remember Cole or what, but I figured we had
to get on with it.

"Well, that explains why no one recognized him immediately."

Av shot me an angry look. I guess that was insensitive.

"What's his name?" asked Digger.

"Blaze."

FOUR

My bleary eyes blinked open and I stared groggily into the dark. Something had startled me out of sleep, and I groaned when I realized what it was—Cubby.

Awake the kid was annoying enough, but asleep he was worse. Every night over the last few months he'd wake me up with his coughing fits, hacking up snot and phlegm over and over in his sleep. It was a common thing in the Ikkuma Pit. Some of the Brothers' lungs just weren't built to take all the smoke and ash flying through the air all day, and Cubby was one of those Brothers. I knew he couldn't help it, but I felt like his stupid coughing was just another reason everyone thought I was so useless, just more proof for Fiver that I was a lousy Big Brother.

I slammed my fist onto my cot and mustered the strength to get out of bed.

I stood on lazy legs and wiped the cold drool from the side of my face, then reached for the little cup dangling from the underside of Cubby's hammock. The hearth fire had died; the quiet hissing of the fading embers and the smell of smoke floated through darkness.

Half asleep, I stumbled towards the back. The water holder sat tucked in a corner beside the Platform—a drink usually helped stop the little rat's incessant coughs. He kept hacking and I could still hear him, his hoarse cough joining the din of snores, groans, and sneezes of all the Brothers.

The muffled call of the pasty creatures sounded in amongst the noises, and I realized they were still out there, waiting. But what for? Blaze, I guessed. If they wanted him so bad, at least make a decision. Either come in and die or go back to wherever they came from. I just wanted that awful screaming to stop.

Then I felt my foot come down on something soft, a sleeping body, and I shifted my weight to my other foot to keep from stepping on it. Too late. My confused lazy legs gave out and I came crashing down on a Brother.

"Argh! What the Mother?" growled the figure beneath me. It was Fiver.

I scrambled off him, scurrying like a frightened Cavy, hoping to hide myself in the dark. A punch from Fiver's big ugly fist was like getting hit by the full force of a raging fire mountain. I wasn't about to take that kind of pain in the middle of the night. He grabbed my leg and pulled me back.

The feathery tickle of his curly hair grazed my hand and I grabbed a fistful, wrenching it.

He growled and grabbed my hand, but I kicked his side. "Oof!" he coughed.

I tried to step over him but my knee hit the edge of the Platform. I heard him shifting in the dark, searching for me, so I scrambled up onto the Platform on my hands and knees. That was when I remembered Blaze. I froze. All I could hear was Fiver's growling.

I felt around me, my hands only ever touching the wood

of the Platform, never Blaze's unconscious body. He wasn't there.

"Shh!" I snapped at Fiver.

"There you are, you little—"

I was afraid Fiver would pounce. My hand shot out in front of me and my palm slammed into his nose. He cried out.

"Shut up!" I said again. "He's gone!"

"I'm bleeding!"

I strained to listen, expecting to hear the stranger shifting in the shadows behind me. I had a sick feeling the two of us would be jumped at any second. But Fiver was groaning and sniffing, and it was blocking the background noise.

"Urgle! I'm gonna kill you for this. I'm— Wait, who's gone?"

Finally the big oaf had heard me.

"Blaze," I rasped.

The two of us stayed frozen in the dark, our ears searching for any sign of the stranger.

Nothing but snores, and coughing, and a mumbling sound.

"Wait, hear it?" I whispered.

The mumbling voice was gruff and deep, unfamiliar, not one of the Brothers.

"I see you, I see you," it hissed, "filthy demon Tunrar. Bah!" It was coming from near the entrance, along with the shuffling sound of feet. Blaze was up and he was moving.

"What's he doing?" asked Fiver.

I didn't know. I wasn't sure I wanted to. But if he was moving, Crow had fixed him good enough. He was feeling better.

I scrambled off the Platform and headed for Crow's sleeping space as best I could. I felt Fiver's desperate fingers touching my back every so often as he tried to follow me through the dark.

Again, the cry of the creatures somewhere in the distance invaded the A-Frame and my head knocked into the post that held up Crow's hammock. My eyes welled with tears and I cursed as Fiver grabbed my arm and moved in close to me. He was panting, his rank breath wrinkling my nose. He was scared.

I reached up and felt around, my hands landing on Crow's sleeping face.

"Hey! Hey!" he whispered. "What are you doing?"

"Wake up!"

"Urgs?"

"Yeah! Get up. Blaze is on his feet."

"What?" Crow was groggy, he hadn't quite come to.

Fiver scoffed in the dark and I heard a scuffle, then a body slammed against my shoulder and pushed me back.

"Hey! Easy!" yelled Crow.

Fiver must have grabbed him and pulled him down off his bed, because in that instant Crow was standing in front of me, his hands on my shoulders.

"What's going on?" he asked.

"Blaze!" snapped Fiver.

"He's up," I said. "Listen."

Crow said nothing for a moment.

"Not the baby, not my baby, can't let them have the baby." The mumbling was faster now, rambling. "What have I done? What have I done?"

At that, I felt Crow move away from me. He was headed for Blaze.

"Hey! What are you—?" I knew Crow wouldn't answer. When Crow was focused on something, everything else fell

33

away from him. I reached back towards Crow's sleeping space and felt around for anything. I felt a heavy pot, and clanged a bowl. Fiver figured out what I was doing and followed suit. Armed with cookware, we tried our best to follow Crow.

It was tough, especially with Fiver's clumsy hands constantly reaching out for me making me jump. I could hear Crow, a long way in front. My best guess was by the fire pit.

Suddenly, a small flame lit up Crow's face.

"Psst!" He motioned to us, waving his little torch.

Thrilled to have light, Fiver and I scurried over to him.

"You better not break those," Crow said when we reached him.

I looked at the charred black skillet in my hand, then the wooden spoon in the hands of Fiver. We looked pathetic.

Crow suppressed a smile and led the way.

We passed the entrance, headed towards the front corner where Av and his Little Brother slept. The mumbling was easier to hear now, Blaze was close.

"Beginning is secrets. . . . Beginning is lies!" Blaze's outline appeared in the light of the torch. He was pacing back and forth, not far from Av and Goobs's sleeping place.

He was shaking his head back and forth, over and over. Crow broke away from me and Fiver, moving in for a better look. "Look at his eyes," he told us.

In the light of the torch I could see Blaze's pale blue eyes, not fixed on anything, like he was looking inside, not out.

"He's asleep," said Crow.

Beside me, Fiver snorted a laugh.

"Stolen secrets!" Blaze went on, pulling at his hair, scratching his neck. "Hidden victory! End to the Beginning!"

"What's the Beginning?" I asked.

34

Crow just shrugged and reached out to touch him.

"Uh . . . ," I whispered, "I'm not sure that's the best—"

As soon as Crow's fingers touched the man's arm, the blank eyes filled with consciousness, wild and confused. He grabbed Crow by the throat and threw him to the ground, torch and all.

Fiver pounced just as quick, jabbing the spoon handle into Blaze's side with his right hand, wrapping his left arm around his neck.

Blaze grunted in pain but never let go of Crow, who was gurgling as he tried to breathe.

Dumbfounded, I couldn't move.

I felt someone grab the skillet from my hand, and Av stepped into the torchlight. He brought the skillet down with an assertive *thunk*, straight onto the back of Blaze's head.

Dazed, Blaze released Crow, who rolled away, rubbing his neck and coughing.

Fiver let go of Blaze and the man stumbled onto his hands and knees, trying not to pass out. Then I caught Av's face: he was catching his breath through his nose, his mouth tight with anger. He wouldn't look at me.

"Way to protect your Brother. Big help there, Useless," panted Fiver. "Thanks for that."

My insides withered. I was useless.

FIVE

I woke to the sweet smell of Larmy pig being cooked up in the fire pit. Pungent herbs tickled my nose. It was the smell of celebration. Excited voices, crackling fire, and sizzling meat filled my ears.

I opened one eye and saw a group of Brothers tending to the fat Larmy roasting on a spit. Crow sat among them, picking at a sprig of herbs.

That was when I remembered Blaze, his giant hand wrapped around Crow's neck in the fading torchlight. My stomach churned and I rolled over, begging myself to go back to sleep.

But I couldn't. All I could do when I closed my eyes was see the night play out again and again. Crow gasping for air, Av unable to look at me. I'd just stood there, like a scroungee. And Blaze's crazy eyes, his crazy words. *End to the Beginning.* Whatever that meant.

The bed began to shake and the pots above me jingled as Cubby scrambled onto my cot.

"What?" I grumbled.

Cubby said nothing. He crawled up onto my legs and sat,

his back resting against the wall as the circulation to my feet was slowly being cut off. I let him stay there, too exhausted and humiliated from the night before to bother with him.

"Digger said we should all be celebrating," said Cubby quietly.

"Celebrate what? Blaze?" I laughed.

"Yeah. The return of our Brother. He's better today. Says those monster things were chasing him for days. Digger's giving up the Larmy pig he was saving for his Leaving Day Ceremony to make this a real big occasion."

Never mind that the man attacked Crow.

"Digger's an idiot."

I turned my head and let my eyes drift over to him again. He was dressed different, I hadn't noticed the new colorful hide draped over his shoulders. One of Blaze's.

The excited cheers of a dozen games taking place outside drifted into the A-Frame.

"So why aren't you out celebrating?" I asked. "Sounds like they're playing Screamers out there."

Cubby said nothing, rocking his legs.

"You love Screamers."

He still didn't respond. I turned over and smacked him on the forehead. "Why aren't you playing?"

Cubby's lower lip was trembling as he tried to dislodge his caught voice.

"Fiver?" I asked. I could only imagine the hideous things he'd said to Cubby after last night.

Cubby shook his head.

"Wasted?"

Cubby nodded.

I kicked the kid off of me and rolled out of bed, ready to go give Fiver's Little Brother what was coming to him.

Wasted was becoming more vicious every day, and in that moment I had every intention of beating the Fiver out of him.

"No! No!" said Cubby, desperately grabbing my arm and pulling me back onto the cot.

"No what?"

Cubby's big eyes darted out towards the Brothers cooking the Larmy, right at Crow.

I felt sick. I was pathetic, useless, and by now the whole A-Frame must have known it . . . and so did Cubby.

He let go of my arm and stared at his fidgeting fingers.

My throat had suddenly gone dry. "What'd Wasted tell you?"

Cubby focused on his dirty fingers, deciding how to answer. I watched them too, having lost the courage to look him in the eyes.

"He said . . . you were a coward—"

A cold wave of shame ran up my left side.

"He said . . . you would've let Crow die—"

A wave up my right.

"He said you were no Brother. And Av"—Cubby's face was streaming with tears—"Av didn't say anything. Av was right there and he—" He looked at me, desperate to understand. "He didn't stop him. He didn't say anything."

His big green eyes pleaded with me, begging me to tell him something, anything—that it wasn't true maybe—but I had no words for him. What could Av say? He'd seen me with his own two eyes, standing there, watching Blaze attack Crow. A Brother wouldn't just stand there. A Brother wouldn't watch his Brother get attacked. A real Brother took care of his Brothers. So what did that make me? Wasted was right.

I lay back down, facing the wooden wall of the A-Frame. "Just go play Screamers, Cub."

He didn't. He stayed on my cot, sniffling. Miserable in our shame, the two of us sat together, unable to face the Brothers, all because I was a coward.

I could hear him laughing—Crow—while he instructed his Little Brother, who was having trouble stripping herbs. I squeezed my eyes tight and there he was, gasping for air while Blaze held him tight around the neck. Blaze. My nostrils flared at the thought of him. The delicious smells that filled the A-Frame and the squeals and laughter outside were all for him. His scar marked him as a Brother, but it was him who tried to kill Crow. Didn't anyone care about that?

End to the Beginning. Those were his words while he slept. How many other lives had he tried to put an end to?

A loud bang suddenly tore through the quiet. I shot up and waited, silently listening. Cubby was frozen beside me, the Brothers roasting the Larmy still as stone. The cheering outside had stopped, everything was at a halt. The sound had been deafening, like the Fire Mountains when they got angry.

But this sound was different—quick and sharp.

Silence.

I got to my feet and headed to the door of the A-Frame.

Outside, everything was still. I looked to the Fire Mountains. The peaks smoldered, spewing smoke and ash just as they always did. No fire, no lava—just the soft rumble they always made.

The familiar call of the deformed creatures from yesterday rang out. They still hadn't left. I could see them at the top of the East Wall, still pacing, watching, waiting. But the noise hadn't come from them.

All the Brothers were frozen in groups—wrestling matches had stopped mid-tackle, races mid-sprint—everyone was staring in the same direction. My eyes followed theirs to Blaze; he was standing beside Digger and holding what looked like a piece of junk from the Landfill.

"Sorry!" Blaze laughed. "It's all right, boys! Go about your business."

There was a quiet murmuring as the Brothers tried to continue with the "celebration."

"Urgle?" Cubby was behind me. "What was that?"

I saw Av in the crowd just in front of Blaze. His Little Brother, Goobs, was bouncing around beside him.

"Av!" I called, running out to meet him. "What happened?"

"Ah, uh—I don't really . . ." He was struggling to keep from looking at me, refusing to meet my eyes, rubbing his chin on his shoulder like he had an itch he was too lazy to use his hand on. I felt my cheeks getting hot. He was embarrassed by me. "Hi, Cub," he said, smiling. Cubby appeared beside me, panting and wheezing from his struggle to keep up.

"Hey, Cubby!" said Goobs, throwing his arms around him in a hug. Goobs had always been overly affectionate, but he was a fast runner and a good friend to my Little Brother. "Did you see what Blaze did?"

"What did he do?" I asked.

"He had this thing!" said Goobs, explaining with dramatic gestures. "And he showed it to Digger. And Digger, Digger was all, 'How does it work?' And, and Blaze, he goes, 'Oh here, I'll show you.' So then, he took it, the thing, that thing he has in his hand, and pointed it towards the East Wall, at those ugly creature things. Then there was this loud

BAM! KABLOW! And everyone turned around and was all, 'Whoooooaaa! What was that?' And Blaze called it a pissle."

"Pistol," corrected Av.

"Pistol," Cubby giggled, trying out the word.

I looked to the East Wall and was surprised to realize there were only two creatures pacing now, not three. "Pistol," I repeated.

"Come on, Cubby, they're starting up another round of Screamers!" Goobs wrapped his arm around Cubby's shoulders, ready to run off. Cubby looked to me, then Av, and I could see he didn't want to leave me alone.

I shrugged. "You love Screamers."

That was enough for Goobs, who dragged Cubby away by the arm, leaving me alone with Av.

Av looked at me a second, then cleared his throat awkwardly.

"What?" I said.

"Huh? Nothing." He shook his head and then walked away from me.

"Hey! Av!" I followed him. "You're not talking to me now?"

"Urgle!" I heard someone bark. All of a sudden a fist slammed into my left cheek and I went down, pain ringing through my head. Fiver was standing over me. "That's for being a waste of space."

With my nose in the dirt, I could still see Av. He was watching me with that same face Cubby had, his eyes pleading with me to do something.

Fiver kicked me in the side. "Quit looking at Av. He's not helping this time."

Another kick pelted my side, the wind completely knocked out of me. "That's for Crow."

Beyond Av, I saw Cubby and Goobs, stopped mid-game, watching the beating with terror on their faces.

"Fiver!" Digger's voice yelled from somewhere.

Another kick. I curled up, trying to block the blows.

Cubby let out a scream.

"This is for your scroungee, you coward," he said, pummeling me with his heavy fists. I didn't fight back. I'd earned this.

The pounding stopped as Fiver was thrown to the ground beside me.

"Knock it off, big guy," said a deep, raspy voice.

I looked up to see the broad form of Blaze, his jaw locked, brow furrowed. "Come on, get up."

I refused his outstretched hand, opting instead to push myself up and stand on my own. Cubby rushed to my side, doing his best to help me to my feet. I wiped the blood from the corner of my mouth and stretched my aching shoulders.

"All right there, kid?" Blaze asked.

I ignored him, shrugged Cubby off me, and looked around at the crowd of onlookers.

"Beat it!" shouted Blaze. The little ones jumped and ran, some started to cry, as the older Brothers calmly scattered to find a game or wrestling match to take part in.

I spun to face him. He had a demented grin on his face, deep red scabs crisscrossing his fleshy lips, his thin nose. This guy and his nightmare was the reason Fiver hit me in the first place, and his sudden attempt at being helpful felt like nothing but a slap in the face. "You know what?" I told him. "I don't need your help, all right?"

He shrugged. "All right."

"Sorry, Blaze," said Digger, pushing Fiver down as he

tried to get up. "These two are always causing problems. You sure know how to ruin a good day, Urgle."

"Go jump in a Hotpot, you Mother seeker!" I yelled.

"Whoa! Whoa!" laughed Blaze. "Let's just keep the tempers in check here. Urgle, I apologize for interfering with your business," he said, bowing with a smirk. Then he turned to leave.

"You make a formal apology like that to Crow?" I said.

Blaze stopped and turned back to me, unfazed. He brushed his hair out of his eyes. "I did, actually. Look, Urgle . . ." He looked to Fiver, still on the ground.

"Fiver," offered Digger.

"Fiver," said Blaze, nodding. "And, uh . . ." He pointed to Av, who was looking the most uncomfortable I'd ever seen him. "Av, right? Look, I know I gave you guys a scare last night. I didn't know what I was doing, and I'm sorry for that."

Fiver and Av nodded, while I glared at him, the metallic taste of my own blood irritating my tongue.

"What's that?" Cubby was pointing at the man's belt, the green stone trinket dangling from it.

Blaze laughed. "That? Nothing. Just my old flint box."

He scratched his neck and turned back to the races beginning behind him, but Cubby had his arm still outstretched, his eyes fixated on the box the same way they fixed on my daggers.

"I like it," he said. "Can I touch it?"

Blaze whipped round, his confident smirk gone, replaced by something else. Surprise, maybe. As quickly as I noticed it, the look was gone and the smirk was back.

"Why not," he said, untying it and gently placing it in Cubby's hand.

Cubby turned it over in his palm, his fingers tracing every edge as though he'd never felt anything so smooth. You'd think he'd been given a flint box that had belonged to Rawley himself, the way he gawked.

"How does it open?" he breathed.

The surprise was back on Blaze's face, and this time it stayed there, mixing with a furrowed brow that said Blaze had lost his patience.

"It's broken," he said quickly. "Here, I'll take it back."

He snatched the box from Cubby and began to fasten it onto his belt again, a tremor suddenly overtaking his fingers. He fumbled clumsily, dropping the green box into the ash. He bent down to retrieve it with a frantic flourish and composed himself long enough to secure it at his waist.

A cry rang out and I looked to the waiting creatures.

Old flint box, my foot.

"What do you plan to do about your friends?" I spat, pointing to the East Wall.

"Just stop it, Urgle," Digger warned.

"Ah, the Tunrar," said Blaze as the creatures released another hideous cry. He fiddled with the pistol thing at his hip and gave his neck a scratch. "Didn't realize how low I was on ammo. Must've wasted all my shots when they were chasing me. Managed to nail one at least."

I had no idea what he was talking about. "Ammo?"

"Anyway, don't worry," he said, ignoring my question. "Tunrar Goblins get bored easily. They'll leave today, maybe tomorrow."

"With you?" I hissed.

"Cryin' out loud, Urgle!"

Blaze smiled. "Nah, not with me." He moved his shirt to reveal his gnarled shoulder, forcing a gasp from Cubby. My

44

nose wrinkled at the sight. "I like to travel without getting chewed on, know what I mean?"

The angry wound bruised blue and black with crusted blood forced me to look away.

Blaze nodded and left us, Digger following him like a scroungee idiot.

SIX

By evening the Larmy was ready. No one had eaten a thing, knowing full well they'd be stuffed on roast Larmy and fenig root after the feast. I had been looking forward to Digger's Leaving Day Ceremony for weeks, not just because I'd finally be rid of the bossy lank, but because Larmy meat was my favorite. I should have been happy to eat it earlier than expected even if I was stuck with Digger a while longer, but my body was still aching where Fiver had kicked me and my stomach was barely keeping down my own spit, so I figured dead animal was out.

Word of my worthlessness had got round to all the Brothers, and they made no secret of talking about me behind my back. Av still wasn't saying much. I spent most of the day on my cot, sleeping. I hadn't even seen Cubby, who was playing somewhere with Goobs.

Digger jumped up onto the Platform as Brothers grabbed their bowls, ready to devour the sizzling Larmy.

"I'm talking!" he called out. "Everyone! Over here! I hope you're all hungry! Mud, Gazer, and Carver have prepared a feast!"

I pulled my blankets over my head. Digger had gone into his "leader" act and I wanted to block out the sound of his arrogant voice.

"As you all know, this Larmy pig was being saved for my Leaving Day Ceremony."

Here it comes.

"But I feel that today is too special to go unrecognized. A Brother has returned. This is truly an important day, and so, Blaze, I offer my Leaving Day feast up, in celebration of your return."

I groaned at the sound of cheers and applause.

"Also!" continued Digger.

Oh, Mothers, there's more.

"Even though this isn't a traditional ceremony, I thought it would be a treat for Blaze, and all of us, to hear our favorite stories of Rawley, the First Brother."

Another round of applause followed this grand announcement, and I was too annoyed to sleep. I sighed and sat up. Figuring I might as well eat, I reached above me for my bowl and Cubby's.

I watched Digger come down off the Platform, shaking Blaze's hand and grinning stupidly. The Big Brothers patted Blaze on the back. They'd been following him in a pack all day, asking him questions about his pistol, those creatures he called Tunrar Goblins, and the world outside the Pit in general. Me, I didn't care. I wasn't ready for the world out there and I knew it was none of my business. My business was the Pit, and it would be till I left. Blaze had left already. Why was he back here at all? Had anybody asked him that?

The Little Brothers were pushing and shoving, crowding around the spit as Crow and Mud filled their bowls with chunks of Larmy meat and fenig root. I didn't see Cubby in the group, or Goobs. Still off playing somewhere—camped out in Cubby's special hiding place, no doubt. I didn't like him climbing up to his little cave alone, and he knew it. It was dangerous, but he never listened. I picked a crusty out of the corner of my eye and hung Cub's bowl up without looking.

Fiver was now on the Platform, cheeks stuffed with Larmy meat as he waited to begin the story. Fiver was the bane of my existence, but I had to admit he was a great storyteller.

"Right!" he yelled out, stretching his legs. He was ready to perform. "'Rawley and the Brothers'? Or 'Rawley Battles His Mother'?"

Boys hollered their preference from all corners of the A-Frame, and I held back a groan when I saw Digger stand up and raise his hands, apparently needing silence.

"We should let Blaze decide!"

He was commanding, not suggesting.

The A-Frame was silent as everyone looked around for Blaze. He was with Digger last I'd seen him, but he'd managed to escape and was now helping Crow and Mud hand out food.

"Uh . . . ," he laughed awkwardly, apparently uncomfortable with the attention. "I like the 'Rawley and the Brothers' story myself."

Everyone cheered and Blaze hurried to fill the last of the bowls in front of him before he ducked into the crowd. I shook my head. Blaze had been here all of one day and already he was doing his best to escape Digger. Fiver clapped his hands together, ready to start the story. "Thousands of years ago . . . when the Landfill was empty and the Slag Cavies ruled the Ikkuma Pit, a boy named Rawley was born to an evil Mother."

Right on cue, a slew of growls and boos rose from the Brothers.

Where was Cubby? He still hadn't come to get his bowl. I scanned the A-Frame for him and was surprised to notice Blaze heading straight for me. His clothing seemed looser, and I noticed he wasn't wearing his belt, the flint box no longer at his waist.

"His Mother and her sisters were the greatest hunters in all the world, but she never fed him . . . or clothed him . . . or taught him to hunt so he could feed himself. She never fed his brothers, either, and her sisters never fed their sons. So Rawley taught himself to hunt—"

"Still sting?" said Blaze, sitting down beside me . . . on my cot . . . *my* cot. My eyes narrowed on him. I hadn't invited him over, yet here he was, sitting on my cot, my space, the only thing that was mine!

"What?" I said.

"Your chin. Still sting?"

I rubbed the spot where Fiver had slugged me earlier and winced. It must've looked pretty blue. Even so, what did Blaze care?

Blaze smiled. "Thought it might. I'm no stranger to a fight myself, though I can't say I ever took one quite so well as you."

I inhaled as deep as I could. *Well.* I couldn't help but think he meant something different. Fiver had landed blow after blow, and I had done nothing to protect myself. I hadn't taken it *well.* I'd just taken it.

All because Blaze had to have a bad dream.

Blaze picked a red piece of Larmy meat out of his full bowl with his giant, greasy fingers and offered it to me.

Mouth watering, I shook my head.

"Not hungry, eh?"

I shook my head again and turned away from him, trying to keep my temper in check. Here he was, pretending to be nice to me and it didn't make any sense. It was his fault my body was bruised, his fault Av wasn't talking to me. He could keep his Larmy. I didn't want anything from him.

"What do you care, anyway?" I snapped.

He grinned, a sideways smirk that made me want to hit him. "I dunno. You just remind me of someone, I guess."

I raised an eyebrow. "Who?"

"Me. A long time ago."

My back stiffened. I don't know what I expected him to say, but it wasn't that. From where I was sitting, Blaze and I had less in common than a Cavy and the Fire Mountains.

He leaned back on his elbow, making himself more comfortable.

I rested my chin in my hands and tried to focus on Fiver.

"I'd almost forgotten, you know, the way it feels here. I haven't felt this . . ." He let his words trail off as he savored the food in his mouth, Fiver's words in his ears.

I waited.

He saw me looking at him and he cleared his throat. "Anyway, it's nice to feel it again."

"Feel what?" I asked.

He smiled, but there was something sad weighing on it, something cloudy behind his eyes as he watched Fiver. "Home."

"And when his evil Mother and her evil sisters decided they wanted no sons, no fathers, no husbands, they led Rawley and all his brothers and cousins far, far away from their home, leading them to die in the fires of the Ikkuma

50

Pit. But brave and clever Rawley would not let his brothers and cousins die—"

Blaze began to chuckle. "Word for word. That's unbelievable."

I turned back to him. "What?"

"The story. It's word for word the same as I remember it." He stuffed another fat piece of Larmy into his mouth and I felt my stomach grumble.

"It's incredible how nothing changes here, how untouched you boys are."

I was insulted and I guess my scowl let him know because he shook his head.

"No, it's a good thing, Urgle."

"When his evil Mother and her evil sisters had abandoned the boys in the Ikkuma Pit, Rawley taught his Brothers all he'd taught himself," continued Fiver. "Then Rawley took a hot ember and burned the inside of his ankle, a symbol of his promise to take care of, and to share with, all his Brothers. And his Brothers made this same promise, and burned their ankles for Rawley. Every day they ate like kings, hunting the creatures of Nikpartok Forest."

Untouched. The word hammered into my brain with Blaze's every smacking chew of Larmy.

"Years later, the evil Mother returned. She had with her another son, a son she did not want—"

"Untouched by what?" I almost didn't realize I'd said it out loud.

Blaze watched Fiver, chewing and smacking. Finally he shrugged. "Things aren't as simple out there, kid. Beyond that forest . . ."

"When Rawley found the baby"—Fiver's voice drifted into Blaze's silence—"he brought him to his Brothers. 'There is not enough room in the Ikkuma Pit for everyone,' he told them, 'and this place has given me all it can.'"

"Beyond that forest what?" I demanded.

"It's madness," he said.

What he meant, I had no idea, and before I thought it I heard myself asking, "What's madness?"

Blaze scratched at his neck, still watching Fiver, mouthing along. I'd seen him do that before, in the torchlight just before he grabbed Crow. *End to the Beginning.*

"'It is time for this man to leave, so that his brother may have the room to grow and learn in the Ikkuma Pit!'"

"What!" I said.

Somewhere outside, a little voice could be heard screaming.

Blaze's icy-blue eyes locked onto mine. "It's war."

The story came to an abrupt stop as everyone became aware of the screams. I barely registered it, my eyes fixed on Blaze. I didn't understand what he meant, and my stomach turned.

"AV! AV!"

Blaze turned away from me, his attention on the doorway.

"AV! AV!"

My heart stopped and I looked for Av. He was on his feet, running to the door. We both knew that voice.

Goobs suddenly appeared, and collapsed on the floor of the A-Frame, sobbing and wailing for his Big Brother.

I watched the door, waiting for Cubby to show, my pulse thumping louder in my ears every second he didn't.

"They got him! They got him!" Goobs cried into Av's arms. "At the East Wall, they got him!"

Not Cubby, I begged. I pushed through the Brothers and

ran to Goobs, who was clinging to Av and whimpering. I could barely understand him. Av looked at me, frightened.

"We were trying to run away from Wasted, he kept yelling, 'Scroungee! Scroungee!' And then the monsters—" He gulped in panicked breaths.

"Who got who?" I yelled. Silence rolled over the A-Frame, as the echo faded and Goobs tried to get ahold of himself long enough to answer.

"Cubby." He sniffed. "The monsters have Cubby and Wasted."

I heard the call of the creatures somewhere in the distance and bolted for the door.

"Urgle!" I heard Blaze yell as I took off outside, running as fast as I could across the floor of the Ikkuma Pit.

Fiver was beside me in an instant, barreling by me, club in hand.

Our bare feet pounded the ground in sync as we charged for the East Wall.

I could see the yellow, ghostly figures of the Tunrar Goblins on a rocky ledge halfway up the wall, Wasted's limp form resting beneath the big one, Cubby kicking and screaming in the clutches of the other.

Fiver roared, startling the Tunrar. The big one shrieked back at him.

Then familiar voices were yelling all around me. Av and Blaze were beside me, bellowing, trying to frighten the creatures off.

Cubby must have heard us because his shrieking became louder, wilder.

I saw the big one drop Wasted and scramble up the East Wall.

Not Cubby.

We reached the rock face and I began frantically climbing. Fiver and Av were flying upwards, they'd be with Wasted any moment. I could hear Cubby above me, he was screaming my name and I momentarily lost my footing, grating the bottom of my foot against the rock.

Below me, Blaze pushed my stinging foot back up and I kept going.

"Oh, no! No!" I heard Fiver crying.

I hoisted myself up onto the ledge and saw Fiver and Av standing over Wasted.

"Crow!" Fiver screamed, tears streaming down his face as he scooped the little body into his arms.

"He's right behind us," said Blaze.

Crow and Digger hoisted themselves up, and everyone gathered around Fiver and Wasted. Everyone but me.

I looked above me and saw the Tunrar climbing, Cubby kicking and punching hysterically in the smaller one's muscular arms.

I climbed, my arms ached and burned, but I had to get to him. They'd disappear into Nikpartok Forest any moment.

When I reached the top of the East Wall there was nothing but dead trees before me, silent and crooked, weaving into each other, impossible to see through.

"Cubby!" I screamed.

He let out a cry, not far ahead.

I ran. My legs were numb with the effort, begging me to stop, but I didn't. Branches whipped my face as I plowed ahead through the thick, brittle forest. The guttural call of the Tunrar sounded somewhere to my left—not far. I couldn't see, the light from the fires of the Ikkuma Pit were behind me, the forest was nearly all black.

I kept running.

Another Tunrar sounded to the right. I stopped and listened.

Leaves and twigs crunched under Av's foot as he caught up.

"One of them is flanking our right," he panted, bent over, gulping in air.

My lungs felt like they were going to burst, and I thought I could taste blood.

There was only silence, except for Av's wheezing. I couldn't hear the screams.

"Go right?" he asked.

I paced back and forth, frantically searching for any sign, any clue as to which way they'd gone. But the damn forest was so black, so dark, I could barely see a thing.

"Cubby!" I cried.

Something shifted to our right; we could hear its labored, sickly breathing. I could see Wasted in my head, what that thing had done to him—his blood, his eyes.

"Cubby!" I begged.

No response.

I threw up.

"Urgs, it's on the right," whispered Av, pulling out his dagger.

I heard it, but I didn't care.

I stayed there, on my hands and knees, smelling my own sour puke, staring into the black.

Then Cubby's desperate shriek rang out.

I was off in an instant, Av yelling after me.

My foot caught and I fell. My hide ripped and I could feel I'd split open my knee. Didn't matter. I scrambled to my feet and kept going, fast as I could.

That was when the big one got me.

The Tunrar slammed into my right side, throwing me into a tree. My head bashed up against it, stunning me a second. It threw me to the ground and was making a sick hacking sound as it clawed at me, trying to pin my flailing limbs.

I kicked and punched with everything in me.

It hissed and slashed at my thigh with its sharp claws.

I grunted in pain.

It pinned my legs and opened its hideous, gummy mouth, the rotten smell of meat on its hot breath.

Wild and furious, I lunged at it as best I could and sank my teeth into its leathery shoulder.

It screamed and bashed my head on the hard ground.

I was dazed, couldn't move.

It circled me, shuffling around through the leaves, hacking and hissing. Then it brought down a huge, heavy fist on my stomach.

I couldn't breathe.

It shrieked with triumph.

The Tunrar raised both fists in the air, and I waited for the rib-crushing blow.

All of a sudden it arched its back and squealed like a Larmy pig, falling on the ground and writhing around.

I crawled away from it, clutching my stomach.

Av ran up and pulled his dagger out of the squealing monster's back, then gave it a hard kick to the head. It went limp.

"You all right?" he asked.

I sat up, still holding my stomach and noticing the hot blood pouring down from my split eyebrow.

I cried. It wasn't the pain, or the blood. It was the silence.

I couldn't hear Cubby.

SEVEN

"Here, let me see," said Av, pulling my hand away from the deep gash on my thigh. He winced at the sight, but I felt nothing. The lump in the back of my throat was swollen and throbbing, I couldn't swallow. I'd lost Cubby. I'd failed my Little Brother.

My stomach heaved and I couldn't hold it in.

Av jumped back and wiped away my bile from his legs.

"Crow!" he called into the dark trees.

I heard thumping feet. As Crow, Blaze, and Digger burst out of the shadows and into the dark clearing, I felt sicker. Images of Wasted, his limp body, then Cubby, his face twisted in terror, flashed through my head. *Not Cubby.*

I stuck my head between my legs and lost myself in violent sobs.

Crow's cold fingers grabbed my leg and flattened it out as he tried to get a look at the gash from the Tunrar.

"Get me a switch from a Sticky Willow," he instructed.

Someone ran off, I didn't know who. Probably Av, because they were back in moments.

I heard Blaze next: "What happened?"

"The thing went at Urgle," said Av, handing Crow a short branch dripping with sap.

"Cubby?" asked Digger.

No one spoke.

Crow leaned into me. "This will hurt," he said.

With a careful eye, he held the oozing stick just over the gash and let several thick black drops fall onto my open flesh. Each drip radiated with a vicious pain, and my body screamed to push Crow away as he pulled the sides of the gash together and squeezed. I didn't care. I'd lost Cubby. I wanted all of it to be the worst pain I'd ever felt, I wanted punishment.

"They'll be headed to the High Temple of Beginners," said Blaze.

His words made no sense to me, like he'd spoken a completely different language.

"What?"

"The Tunrar and the kid."

I looked up at him. "What do you mean?"

"They won't kill him." He was so matter-of-fact, as if we should have known.

Again, I thought of little Wasted.

"But Wasted . . . ," said Digger.

Blaze shook his head. "Wasted was for them. They're saving Cubby for the Beginning."

We looked to one another, confused. I could hear my pulse in my ears, hear the grumbles of Blaze in the darkness: *End to the Beginning.* Hope and dread throbbed in the pit of my stomach.

"The Beginning?" I asked.

"Look," explained Blaze, "Tunrar Goblins are servants of the Beginning. Whenever they feed, whenever they take,

58

they are bound to give back to it. So if they fed on Wasted, they have to save Cubby for sacrifice."

"Sacrifice?" asked Av.

"The Beginners' High Temple is where they'll head. They'll take the boy to the priests there."

We stared at him blankly.

"Their home," said Blaze.

"Where's the Temple?" I demanded.

"Other side of the Abish Village, tucked away somewhere in the Baublenotts."

"No!" I yelled at him. "How do I get there?" I had no idea what these places were, but I was on my feet and brushing Crow off my leg, ready to sprint in whatever direction Blaze pointed me. My angry cut pulsed with pain and I wavered. Av put a hand on my shoulder to steady me.

"The Abish Village . . . to the—" Blaze stopped when he saw my face and sighed. "You are going after him completely blind."

He was right. Every word out of his mouth was new to me, devoid of any meaning. I was blind. I knew nothing of the world outside the Pit, and what was more, I was the least ready of anyone to leave it. I wanted to scream at Blaze, his blue eyes pitying me and my ignorance. I wanted to hit him, make him say something that I understood.

He shook his head and sat against a tree, his hand rubbing his neck. Watching him, I understood one thing: I needed him.

"Show me," I said, my voice trembling.

"Urgle—" Av started, eyes wide at the very idea.

Blaze had a knife out, his eyes following the blade as he thought. It glistened for a moment in the moonlight. I looked up through the crooked branches and shivered when

I didn't see the thick black smoke of the Fire Mountains. There was only naked, night sky. I'd never seen the moon before, a blotchy, pasty orb, alone in an expanse of empty blackness. Once I had Cubby back, I never wanted to see its blue glow again.

"A Beginners' Temple isn't exactly a place I want to be, Urgle," he said.

If I could have killed him in that moment, I would have. It was *his* fault the Tunrar came, *his* fault Cubby was gone. And here he was telling me what he wanted or didn't want? Searing hate pulsed through my flesh and I stomped on his ankle. He let out a snarl as Digger shoved me away from him and Av was by my side, arm out to hold me back.

"We helped you when you needed us!" I bellowed.

He looked at me, his eyebrow arched with amusement.

Av pressed harder against my chest to keep me back.

"I am a Brother," said Blaze, revealing the ankle I'd slammed with my foot. His scar was almost white in the moonlight. "I'll take you to get the boy back. But once I get you to that Temple, you're on your own."

"I'm going with you," said Av.

A lump formed in my throat. He didn't have to, but I was relieved Av would be with me.

"Uh, bad idea," said Blaze, getting to his feet. "The Baublenotts are tough going. Keeping my eye on one of you is going to be hard enough."

"I can take care of myself," Av snapped.

"I'll go," said Digger.

Digger had the same opinion about Cubby as Fiver, though he wasn't as vocal about it. What did he care if the little scroungee was dead? Surprised, I turned to face him, and when I did it all made sense. He was standing straighter than I'd ever seen him, shoulders back. He was showing off for Blaze.

"We don't need you," I spat.

"Makes more sense for me to go than Av," he said. "It's almost my Leaving Day. Better for you to have two grown men helping to get Cubby back than just one."

Two men. What a moron.

"Crow, you have to go back, take care of Fiver." Digger's leader voice was out again. "And tell the others what we're doing."

So everyone knows what a hero you are, I thought.

"Crow?" said Av quietly. He was looking at his feet, kicking lightly at the dirt. "Would you look out for Goobs for me?"

I felt my stomach churning again. I hadn't even thought of Av, what he was leaving behind in order to help me.

Crow nodded and Av patted his back in thanks. Then Crow turned to me and grabbed my hand. "Good luck, Urgle."

I nodded, feeling the lump in my throat rising as he disappeared back into the shadows of the forest, back to the Ikkuma Pit, back home to the Brothers.

"Well," said Blaze. "Ready?"

For the first time I was aware of a chirping sound all around me, the rustling of the trees in the darkness as the cold wind slithered through their branches. I shivered. I'd never been this cold. Even with my Brothers standing there with me, I was overwhelmed by the feeling that I was alone.

EIGHT

It was morning when we finally emerged from Nikpartok Forest and found ourselves trudging through endless rolling hills of long grass. The sun lay low in the sky, scorching my eyes. I had to stare at my feet to avoid the pain, but my legs up to my waist were hidden by the thin grass swishing as we forged ahead.

"This is impossible," Digger whined behind me. "My head is killing me and I can't see anything!"

Several paces ahead, Blaze was hacking at the grass with a long blade.

"It's because you're used to the Pit being so dark," he said. "Most places don't have the smoke cover you boys have grown up with. Takes a while but you'll get used to it."

I hoped he meant the sun and not the ache in my head.

"One day, you might even enjoy it."

I doubted that.

The pulsing in my head thumped to a rhythm that matched the throbbing where Crow had patched up my leg. There was nothing to be done about that either.

I looked over at Av. He was waving his hands around his head.

"What's wrong?" I asked.

"Buzzing," he growled, swatting and clawing at the air.

"The bugs?" said Blaze. "They should go away once we hit the village."

Digger stopped in his tracks and hung his hands pathetically. "When's that gonna be?"

"Not too far."

My head turned from left to right, and all I could see was rolling hills of long grass. Waves of bright green opened out beneath a sky the color of Blaze's eyes. It looked so strange, like they didn't belong together, the green and the blue fighting to overtake the horizon.

The ache in my head throbbed and I looked at my feet, trying to find relief from the brightness.

"Ugh," Digger growled, "how long does it take to get used to it?"

Blaze shrugged. "Not long."

"How long did it take you?"

He paused to think. "You know, I don't know. I don't remember any of that sort of thing bothering me."

As the buzzing Av was talking about made its way to my ear, I found that hard to believe.

"It's the loneliness that gets to you more than anything."

None of us said anything, too distracted by the brightness and the buzz. But Blaze went on. "You're lucky, actually, being out here with each other." His blade struck the grass with an angry slash. "All I could do was cry the first few nights. It was the scariest thing, sleeping alone."

With a final swat, I managed to make contact with the

buzzer and the noise stopped. Sleeping alone. I'd never thought about it before, and I realized I'd never slept alone. Every night of my life had been spent in the A-Frame, with Cubby sleeping above me for the past few years. Where would he sleep tonight?

"Did you boys, ah . . . ?" Blaze paused, his eyes on his feet as he forged ahead. "Did you know my Brother?"

"Cole?" said Digger.

I bit the inside of my cheek and looked to Av. He was kicking at the grass, and gave me a quick glance before he bent down to inspect something by his feet.

"Yeah, we knew him," said Digger.

Blaze nodded and bit his lower lip. He looked like he was going to say something else, ask how Cole died maybe. It had been something with his insides; there was nothing Crow could do for him. He cried and screamed for days, no matter how many tonics Crow forced down his throat for the pain. Finally, he just stopped. But Blaze didn't ask. Just one nod and that was it. If it had been Cubby, I wouldn't ask either.

Cubby. My stomach twisted at the thought of him out there by himself.

Av stood up with some kind of root, giving it a careful sniff. "You ever run into anyone?" He gave it a lick then spat, tossing the root away. "Brothers, I mean."

Blaze just shrugged. I guessed that was a no and my stomach twisted further. No. How big was it out here? How far away could those things take Cubby from me?

"So you mean," said Digger, "you didn't find your Big Brother?"

Blaze shrugged again. "I never really looked."

Digger's whole face seemed to sag and it was no se-

64

cret why. Digger had been really close to his Big Brother, Steamer; they even talked and moved the same. He'd mentioned more than once that he planned to find Steamer after his Leaving Day. I never understood it. Things hadn't been that way for me and my Big Brother.

Without noticing, I quickened my pace and I passed by Blaze.

"Urgle?" he said. "Wait up."

With a few more steps, my legs were free of the cool long grass and I stood on a wide dirt pathway.

In front of me were dozens of little wood and stone structures, like the A-Frame but cleaner, bigger, sturdier. Hordes of men, burly and covered in colorful skins, moved in and among them, undisturbed by the blinding light of the sun. So many. If my eyes tried to focus on one single person, five, six, and seven crowded my view of them.

"Abish Village," said Blaze. "Other side of that we start on the Baublenotts."

"And that's where the Temple is?" I asked.

Blaze nodded and led the way.

There were people everywhere. Men behind cluttered stands lined the streets, shouting in grumbles to one another, to Blaze, and to the rest of us.

"Who are they?" Av asked.

Blaze raised an eyebrow. "It's an Abish village. Behold, the Abish."

What I beheld, I didn't like. The Abish were fat and loud and stunk of sweat; they were like Larmy pigs. They shoved by as though they didn't see us at all, and on each face that passed me I searched for something familiar, something like us. I didn't see anything. Their faces were fatter, hairier. They looked tired and hard.

"Think we'll find one of the Brothers?" asked Av beside me.

I shook my head. I doubted we'd find any Brothers living among men like these.

A man with a feathered garment on his head rammed into Av with his swollen belly. Av leaped back into a crouch, dagger drawn, and Digger and I readied ourselves for a brawl.

The man stared at Av a moment, then threw up his arms and made a "Bah" noise before stumbling off in a different direction.

"Hey! Hey!" Blaze rushed over to Av and tried to pry the dagger out of his grip. "Put that away, will you? Wanna get us arrested?"

Av didn't answer, I guess because like me he had no idea what that meant, though Blaze didn't seem to be waiting for us to respond. He pulled a pouch from his pocket and began counting a handful of silver pieces as he continued farther through the crowd.

Av looked to me, his wild eyes making it clear he didn't want to venture into the masses. Neither did I. I shrugged my shoulders, defeated, and followed after Blaze.

Children shrieked and giggled as they ran by and through our legs. Large, rusted metal objects rattled as they plowed through the streets. I recognized some from the Landfill back home. They hissed and roared as they thundered by, the people they carried shouting at everyone to get out of their way. I could see Digger ahead of me, cowering behind Blaze with his eyes shut tight, his hands over his ears. Sharp whistles cut through the air as men waving colorful fabrics fought to get my attention; the jingling of trinkets and screams and cries of babies surged and waned as people moved by me. I'd never heard noise like this, and a new panic swelled in my chest.

Blaze stopped by a stand and spoke to the boy behind it. I wanted to know what they were saying, what Blaze was up to, but the words were not mine and I wondered where Blaze had picked them up. Did all Brothers who left learn how to speak with the words the Abish used? Or just Blaze? Spongy, golden-brown bricks were lined up along the table, and their sweet scent mercifully overtook the smells of sweat, spice, and dirt that had been assailing my nostrils. The boy handed Blaze two of the sponges, and Blaze gave him several silver pieces in exchange.

A man behind the stand to my right was barking at me, waving something as if he needed me to take it from him. It was bright and orange, and when I looked closer it looked like Blaze's flint box. All the trinkets at the man's stand looked like Blaze's flint box. Different colors and sizes all dangled from hooks and lined the walls. Cubby could have had any color he wanted. The man grunted again and I reached out to take it, to keep it for when I got Cubby back.

Blaze's hand shot out and grabbed me by the wrist. "No, no. He wants you to buy it."

"Buy?"

Blaze rolled his eyes and shoved the flint box at the man. "Trade for it," he told me. He said a couple of words I didn't know, and the man reached down, pulling out a dark colored bag. Blaze turned it over, dumping out some shiny-looking stones. With a nod, Blaze flicked the man another piece of silver.

I saw Av standing in the middle of the street. He was being bombarded by another large Abish man offering him objects that looked a lot like Blaze's pistol.

"Hey, no!" yelled Blaze, Digger still clutching to his back, which left me to be the one to collect Av.

Higher voices screeched around me, strange words flooded the air, and the ache in my head was becoming a pounding pain. The light, the loud noises, the weird smells—I threw my arms around my head, covering my ears and eyes for a second of relief. Suddenly I felt someone pulling on my arms, then tugging at my back. There was a smell, dust and body odor, choking my throat. I opened my eyes and found myself surrounded by several drooping creatures pawing and droning at me in crackly voices. Crevices and lines dragged down their faces, heavy bags and flaps of skin sagged around their eyes and mouths.

The fattest dangled a string of feet that looked like Cavies' in front of my face—bright, vivid colors I'd never seen. I pushed it back from me and reached for my knife but it wasn't there. I cursed. I'd left everything behind at the Pit. Others moved in, grabbing at the air around me, wailing and singing.

I wanted to run, but everywhere I turned another creature had its hands out to grab me. Their circle tightened and I screamed for Av but I couldn't even hear my own voice over the sound of their screeching chants.

"Clear off, you old crones," said Blaze, reaching through the creatures and pulling me towards him.

I clutched to Blaze as I caught my breath and watched the hideous group disperse.

"You all right, Urgs?" asked Av, jumping as people brushed past him.

"What the Mother were those?" I gasped.

Blaze unclenched my hands from his forearm. "Abish women."

My heart stopped. As I watched the fat one shaking her string of colorful Cavy-like feet at passersby, I felt my headache pulsating and every image of the Mothers I'd ever thought up warping and changing. In my head, they'd been like us—bigger maybe, nasty and mean too, but still like us. Never had I thought they'd be like this, like some creature from Cubby's nightmares.

I looked up at Blaze; he was smirking. "Old ones, for sure," he said. "Really old ones. But women just the same."

"How'd they get like that? Get all"—Digger's face was twisted, he looked in worse shape than me—"all melty?"

Blaze threw back his head and laughed. "Wrinkled? It happens. Live long enough, you'll look like that one day."

My stomach churned and Av and Digger went white.

"Come on," said Blaze. He thumped me on the back twice, and reluctantly I followed him deeper into the village.

We hadn't walked far when the crowds of people thinned and the buildings of stone and wood seemed to close in on us. They shaded us from the sun, and now that I wasn't squinting my eyes felt swollen and tired.

"I think we should have a break," Digger said, sitting down on the side of the road.

Av and Blaze stopped to look at him, but I kept moving.

"No," I snapped.

"We've been on the move since last night! We can't keep going forever."

"Rest, then," I told him, continuing to follow the road through town. I couldn't have been happier to leave him behind.

"He's right," said Blaze.

I whirled around in time to see him taking a seat beside Digger, who had a maddeningly smug smile on his face.

"I don't have time to stop!" I yelled. "We might be able to catch up to Cubby!"

"Look, Tunrar won't go through this village," Blaze said, pulling out his pistol. "They've had to go all the way around and enter the Baublenotts from the east, which is tricky. We're making good time, Urgle."

I scowled but Blaze didn't seem to care; he was filling the pistol with his new fancy stones.

I looked to Av, hoping for some support, but he was watching the road behind us.

"I think someone's coming," he said.

With a click, Blaze shoved the pistol back into his belt and got to his feet beside Av.

Beyond them I saw a rickety wooden contraption coming up the road, pulled by a large, fat creature with a droopy mouth I didn't recognize.

"What sort of creature is that?" asked Digger, licking his lips like he planned to spear it.

"Sibble Cow," said Blaze.

A group of children ran along the front and sides of the contraption, more riding on top.

The contraption jingled and rumbled, and the creature, a Sibble Cow, groaned in protest as the children struggled to pull it along the road. They began to wave and squeal, smiling when they saw us. Av couldn't help himself and tried to hold back a chuckle.

"Don't encourage them," said Blaze. "They'll rob you blind if you let them get too close."

"What exactly are you worried they'll take?" I said. None of us had left the Pit with anything more than a weapon or two, or nothing at all in my case.

Several of the children, giggling and laughing, ran over,

speaking in more words I couldn't understand. They reached out, pulling at my clothes, inspecting my fingers, grabbing and touching.

Blaze roared at them, and the children screamed and ran after the contraption as it rumbled by.

Only one stayed behind. The child couldn't have been more than six, long sandy-colored hair flowing down to his elbows, his colorful clothes blowing around his knees. I'd never seen a child so clean; he didn't look like a person should.

"A girl?" asked Av quietly.

The child giggled.

"She's wearing a dress," said Blaze. "She's a girl, all right."

My body went rigid, and I could feel Av and Digger tense too. A girl. The preferred baby. Someday a Mother. Her big brown eyes sparkled at all three of us, ignoring her companions disappearing in the distance.

She waved a little hand.

None of us moved.

Having got no reaction, she sighed and looked at her feet.

Blaze yelled something at her in words I'd never heard, trying to shoo her away, but she ignored him. She glanced at Digger, then Av as she twirled a strand of hair on her little finger. Then her brown eyes focused on me, and her smile faded.

Uneasy, I looked to Av and Digger, who stood still as stone.

The girl walked right up to me and I moved back. She had her hands out to touch me and I braced myself, as if a single touch would burn.

Her cool little hands grabbed my left one and she opened it up, staring at my palm.

I tried to pull away but she whined and pulled harder.

"What's she doing?" I said, struggling to sound calm.

Blaze rolled his eyes. "She's reading your palm."

"What?"

Her fingers tickled as she ran them up and down the creases of my hand. Then she gasped and dropped it.

When she looked back at me, her eyes were filled with tears.

She spoke, her melodic voice blurting out a string of strange words. When she realized I couldn't understand she turned to Blaze, urgency drenching every quick little sound.

Blaze scratched the base of his neck, his brow knotted as he listened.

A numbness seeped into my hand. I didn't have the words, but I could read her tone, read Blaze's face. Whatever she'd read on me hadn't been good.

"What's she saying?" Av asked.

"Nothing," he said. Then he yelled at her in her own tongue, but she screamed over him, begging him to listen.

"She's a crazy Abish girl," he said. "Fortune-tellers and liars, the whole lot of them."

Her big brown eyes fixed on me again, and I had the sudden urge to give my hand back to her. Liar, Blaze called her. What did she have to lie about? Blaze scratched nervously at his neck and I wondered who the real liar was. I looked back at the girl. She sighed dramatically, seeing there was nothing more she could say to me, and her frightened expression melted away until she wore the same happy face she had when she'd first waved at us. She shrugged and waved again, then turned and ran off after her friends.

The four of us stood baffled, watching her skip down the road and around a corner.

"But what did she *say?*" asked Digger.

"She said you're ugly," Blaze snapped.

I looked down at my open palm, trying to see whatever it was she'd seen. Nothing. I couldn't see anything on my skin. In my brain, there was only Cubby.

"We're not resting," I said.

"No," agreed Blaze. "We should keep moving."

NINE

The sun's mind-numbing glare had died to a soft orange glow, reminding me of the Hotpots back home.

I traced the lines on my hand as we walked, my mind on Cubby.

An elbow bumped mine and I looked up to see Av walking beside me.

"Are you all right?"

I put my hand down quickly and nodded.

"It hurt?" He gestured to my hand.

"What hurt?"

He grinned. "You should wash it."

I smiled. Just this morning I would have expected a single touch from a Mother, even a little girl, to burn. It hadn't burned. But still, a feeling lingered on my palm where her fingers had touched me. Maybe Av was right, maybe a rinse would help get rid of it.

"What do you think she told him?" Av asked, nodding to Blaze who walked just a few paces ahead.

"I dunno," I said. "She looked pretty upset."

She looked horrified and I had no idea why. How she

could learn anything about me from staring into my palm, I'd never know. But she'd been frightened, that much I understood. By what? Blaze knew. I couldn't stop worrying that it had something to do with Cubby.

"Hey," said Av, and he smacked my hand where my fingers were probing the lines, "she got over it pretty quick too. You saw her; she was smiling when she left."

That was true. Liars, Blaze had said. And maybe she had been lying.

The Abish dwellings came to an abrupt stop, the road curving around and leading us back the way we'd come. Beyond it, more rolling green hills.

"Where are we now?" I asked.

Blaze stepped across the curving road and into the thick, tall grass.

"End of town." He pointed straight into the rolling hills. "Baublenotts are just off that way; we should be there before it gets dark."

"By Rawley," breathed Digger from somewhere behind me. He'd been dragging his feet the whole time and had fallen pretty far back. Some leader. He'd been deadweight from the start. "What the Mother is this ugly thing?"

I turned and when my eyes found what he was looking at, I nearly fell backwards.

A monster, a giant hideous yawning monster towered above the village, its hideous gaping mouth silently screaming out into the distant hills. Av steadied me before I could go down.

"It's a Shibotsa," said Blaze. "Abish superstition. Let's go."

Its arms reached the sky, crooked skinny things, and as I stared at the claws I could see they were branches. The legs were hidden by the large sheets of flowing, fraying fabric that clothed the thing, but I could see a small part of its legs poking out the bottom. They were logs.

"They made this thing?" I asked.

Blaze nodded. "It's supposed to be an angry spirit. Keeps trouble away."

Av lifted the Shibotsa's skirt and inspected what was underneath. "Spirit?"

"Like, I dunno, a monster, I guess."

Blaze had already turned his back on the beast, completely disinterested, and started making his way through the long grass.

"What kind of trouble are they keeping away?" I asked him.

At that Blaze stopped and turned back. He clicked his tongue three times while he rubbed his neck, trying to decide how best to answer. "The war."

He stood there and I waited.

He sighed, realizing I didn't know what he meant. "Let's just say the Abish want to keep out someone else's fight."

"Whose?"

He smiled, and a laugh that sounded more bitter than amused escaped him. "The Beginning's."

There it was again. *The Beginning.* I could feel my brow go heavy. What did that mean? What kind of trouble comes from the start of something?

"So this thing," said Digger, kicking at the base of the Shibotsa, "is gonna fight off something for the Abish?"

"Of course not. It's just a symbol, just—" Blaze let out a groan and ran his fingers through his hair. "It's a warning to anyone who would come and cause problems here. Did your Big Brother ever tell you he'd get your Mother to take you back if you didn't stop misbehaving?"

All three of us nodded. Every Big Brother has said that at least once to their Little Brother. I felt a pain in my gut, knowing I'd said it to Cubby enough times. He never believed me, though.

"Well, the Shibotsa here is like the Mothers. If you cause trouble, she'll come and get you. Make sense?"

It made sense enough for Digger, who abandoned the Shibotsa and made his way into the grass after Blaze. It didn't make sense completely for me.

"This . . . Beginning," I said. Blaze watched me as I tried to figure out what I wanted to ask. "It's a people?"

Blaze sighed. "It's more like an idea." He rubbed his neck and looked down at his feet.

"I don't understand."

"I told you it's not so easy out here," he said with a sad smile. He turned back to the rolling hills and headed out towards the Baublenotts.

This was how Blaze liked to talk, lots of words but never saying anything. It was frustrating, and I was getting tired of him just telling me what I felt was only part of the whole story. "Hey," I barked, making him stop. "But what *is* it?"

He clicked his tongue obnoxiously, staring up at the Shibotsa for what seemed like hours. Then finally: "You have Rawley, right? He's a real Brother, right?"

I nodded, and Digger and Av joined me.

"Have you ever met him?"

Digger laughed. "He's been dead forever. No one's met him."

Blaze looked to Digger. "So how do you know he's real?"

"B-because," Digger said, "because he's Rawley. Because he was the First Brother. He just did . . ."

"But you've never seen him, right? You don't *know*."

"He's dead," I said, annoyed that Blaze was doing his confusing talk again. "We just know."

"No," Blaze said. "You don't know. Not really."

"What's your point?" Everything that came out of his mouth was frustrating, like he thought we were stupid.

"My point is, the Beginning is lots of people's Rawley story. It's something they tell themselves they know."

Untouched. That was what he called me when he sat down on my cot. He was right. Everything in this world outside the Pit was so confusing, so frustrating, so loud. How could any Brother survive on his own? My stomach twisted. How could Cubby? He was so small, so kind. This world was too ugly for him, and now he'd seen it. If I got him back, would he even still be like he was?

I quickened my pace and followed after Blaze. I had to get him back, and do it fast.

TEN

We stalked the fringes of the Baublenotts for hours, back and forth, while Blaze prodded the waterlogged earth, humming and hawing, deciding on the safest entrance to the still marsh.

I was losing my patience with him. This was taking too long.

Av and Digger sat together on a large slab of rock with their heads in their hands, bored and tired, while I paced around, unable to hold still.

Blaze stopped in front of a large pool of water and sank the large stick he'd been walking with for the hundredth time. The stick stopped halfway, and Blaze pushed and wiggled it cautiously.

"Well?" I asked.

Blaze ignored me and stared ahead into the green swamp. The sun was almost gone, the water still as glass, large rocks and vegetation poking out in patches.

Blaze stepped into the pool and he sank up to his knees. He prodded again with the stick, then cautiously took another step.

Av perked up and watched Blaze hopefully, while Digger's head bobbed as he fought sleep.

"Can we go now?" I pressed.

Blaze kept on ignoring me. He was silent and watchful, staring into the marsh.

"Nope."

Av sighed, resting his chin back in his hands.

Restless, I slid down the muddy bank to the edge of the pool.

"Blaze!" I barked, crouched in the mud behind him.

He whipped his head around and shot me a vicious look, a finger to his lips, then went back to watching the dead marsh.

"Blaze," I whispered, "this is as good a place as any! Let's just go!"

Blaze poked at the floor of the pool again, then nodded.

"Yeah," he said. "We'll go in this way."

I let myself collapse in the mud with a breath of relief. "Thank Rawley."

Blaze hoisted himself out, back onto the bank, and walked over to Av and Digger's rock. Digger was now fast asleep and Blaze smacked the back of his head. Startled, Digger yelped as he fell off the rock.

"Have a bite and we're on our way," Blaze instructed.

I sat up. "You're kidding!"

"Uh, no."

"No, no, no," I said, scrambling to my feet. "There's no time to forage or hunt for food. If you see something as we go, fine. But we can't stop; you took hours finding a way in!"

"No one's foraging," he said, pulling out the spongy golden bricks he'd taken from the boy in Abish Village.

He broke off a huge crumbly piece of the first and stuffed

it in his mouth, then handed a piece to Digger, who waited with an outstretched, greedy hand.

He handed a piece to Av, who sniffed at it suspiciously. "What is it?" he asked.

"Some kind of Abish cake," said Blaze through stuffed cheeks. He threw me the other brick and I caught it. I broke off a small piece and sniffed. The smell, different and spicy but still nice, made my ravenous stomach growl. I was starving. I looked at Av. He had taken a bite and didn't seem to be enjoying it, his face scrunched up as he chewed.

I touched it lightly to my tongue. It was pleasantly sweet. I popped the piece into my mouth. I'd never tasted anything so sweet or moist. What was Av so repulsed about? I took a huge bite out of the brick.

"It's just flour and sugar," Blaze went on. "Some egg in there, bit of wolf urine."

I choked and spat it out.

"What?"

"Oh, I doubt there's any real wolf urine in there," he laughed. Relieved, I went back to eating. "Abish have all kinds of cakes for different things, sell them to outsiders as remedies for heartache, bad luck, and such. Wolf urine supposedly makes people strong, agile, fearless. With the war going on they sell tons to frightened soldiers and their worried families."

I took another giant bite, but Av was still unconvinced.

"I doubt the Abish risk taking on a wolf every day to make cakes that they only sell for a couple of silver pieces," said Blaze, and I nodded in agreement. "Probably just take it from local dogs."

I stopped mid-chew and glared at Blaze.

"It's good for you," he said, then winked.

"What's a soldier?" asked Digger as I wrestled with my painful hunger and the sudden urge to gag.

"Soldier?" said Blaze. "It's a person who, I dunno, fights for . . . whatever someone important tells them to, I guess."

"Fights what?" said Av.

"Other soldiers." Blaze was shifting in his seat. "Other soldiers who are doing whatever some other important person told them to."

"Why would they do that?" asked Digger.

Blaze was quiet a minute, struggling to figure out an answer. I watched him scratch his neck for the hundredth time that day, and caught sight of a blue mark on his skin, half hidden by his shirt. The blue was bright and rich; I'd never seen such a color on skin.

"Put it this way," he said finally. "Let's say you met Rawley, the First Brother."

"I told you, he's dead," said Digger.

Blaze rolled his eyes. "If he wasn't dead. Say he came to you and told you his Mother was coming to the Pit, to take over, and he needed your help to fight her. Would you do it?"

"Yes," said Digger. Av and I nodded.

"That's a soldier," said Blaze.

"Someone who helps Rawley?" asked Digger.

"No," said Blaze. "They've all got their own Rawleys."

"Who?" I asked.

Blaze sighed. We were exhausting him with questions, and I felt nervous that there was so much we didn't know.

"Look," he said. "For some soldiers, the Beginning is their Rawley . . . and for others the Beginning is their Rawley's Mother."

I didn't understand, and by the look on Av's and Digger's faces they didn't either. This Beginning, this idea, was growing more frightening all the time. How could it be so awful to one person, how could it take away Cubby, and still be as good as Rawley to someone else?

Blaze was facing the still marsh, his pale blue eyes looking like they did the night he'd been sleepwalking—looking inside, not out. I watched as his hand slowly reached for his belt, where the flint box had once been, only to remember it wasn't there. He scratched at the blue mark on his neck again, almost like he had to whenever he talked about the Beginning. A question rolled around in my mouth, begging me to ask it, but I wasn't sure I wanted to know.

"What's the Beginning to you?" I asked.

Slowly he looked at me and I glanced at his neck. He moved his hand away and got up, but it was too late, he knew I'd seen it.

"It's nothing to me," he said. "I don't care either way." He picked up his stick, slid down the muddy bank, and stood beside the first pool. "Should we get moving here or what?"

I bit the inside of my cheek. He was lying. He had to be. The Beginning was something to him. A big something. Even if he refused to admit it.

Shoving the last piece of Abish urine cake in my mouth, I got up and followed. Av threw his cake away and slid down the bank, while Digger yawned and stretched, reluctantly joining us.

"Here's the deal," said Blaze. "You step where I step, nowhere else."

We nodded.

"I mean it. There're sinkholes, caverns, black water. Only step where I step."

We nodded.

"You do what I do. If I start running, you run. If I hide, you

83

hide. Exactly what I do. If I start running in circles singing 'Wamby the Wiggly Wooga,' you'd better be doing the same."

Digger snorted.

"And keep quiet. We don't want to attract any attention."

"From what?" asked Av.

"Anything."

Blaze turned his back on us and slid into the pool.

I looked out on the marsh and the still, quiet surface of the water was no longer sleepy and dull, but alive, waiting for me. I thought of the Hotpots, of how dangerous they were, but at least they didn't lie. Their orange glow and intense heat gave you fair enough warning. If you were dumb enough to get too close, well, the Hotpot did its best to tell you not to. But these quiet pools, they kept their dangers secret.

Blaze, watching me standing on the bank, nodded for me to follow and I let my foot sink into the water, a nagging itch overtaking my palm where the Abish girl had touched me.

The water was freezing, and a jolt of pain from my Tunrar wound rippled up my thigh like a cold burn. My bare feet met the bottom, swallowed by several inches of mud. I had to wrench my foot with every step to dislodge it and my calves quickly started to ache.

Every five steps there was new terrain. The water would drift around my ankles at one moment, next thing I'd be up to my waist. Large slabs of pink-speckled rock sat in random places, shrubs growing on and around them. Blaze would carefully lead us across slippery surfaces, pointing out the crevices—large black gaps in the rock that led down to nothing but darkness.

Everything was damp and wet, even the air, and I felt a chill seeping into my bones as the night washed over us. Av walked behind me, his teeth chattering. The Ikkuma Pit was hot, sticky. Its air pressed against your skin, engulfed you, hugged you. In the Baublenotts, the air was different: thin and cold, unwelcoming.

Something howled in the distance and my heart stopped.

"Tunrar?" I whispered.

"Wolf," said Blaze and Digger at the same time.

We moved on in silence. The disturbed water laughed at me as we waded through, the pools of the Baublenotts giggling at our weary effort. I shivered.

"Hey," whispered Digger. "Wait."

Av and I turned to see what his problem was, but Blaze kept going, prodding at the ground before taking a step.

"There's something behind us," said Digger, looking back the way we'd come.

Av and I watched.

The marsh was well lit by the moon; silver light reflected off the still water. There was nothing to see but rock and vegetation.

"You're fine, Digger," sighed Av, turning miserably to follow Blaze.

Digger looked back at me. "I was hearing something, a person. I'm sure of it."

I shrugged and motioned at him to follow.

He jerked but didn't move.

"What are you doing?" I asked.

He ignored me, shifting his hip awkwardly and scowling at the water.

"I can't—" He twisted his knobby legs. "My feet are stuck."

I looked back to Blaze and Av. They weren't far ahead but they were still moving.

"Twist them out," I said. "Let's go."

"I'm trying!" Digger snapped.

I sighed and walked back to him. It was only four steps, but I was so tired that I cursed at the knowledge that it was four steps I'd have to take again.

"Gimme your arm," I said.

Annoyed, Digger slapped the water. "What the Mother is that gonna help, Urgs? You need to grab a leg."

I didn't like his tone and considered leaving him there. I settled for splashing him instead, and smirked as he growled. I bent down and grabbed a leg, the water swallowing me up to my neck.

"Ready? Go."

I pulled as Digger wiggled; we both grunted with the effort.

We heard Blaze whistle and stopped.

Av and Blaze had their attention to the west. Blaze pointed to his ear and Digger and I listened.

There was a faint whispering noise, or a sizzle. I'd never heard anything like it but it was coming our way.

The sound surged, then grew faint, another surge, then faint. Digger and I watched Blaze.

The whispers suddenly became a loud, violent hiss, and Blaze threw his stick and took off running as best he could, Av hot on his heels.

"Come on!" I yelled at Digger.

I tugged and jerked at his caught leg and it trembled with his own desperate effort to pull it free. He grabbed onto me to steady himself as he strained, his fingernails digging into my back, begging me not to leave him.

With a sudden jerk the leg came free and I fell back into the pool, submerged up to my neck. Digger grabbed me and hauled me to my feet.

The two of us trudged after them, frantically searching

for Av and Blaze. They were gone, and I had no idea where Blaze had stepped, but the hissing was louder, closer—I couldn't worry about his path.

The water was so deep and thick with mud that we were getting nowhere fast, and I thought my pounding heart would burst from my chest any moment.

I stopped and grabbed the nearest log for support. I clutched my chest and gulped in the damp night air.

There was no sign of Blaze ahead. To the west, a small cloud was closing in, the hissing sound coming with it.

Digger leaped out of the water onto a giant hill of pink rock. He reached out for me and I grabbed his arm. He hauled me up and we ran.

Legs free from the mud and water, it felt like flying.

Digger was in front, yelling at me to move faster.

I tried. I pumped my legs and nearly slipped a dozen times on the slimy, wet rock.

Digger let out a scream and disappeared down a crevice in front of me.

Before I could stop myself, I felt the rock beneath me disappear and I fell too.

I caught the edge of the rock.

My arms trembled and it was all I could do to hang on. I tried to pull myself up but my body couldn't do it.

"Digger!" I screamed.

I heard him below me whimpering in pain.

"My leg!" he called. "I think I broke my leg!"

The hissing was louder. I couldn't turn around, but I knew what I'd see. The cloud was coming.

"Blaze!" I shrieked.

I tried to pull myself up again and cried out as I nearly lost my grip.

I closed my eyes tight and saw Cubby's face, his body trapped in the arms of the Tunrar, his little hands desperately reaching out for me.

"BLAZE!" I shrieked again.

It was then I heard a familiar roar and wondered if I'd dreamed it.

I hadn't. A pair of hands grabbed my arm and pulled.

Digger had definitely been seeing someone.

"Gotcha!" said a voice.

I opened my eyes and saw the big ugly face I thought I'd never be happy to see.

"Fiver?"

Fiver pulled me out of the crevice and I gripped onto him, hugging him for the first time in all our lives together.

Av and Blaze were rushing towards us, Av nearly stopping mid-sprint when he saw Fiver.

"Come on!" Blaze yelled.

The cloud was even closer, and I knew what it was now: an angry swarm of some kind of insect.

I ignored Blaze and threw myself to the ground to look into the dark hole for Digger. I couldn't see him.

"Move it, Useless!" Fiver begged.

"Digger!" I cried. I reached frantically into the darkness. "Can you grab my hand?"

The swarm was nearly on us, dancing and pulsing. Fiver grabbed me and pulled me back. I saw the cloud, black up close, its angry din numbing my ears. We ran down the slope of the stone towards Av and Blaze, and I turned my head back every three seconds to the swarm.

Av grabbed me when I reached him, my legs nearly giving out.

The thick swarm hovered over the crevice.

"Urgle!" Digger shrieked. "Come back! Urgle!"

"Digger!"

Blaze jumped on top of me, his hand covering my mouth.

The swarm disappeared into the crevice and Digger began shrieking, screaming.

"What's happening?" Av demanded.

"They're eating him," said Blaze.

I struggled under Blaze and he let me up.

Av, Fiver, and I ran to help Digger, his wails of agony carving into my brain.

We stood at the edge, staring into black, hopeless, the crackling hiss of the swarm mixing with the shrieks of Digger.

He wasn't calling for me anymore, he wasn't even saying words, just screaming, screaming, and I had to get him out.

"Help me!" I said, grabbing Av by the arm, steadying myself as I tried to climb down to get to him.

Suddenly Blaze was beside us, pistol in his hand. He grabbed me by the back of the neck and threw me away from the edge. I landed on my back and watched as Blaze pointed the pistol into the crevice.

"What are you doing?" barked Av.

With a loud bang, Digger's screaming stopped.

The only sound was the crackling hiss of the swarm.

"Let's go," Blaze said. "We need to get as far away from here as we can before they finish him."

ELEVEN

Death took Brothers in the Ikkuma Pit often, and we were used to it. Little boys around Hotpots with too much courage, or sometimes too little, often fell in. Illnesses that Crow couldn't treat sometimes took infants. Hunting accidents were rare, but not unheard of.

Digger's death had been different. It hadn't been an accident.

We walked through the night, none of us speaking, trying to wrap our heads around what we had just witnessed.

"How—?" rasped Av suddenly. His eyes were puffy from tears, focused on nothing, his face worn and ghostly in the moonlight. He was hunched, dragging himself along, and I felt my body doing the same. "How—?" he tried again, and swallowed hard. His eyes shifted towards Fiver, but still he did not look at him. "How did you find us?"

Fiver cleared his throat and shook his head, his damp curls dripping from the wetness; he too refused to look at anyone. "Wasted is dead. I wanted—" He struggled to keep his voice steady. "I want the Tunrar dead. I just followed your trail. Useless over there doesn't exactly hide his tracks."

I didn't care why Fiver was there, why he'd saved my life. I just knew if he hadn't, I'd have fallen in with Digger.

"Thank you." I didn't even recognize my own voice. It was hoarse, just as exhausted and worn out as the rest of me.

Blaze was twenty paces ahead of us. He marched through the Baublenotts just as alert as ever, Digger's death affecting him less than the cold night air.

"He didn't let us try," whispered Av. White circles of moonlight reflected in his hard, puffy eyes. He was glaring at Blaze and breathing through his teeth, his jaw locked. I could see the anger raging inside him, in Av, the boy who never lost his temper. I didn't recognize him. He was wild and seething.

"Av?" I placed a hand on his shoulder and he jerked away from me. I jumped back, afraid for the first time he might turn on me.

"Not even *try* to save him!" he hissed. "Who is this guy, Urgs?"

He was looking at me now, rage and fear distorting his brow.

"You were right, back at the Pit; we don't know anything about him. Where'd he come from? Why were those Tunrar things after him in the first place? He hasn't told us anything. And we what? Follow him without question?"

I had to turn away from that accusing glare. He was right and I had no response. All I knew was I needed Blaze. Blaze could take me to Cubby . . . I hoped.

Av ran in front of me. "Aren't you watching him? The man is a nervous wreck!"

"What are you talking about?"

"Mention the Tunrar, or the Beginning, and the guy fingers whatever that mark on his neck is. It's like a tic!"

I knew what Av was getting at and I didn't like it. The pieces of Blaze that were coming together in my head were making a picture I wanted to ignore. Had to ignore. But it was getting harder all the time. I felt the world around me straining, ready to break.

"How do you know he's not one of them? Huh?"

"Because the Tunrar were trying to kill him," I hissed.

"He killed Digger," said Fiver. Fiver was tired but he was calm, not on the edge of control like Av. "It wasn't the swarm. It was him."

In my brain I could still hear the hissing of the quiet after Digger's screams had stopped.

"The Piq Flies killed him!" I heard Blaze call.

The three of us turned to see him silhouetted in the moonlight.

"He was still alive," snarled Av.

"He was dead!"

Av said nothing, but his fierce eyes were locked on the dark figure of Blaze. I knew Av better than myself, but not like this—those eyes, that rigid body, clenched fists. Av was the good one. Out of all of us, Av was always the good one. For Av, there was right and there was wrong, there was no in-between. Digger's death had been wrong. There was no way to fix it, to make it right. And for Av, I knew that meant Blaze was nothing but wrong.

The water laughed in the eerie silence as Blaze waded through it, back towards us. He stood in front of Av, confident under that wild glare.

"I saved him," he said. "I ended his pain."

Av threw a punch, taking Blaze by surprise and sending him on his back in the muddy water. Av launched himself on top of him, screaming savagely, pounding with fury on Blaze's wounded shoulder.

Blaze bellowed in pain and flailed his limbs, struggling to get a hold on Av, but it was no use. Av landed blow after blow, while Blaze splashed helplessly.

I watched in disbelief. Fiver took a step back, seemingly impressed by Av's ability to take down a full-grown man when he was so upset.

Av's hands grabbed Blaze's neck, and with one violent shove Av plunged Blaze's head under the water.

"Av!" I yelled. "Stop! Av, stop!"

He didn't hear me. He was miles away from me in a fit of anger. Somehow, I just knew he wouldn't stop until he'd made it right the only way he could. He wouldn't stop until he killed Blaze.

I thought of Cubby, his cheeky smile and wheezy laugh. I needed him back, and that meant I needed Blaze.

I threw myself onto Av, knocking him off the drowning man, and the two of us landed side by side, face-first in the mud.

Blaze flew to his feet, coughing and sputtering.

I reached for Av, and again he shrugged me off, staying on his hands and knees in the mud and struggling to get ahold of himself.

"Do you know what Piq Flies do?" Blaze shouted. "They eat you from the inside out! They go in through your mouth, your nose, your ears, eyes! They eat and eat and you can feel them ripping at your flesh!"

I watched Av dry heave and winced at the memory of Digger's shrieks.

"Did you want him to feel that?" Blaze shouted again.

"He was alive," Av groaned.

"What did you think you could do? Pull him out of there? Then what? Didn't you hear him?" Blaze was yelling at us, frantic.

"Stop it!" I begged.

"He was in agony! Even if we got him out, they'd still be inside him!"

"Stop!"

"His lungs, his throat, his ears! Eating!"

Av heaved again.

"The second they swarmed him, he was dead!"

I watched Av squeeze his eyes and grit his teeth. Tears rolled down his cheeks, streaking his dirty face.

"He was dead," Blaze finished. "And I saved him." He pulled his long sopping hair back off his face, scowling at us. "You want to know the truth?" He laughed bitterly. "She told me he'd die."

My palm tickled and I got up, slowly. "She?"

He laughed again, but it was obvious he didn't find it funny. "The Abish girl. The crazy fortune-teller."

"What?"

"I didn't tell you because I didn't want to scare you, but that's what she said."

"It was *my* hand!" I protested.

Blaze nodded and shrugged. "Let's just say she didn't see a lot of good coming out of this little adventure of ours, all right?"

My knees were shaking, but I forced myself to sound as firm as I could. "What exactly did she tell you, Blaze?"

"Nothing very encouraging." He turned away from me and wiped at the mud on his trousers.

"Stop telling me what you want me to know and tell

94

me what I'm asking you!" I grabbed his arm. "What did the Abish girl tell you?"

"That your Brother's dangerous!" he shouted.

I let go and stepped back from him. I looked to Av—he was just as confused and frightened as me.

The Baublenotts fell quiet again and I thought of Cubby. Had the Abish girl seen him somewhere in the lines on my hand?

"Cubby? Dangerous?" asked Fiver suspiciously.

Blaze shrugged. "I don't—" He was calming down, regretting having said anything. "I don't know. I had a hard time understanding."

"Right," said Fiver.

"My Abish isn't that great. A lot of it was just gibberish."

I felt a hand hit my leg and saw Av reaching for me. I grabbed him and pulled him to his feet.

"Just stop talking, Blaze," he sighed. "No more. Take us to the Temple. That's all you need to do."

TWELVE

It was a silent hike through the Baublenotts after Av attacked Blaze. Silent and cold. I couldn't even look at Av, afraid he'd ask me for more answers, afraid I'd have to admit he was right. We couldn't trust Blaze. But for Cubby, what other choice did I have?

I stared at my palm again, and even in the darkness I could see something was wrong with the skin. My fingers were shriveled and splitting, and they shook as I tried to inspect them. My whole body shook; I was shaking all over and my limbs were starting to feel numb. I could feel the seal from the Sticky Willow losing its grip on my skin, the water washing away the stick. Every part of me was soaked; my skin felt cool and clammy to the touch. It was the Baublenotts. I could feel it draining my strength from my body. It didn't want me.

"You all right?" called Blaze.

Before I could answer him, my right foot sank unexpectedly and I lost my balance, falling into Fiver. He grabbed me by the arm, steadying me on my feet. I could hear the chatter of his teeth.

Beside me, Av was trembling too, hugging his arms tight to his naked chest, hunched over and breathing through his teeth. We were not all right.

It was like the Pit. It chose who to keep and who to kill. It chose to keep Rawley, keep my Brothers and me, and all others were intruders. But to the Baublenotts, we were the intruders.

"We'll stop," said Blaze. "I'll find us someplace out of the water to warm up."

I wanted to tell him no, but my mouth was shaking too much, and I had trouble getting the words out. "B-but," I stammered, "we can't stop!"

"You've been in the water too long. The cold can kill you just like anything else, Urgle," said Blaze. "What good will you be to your Brother dead?"

We marched a long way before Blaze was able to find a dry enough spot for us, and by then I could barely walk straight anymore. Any problem I had with stopping was long gone. I crawled out of water that was up to my waist and onto a slippery stone surface. The spot Blaze had picked was a large grouping of pink-speckled Baublenott rocks surrounded by drooping trees and thick brush. The stones were damp, but well above the water, and I immediately felt relieved to be standing in the open air.

Av and Fiver were standing close to me, the three of us watching as Blaze approached a giant pile of dark stone off to our right. The large stones were smothered in moss and vines, and Blaze set to work picking off chunks and collecting them in his arms.

"Toss me that knife," he ordered. Av made no move to do it, hugging himself and glaring as his teeth clattered together. Blaze didn't seem to care much, and marched up to Av, pulling the dagger out of the waistband of his Larmy skin. Av said nothing, but their eyes met for the briefest moment, and if Av hadn't been so cold, I worried he would have attacked Blaze again.

Blaze undid his outermost skin, a heavy, dark hide with sleeves. He handed it to me.

His bare arms were thicker than my legs.

The hide was way too big for me and I held out my arm for Av to come closer. He jerked away, refusing to touch anything that came from Blaze.

Blaze didn't notice—he was heading for the surrounding droopy trees.

"What are you doing?" I asked.

"You need to warm up," he said. "I'm starting a fire."

"Everything's soaked," said Fiver.

"Yeah, everything is." Blaze was at the edge of the stone floor, touching the sides of one of the droopy trees. Apparently dissatisfied, he moved to the next. "Pay attention: these are Bauble Weepers," he said, digging his knife into the dark black bark of the tree. "Lots of layers to the bark." A piece of the bark peeled off with the knife like dead skin, and Blaze ripped it away with his hand, throwing it into a nearby pool. "Peel away enough," he said, "you'll hit the dry stuff."

With a grunt he pulled away more bark, discarding what he didn't want. After a couple more pulls he got to the bark he wanted to keep. It was white and thin.

"Come sit down," he said, making his way back to the moss-covered stones. None of us moved at first. I still didn't trust him, none of us did, but the promise of fire when everything was so wet was too tempting, and I joined him on the ground.

Blaze lay his Bauble Weeper bark down and picked up his moss, squeezing a large bunch of it between his hands. I watched him work, though I thought it was a wasted effort when I saw the water dripping out of the moss.

Blaze reached behind him and pulled out a bladder bag from his belt. He reached in and took out a chunk of rock.

He ran Av's knife along the edge and a spark flew.

"What is that?" I asked him. I already knew what it was.

"Flint," Blaze said, focused on his work.

Flint. He kept it in a bladder skin. I remembered Cubby's little fingers, reaching out for the smooth green trinket dangling from Blaze's belt. He said it was a flint box. If his flint was here, what had he done with the box?

I glanced over at Av, but he hadn't heard it, too focused on the strange tinder Blaze had collected. Fiver was picking at the bark. After a few sparks the fire was well on its way. Av and Fiver sat with their noses practically roasting on the flames, obsessively studying every piece of juicy Baublenott that had gone into creating it. No Brother could make fire when it was wet; there had never been a reason to. The Pit was so dry no one could believe a fire would start around so much water. I could just imagine the looks of amazement on the faces of the Hunting Party when Av and Fiver showed them they could do it.

The heat immediately went to work, breathing life back into my limbs and drying my cool, damp skin. But still, my insides felt cold, my gut sloshing with a chilly feeling that Blaze was hiding more from us.

As the rest of me tried to warm up, there was a burning in my thigh. With the light of the flames I could see that my Tunrar wound was half open. Black bits of Baublenott filth clumped inside the flesh and my nose wrinkled.

"You need to tie that up," said Blaze, nodding at my leg. He undid his belt and held it out to me.

I waited, wondering if he knew I'd noticed it was missing his flint box.

"Go on," he said.

I took the belt, and his focus went back to the flames. He didn't know.

I pulled the belt as tight as I could, and the sting forced a hiss from behind my teeth. At least it was covered now.

The fire popped and cracked, dulling the creature sounds of the Baublenotts. Staring directly into the flames, I could almost trick myself into believing I was in the A-Frame.

"We should build one for Digger," Av said, his eyes glowing in the firelight. "Send him off to Rawley proper."

I shivered and rubbed my arms. Av was right. We'd just left him, with no way for Rawley to find his fire. The Brothers say there's a fire, a flame that belongs to the Pit, burning inside each of us. When Cole died, we all took him outside and laid his body on the ground. Crow lifted his head back gently and opened his mouth wide, so Rawley could see his flame, so Rawley could find him and take care of him. That's how it is for all Brothers. Except for Digger. We'd left him, not making sure Rawley could see his flame.

Av was on his feet, and headed for the Bauble Weeper Blaze had stripped. Fiver sighed and stood up to help.

Blaze began pulling at the moss behind him, gathering it up for Av, when Av hurled a stick that connected with Blaze's hand.

"Don't!" he snapped. "His *real* Brothers will do it."

Blaze gritted his teeth, massaging his hand where the

stick had struck it. I watched Av and Fiver in the darkness, their backs to me and Blaze alone by the fire.

I held out my hand to him. "We'll need Av's knife."

Blaze tossed it to me, focused on the damage to his hand.

"And your flint."

He slapped it down in my palm and leaned his head back against the dark moss-covered stones.

I lowered my voice. "What happened to your flint box, Blaze?"

He stayed leaning against the stone, but I could see him tense, see his jaw lock. His eyes shifted over to me. "I lost it, I guess."

I stared at him, daring him to make me believe that.

"Probably when your friend jumped me," he said.

I kept on staring and he stared right back. He didn't have the flint box when Av attacked him. He didn't have it in Abish Village, even. He was lying.

He sat up, waiting for me to ask more, his eyes locked onto mine.

"Urgle." It was Av. I looked up and he and Fiver stood in front of me with arms full of Bauble Weeper. "Are you coming?"

"Yeah," I said, and Av and Fiver made their way across the rocks to find a spot to say goodbye to Digger. I took off Blaze's heavy hide and handed it to him with one last narrowed glare. This conversation wasn't over, and I wanted to make sure he knew that.

"Take some of the moss," Blaze said. "Squeeze it out, it'll make a proper flame."

I knew Av wouldn't want me to, not if it was Blaze's idea. But he'd used it on his fire and it was crackling and glowing nicely. We needed a nice flame for Digger.

Without acknowledging Blaze, I pulled away enough moss from the stones at his back to fill my arms, and left him to sit alone by the fire.

I could see Av and Fiver, shadows in the dark, setting up far from Blaze. As I walked over, I could feel the weight of the flint and Av's dagger in my hand. Poor Fingers. The dagger I'd made him would never find its way to his Big Brother's hand now. I'd have to give it to him when we got home.

And then I'd finish Cubby's.

I handed the flint to Av, and after a few unsuccessful attempts Digger's fire lit up our faces and burned warm and bright.

"Think Rawley will find him?" asked Fiver.

Av didn't say anything, just wiped at his face with the back of his wrist and I could see his eyes were wet. I hoped so. The thought of Digger alone in the Baublenotts made my throat start to swell, and I swallowed hard. But that was Rawley's job. He came for all of us, took care of all of us when the time came. He'd find Digger. The fire was bright, the flames were big. He'd come.

"When it was Wasted—" Fiver stopped short and cleared his throat, pretending to hack something up, then spat at his feet. "When it was Wasted, Crow told me I should, ah—" He stopped again, kicking the spot where his spit had landed. His chin was pressed to his chest, but even still I could see it quivering. I felt a sudden sting in the pit of my stomach. Fiver had done this before, for Wasted, his Little Brother. And none of us had been there with him.

Fiver let out a breath and looked to me. "He told me I should say something to Rawley. Ask him to come, and that I should"—he shrugged—"I should tell him the kind of things Wasted liked, so he'd know."

By the fire, I could see flames reflected in his glossy eyes, and my own started feeling hot, knowing it could have just as easily been me who spoke to Rawley.

Av shifted on his feet and let his hands fall behind his back as he stared into the flames. "Rawley," he started, his voice heavy and dry, "this flame is for our Brother, Digger. Digger really likes setting snares; he was always very good at it. He had a Little Brother named Fingers." Av stopped and wiped at his eyes again. "But he looked after everyone. Sort of tried to be a Big Brother to us all, I guess."

I'd never thought of it like that, but Av was right. He'd bossed us around, but really he was just trying to take care of us all.

I looked up into the sky—wisps of silver-lined clouds drifted in a black sea of stars—and I wondered if that was how Rawley would find our Brother, if he'd ride it to Digger's lonely spot in the Baublenotts and take him away. And Cubby. He was alone in the dark somewhere. Would Rawley watch over him? I squeezed my eyes tight and swallowed again. I made a silent wish to Rawley, begged him not to come for Cubby. Not now. It would be me who came. It had to be me.

THIRTEEN

When the flames had finally dwindled on Digger's fire and the embers were cooling, the smell of roasting meat drifted lightly on the breeze. My stomach growled and I looked over to Blaze's fire. The flames were still high, and they were licking at something Blaze was roasting over it.

"We'll be at the Temple in the morning. You should eat something," he called out to us. "Come have some Marmos."

I didn't know what Marmos was, or where he'd got it from, but the smell was enough to tell me I'd like it, and I started to make my way over. Fiver was already ahead of me.

Av didn't follow. I turned back to see him, his arms crossed and trembling in front of Digger's dying embers.

"You should eat, Av."

"I can hunt for myself," he said. "I don't need *him* to take care of me."

If anyone knew Av didn't need someone to take care of him, it was me. But he hadn't eaten anything but a nibble of the Abish cake. He had to be just as hungry as I was. And the cold was seeping in again. I could hear his teeth starting to rattle together.

"At least come warm up," I tried. "We'll have to get going soon. You might as well be dry."

He bounced on his knees and stared at the cinders, deciding whether or not to listen to me. I could tell he didn't want to. We'd all been shocked by Digger's death, but it was weighing on Av the most. Digger was Av's Brother, my Brother. Digger was one of us. It was the "us" part that Av was always reminding me about. It was what we were, what we had. We were Brothers. And Blaze took Digger away from us. How could I ask Av to trust him?

"You're right," I told him. "About Blaze, I mean."

He looked at me. That was a good start. He'd been so mad, so different. Av hated Blaze, and Av never hated anyone. But I needed Av to put up with him, just a little longer.

"I don't trust him either. But he's all I've got to get to Cubby, Av."

Av bounced on his knees again, not saying anything. Just talking about Blaze made him so furious. I hated seeing Av so unlike himself.

"At least use him for his food," I said, hoping to get a laugh. "Might as well get something out of being around him."

He didn't laugh, but the corner of his mouth twitched, and that was enough for me. He dropped his arms and stepped away from the fire. "Let's hope Marmos is better than Abish cake," he grumbled.

I grinned, happy to hear him sound more like the Av I knew, and we walked back together to where Blaze was sitting with Fiver.

They were mid-conversation, Fiver prodding Blaze with more questions. Fiver bit into the back side of some roasted bird, his cheeks stuffed as he talked. "So she's his Mother?"

105

he said, staring up at the dark moss-covered stones at Blaze's back.

By the light of the fire, I could see faces where I'd pulled away the moss. They were carved into the stone. Six young faces, one on top of the other. The second from the top caught my eye—a girl with a gentle smile.

Blaze shook his head, poking at the fire. "She's his sister."

He handed me a stick with a sizzling roasted Marmos skewered on the end, and I tore off a crispy leg, then passed it to Av.

"I'll bet I know which one their Mother liked best," said Fiver, picking a bone out of his mouth.

"There was no Mother," said Blaze.

"How's that?"

Blaze yawned and rubbed his eyes. "It's just an old story."

Fiver went on chewing, watching Blaze expectantly. As a storyteller, Fiver couldn't resist adding a new adventure to his memory, a new tale to tell the Brothers.

Blaze shook his head and stood up beside the stones. "There's about a hundred different versions," he started. "There's thousands of pillars just like this one, in every village and city, but they're all different in their own way, and so is the way they tell it."

"So what's the story?"

He took a deep breath and stared at the stones as though he was exhausted just thinking about it. He let his hand rub the base of his neck. "Basically, six babies were said to be born out of the fabric of the earth, three sets of twins. Folks call them the Sacred Six."

"What's that mean?" Fiver asked.

"They were gifted." He pointed to the two faces on the bottom. "See here, these three dots?" There were three

106

dots marking their foreheads. "That means these brothers were born of the desert. That's Keely and Hines. People say they had the power to make things grow. They could make the crops obey them—that was their gift." He moved up to the next two faces, three diagonal lines marking their foreheads. "And here the lines mean these were the brothers of rock and ice, Amid and Azul. They were gifted in moving the earth, carving canyons and raising peaks."

His hand moved up to the girl's image on the next set, his fingers pausing on her round cheeks. Her forehead was marked by three circles, like ripples on water. Blaze ran his thumb along the rough line. My eyes drifted to the face of the twin brother above her, and only now did I notice it had been scratched out.

"And them?"

Blaze sighed, leaning against the stones with one hand, his other brushing hair out of his eyes. "Those two are the water twins. Their gift was water; they could manipulate it to their will, according to the story. That's why they've been put at the top of the pillar here, I guess. Folks say they were born right here, out of the waters of the Baublenotts."

"What happened to her twin?" asked Fiver, pointing at the scratched-out face.

"Some people don't like him much," said Blaze. "According to some people, he caused a lot of problems."

"For who?"

Blaze's hand went to his neck and Av looked to me. I bit into the flesh of the warm Marmos, waiting for Blaze to go on.

"Well, these guys, for one," he said, waving at the faces below. "He wound up killing all of them, except his sister."

107

I stopped mid-chew and Fiver sat up straight. "Why would he do that?"

Blaze sat down and poked at the fire. "He wanted to take her sons away from her."

"So?" said Fiver. "What'd she care? Probably didn't want her sons in the first place."

I nodded. That was how Mothers were.

Blaze smiled. "Yeah, that's what I said when I first heard the Sacred Six story. She wanted him, though. She fought hard to keep him."

"Did she? I mean, did she keep her son?" I was surprised to hear Av speak, surprised he'd want to listen to anything Blaze had to say.

I glanced over at Fiver, and his eyebrow was up. I knew how Av's question must have sounded to him. In the Pit, a question like that sounded like something a Mother seeker might say.

Blaze shrugged. "Not with her. She hid him," said Blaze. "Hid him where no one would find him. No one ever did."

I looked at her quiet smile, the tiny dimples on either side of her mouth. Her eyes were black, blending in with the color of the rock. They were empty stone, but there was something there, maybe it was the fire, something that made me feel like she knew we were talking about her.

"What was her name?" I asked.

"Belphoebe," said Blaze.

"And him?" asked Fiver, motioning to the scratched-out face with the leg of his Marmos.

Blaze sighed, his voice heavy. "Ardigund. His name was Ardigund."

The stone was scratched out so badly all I could make

out was the shape of his left cheek, a single dimple just like his sister's still intact. "What happened to him?"

Blaze bent down and picked up a loose rock. He stood up and smashed it into the scratched-out face, several pieces flaking away where he hit it. "He found the Beginning," was all Blaze said.

He stood there, staring at the twin without a face, his fists balling at his sides. There was hate inside him, but why? What had the Beginning done to Blaze that had him so angry?

"Did you?" The question fell out of my mouth before I could stop myself. Blaze turned, his brow knotted. "Did you find the Beginning? Is that why you hate them?"

Blaze dropped his head, and a laugh that was steeped in something black escaped him. I didn't care if he thought it was ridiculous. He knew so much about them, knew so much about us, and Cubby's life depended on everything he knew.

"Why are you even here, Blaze? Why help us?"

He raised his head to that, his lips tight. He squatted down by the fire and looked at me with those cold blue eyes. "Listen to me, because you need to know. Living outside the Pit, you have to be a lot of things if you want to survive. You've got to be a hunter, a warrior, a soldier like those men we talked about, husband, father. Some stick, some don't." He pointed at me, making sure I was really listening. "One thing I've always been is Ikkuman."

I felt pain in my throat, a warm rush to my cheeks.

"I'm a Brother. We take care of each other. That's why I'm here, Urgle. And that is why I'm getting you to that temple."

I nodded and looked away, fidgeting with the belt he'd given me to cover my leg. I wanted to believe him. I wanted to know for every one of us, not just that Blaze was telling the truth but that after all of this, after everything, somehow we'd still be us.

FOURTEEN

The Beginners' High Temple was a sight I'd not been prepared for. In the morning, Blaze led us deeper into the Baublenotts, where we came to a wide river. Loads of rushing water flew past us and spilled over the edge of a cliff. "The Falls of the Faithful," Blaze called it. At the edge of the falls, in the middle of the river, sat the Temple. It was a large stone structure of rich blues, greens, and reds.

Blaze had done what he promised; he'd taken me to it. But still, I didn't know what to think. He was a Brother, it was so easy to forget because of how confidently he made his way through the world outside the Pit, but he'd said it himself, he was a Brother. And Brothers take care of their Brothers. He'd done that. He'd brought us here. But then there was Digger. And the lies. He lied about his flint box, I was sure of it. How could I trust him? I could see plain enough that Blaze's speech hadn't made much of an impression on Av, who'd been ignoring Blaze all day. Blaze killed Digger. That was the truth as far as Av needed to know it.

Rushing water spilled through the base of the Temple, flowing through the open doorways while Tunrar sat on the rooftops, bathing in the sun, their hideous cries fighting the thunderous volume of the great falls. The weedy vegetation of the Baublenotts grew in and around its turrets as if trying to hug the evil thing.

"How are we supposed to get to it?" Av yelled over the noise.

Blaze scratched at the blue mark again, and I felt my stomach twisting.

"Well, the docks are pulled back," he shouted. "See those long wooden things?" He pointed to several long, flat structures that sat parallel to one another, the current slamming them violently into the base of the Temple. "Normally those docks attach to each bank of the river. Seems they don't want visitors."

"What do we do?" said Fiver.

"Swim it."

I watched the white water barreling past us, listened to its angry roar and felt my jaw lock. I'd known it. As soon as Blaze scratched his neck, I knew he'd tell us this.

"It's not possible," said Av.

"It is," said Blaze, nodding.

"Oh yeah? You done it?"

Blaze made no reply. His eyes were on the water.

"You've done it," Av said incredulously.

Blaze said nothing, his gray-blue eyes now watching the Temple.

"Blaze?" I said. "Have you swum this?"

"What?" Suddenly he was back from wherever his mind had gone, focused on us. "No. No, I haven't."

"But you've seen it done?"

He nodded.

"He's lying," Av spat.

Blaze's eyes flashed to Av. "Kids younger than you have done this swim and I've seen it."

"And drowned!"

Blaze withdrew into himself again, staring at the water. "Some make it," he said quietly.

There were memories inside his head, ones he'd never share, and I wondered if I even wanted to know. Fiver moved in beside me, his back to Blaze.

"What do *you* think?" he asked.

I couldn't remember a time when Fiver'd ever cared what I thought about anything. Even still, I had no idea what to think. Cubby was right there, in that temple. All that stood between me and him was this raging water, and I'd never swum before.

"Can you swim?" I asked him.

Fiver shrugged. "Once or twice I gave it a shot when the Hunting Party went out."

I nodded. Av had told me about swimming with the Hunting Party; he'd said none of them had been terribly good and I didn't think the water had been like this.

Av was crouched by the side of the river, watching me and Fiver expectantly.

"Cubby's in there," I said finally. "I'm going."

"Going," Fiver said, nodding. "Wasted's dead. I owe it to him."

Av stood up and wiped a drip from his chin on his shoulder. "Cubby's in there," he agreed regretfully.

"In that water," Blaze said, "you fight with everything you've got in you. Understand?"

I nodded.

"Everything. That current is going to sweep you right over those falls if you let up for a second."

Fiver and I nodded.

"What are you still doing here?" said Av. "You got us to the Temple, now go!"

When Blaze looked at me, I hardened my face and made sure he knew I agreed with Av.

"Goodbye, Blaze," I said. Fiver crossed his arms and stepped in beside me. We didn't trust Blaze. It was time for him to leave us.

Blaze smiled sadly, and nodded.

"Take care, Brothers," he said.

I stood and watched him go, a twinge of regret pricking my brain.

He stopped and turned back, motioning for me to follow.

Fiver and Av were crouched by the water, preoccupied with deciding how best to approach the Temple.

I hurried over to Blaze.

"What?"

"Look, I know this is your Little Brother and all," he started, "but I need to say this to you. If you make it across, make it in there, and you see him—"

I felt a sudden surge of panic. "Will he be dead?" I blurted out.

"No, no."

"How do you know?"

"Just—if you see him, think a moment. You need to ask yourself this, and . . . you may not like your answer."

"What?"

"If it turns out you can't have him, if you can't take the

boy outta there"—he bit his lip and looked away—"is he better off there than, than with Rawley?"

I took a step back. "What? What do you mean?"

"I mean," he said, his eyes boring into mine and hiding something more behind them, "he's better off not breathin' than breathin' in that place."

I took another step back. "No. I—" I couldn't understand what he was saying. I wouldn't. Cubby was coming home with me. "Why would you even say that?"

Blaze pointed to my hand, and I looked at my palm. "Just take that second to really think. A lot depends on your decision," he said.

I felt dizzy a moment. I thought about demanding that he tell me what the Abish girl had told him, but the look on his face stopped me. I suddenly didn't want to know—in fact, I was terrified.

"If you get in there, ask to see Gorpok Juga. They won't say no after you've made that swim."

"How do you know all this?" I asked.

"If they ask you questions, be brief with your answers, you understand? The less they know about you, about any of us, the better."

I nodded.

"And don't mention my name. It won't make you any friends in that place."

"Were you one of them?"

Blaze laughed and pulled aside his shirt, revealing the blue mark, the whole of it for me to see. It was raised and bubbly, the blue had been seared into his flesh. "See this?" I stared. The symbol was one I'd seen before, three circles like ripples on water. I'd seen it on the forehead of the girl in the stones, the girl called Belphoebe. But this was different. A line ran through the whole of it.

"It means I'm not anything. Not to them."

It had to mean something. "One decision," Blaze added, scratching his neck. "Make sure it's the right one."

At that he turned and walked away into the Baublenotts, leaving us to get Cubby back on our own.

FIFTEEN

I stood trembling on the banks of the angry river, my Brothers on either side of me. Av and Fiver looked confident and ready like the great hunters they were—Av tall and lean, broad shouldered, Fiver thick and muscular, eager to attack the water.

I wasn't strong like them, or fast. I was useless. I breathed deeply, trying to get a hold of the terror that was overwhelming me. I'd come this far for Cubby only to drown and be thrown over the biggest waterfall that I suspected had ever existed.

Before I could muster my courage, Fiver dove in. The raging torrent swallowed him up, and I closed my eyes. I couldn't handle the death of another Brother, not now.

I heard Av laugh beside me. "Look at him, Urgs!"

I opened my eyes and saw Fiver fighting against the water that struggled to throw him, to carry him away, but he kept swimming. He was swallowed in a flood of white, then reappeared, forging ahead. He was doing it.

Emboldened by Fiver's success, Av leaped in.

"No, wait!" I yelled. I wasn't ready. I couldn't do this.

Av's head appeared above the racing flood, sputtering and coughing, but he was fighting with all his strength, following Fiver.

A Tunrar atop the Temple let out a loud shriek and my stomach knotted. I saw it standing at the edge of the roof, its head bobbing up and down as it watched Av and Fiver eagerly, excited to witness their deaths.

I saw Cubby in my mind, then the gummy mouth of the Tunrar that had beaten me senseless in Nikpartok. I felt a swell of rage and plunged into the waters too.

The force of the water was crushing and I kicked and pulled furiously at it, fighting to reach the surface. My body was thrown forward, then pulled back, the racing current unable to decide if I should live or die.

My head surfaced and I gasped for air. Water crashed down on me, and my body spiraled and turned, dragging me closer to the falls.

I surfaced again and gulped for air. Water ambushed my mouth and lungs, and I coughed and sputtered, kicking and clawing for the Temple. In that moment I was all alone, desperate to stay alive. I couldn't see anything but white, and the occasional deep blue and greens of the Temple.

I was so close, I had to do this. I lashed out at the water, forcing my way through. White engulfed me again, this time slamming my injured leg against the riverbed. I felt the water carry me farther down, closer to the falls, and I refused to go, kicking through the pain. I'd deal with it later; I couldn't let myself feel it now.

In front of me I could just make out the wood of the docks crashing against the Temple. I reached for it and missed, the current dragging me farther away. With the last bit of effort in me I went for it, and my arms wrapped around the wooden railing. I tried to catch my breath, lungs bursting, as the water rushed over me and the dock. My leg was throbbing, but I was alive.

"Look at you, Useless!" Fiver clung to the front of the second dock, not far from me. "I thought you'd be a goner for sure!"

I glared at him, but he was grinning ear to ear. My scowl broke and the two of us laughed.

"Where's Av?" I called.

Fiver looked around him, and I did the same. Suddenly frightened, I looked at the water behind me that was pouring over the edge of the falls and scanned for any sign of him.

"Wanna give it another go?" There was Av, standing on the stone of the Temple. He was sopping wet and smiling.

Relieved, I hauled myself onto the wooden dock that was being jostled by the current. I reached for Av, who gave me his hand as I climbed over the railing and set my first foot on the wet white marble floor of the Beginners' Temple.

SIXTEEN

The water tirelessly swamped our feet, rushing over the marble and beating at the massive golden doors before us.

Av and I clung to each other for balance, the strength of the current pushing at our ankles, threatening to knock us over.

"Mother seeker!" Fiver cursed over the thunder of the rushing water as he fell over and his body was slammed up against the doors.

Av and I scrambled to help him to his feet as one of the golden doors opened slightly. A voice growled at us in words we didn't understand from somewhere behind it.

Av looked at me, his hand on his dagger securely fastened to his Larmy skin, and nodded. He was with me. Cubby was inside. Whatever waited for us behind those doors, Cubby was inside. I took a deep breath and placed my hand on the door, pushing it open wider.

As soon as I did, the door flew open and two large Tunrar pounced, landing on Fiver and Av, holding them down in the pounding water. Av cried out, the scream quickly fading into a gurgle as the Tunrar shrieked and gave his head another slam.

A hard metal point pressed at my chest and in front of me stood a large, broad man. He was slightly melty, not as extreme as the Abish women, but still, his face was worn. His long white hair was braided and wrapped around his neck several times and he was snarling. My mind reeled when I saw his forehead, the familiar blue mark staring back at me. He pressed his shiny blade harder into my skin and spoke with a calm voice that didn't match his hard expression. I trembled when I couldn't understand what he'd said.

"Gorpok Juga!" I blurted out, suddenly remembering Blaze's instructions. "Get me Gorpok Juga!"

The man raised an amused eyebrow. "Ikkuma?"

"Yes! Yes!"

The man smirked and snapped a command at the Tunrar. They released Av and Fiver with a violent shove and disappeared behind the man back into the Temple.

Av and Fiver got to their feet beside me, Av rubbing the back of his head, Fiver wiping blood from his nose. I saw him reach for his knife, ready to chase after the Tunrar and get his revenge, but I stomped on his ankle. He growled and glared at me, but I couldn't let him ruin my one chance to get Cubby back.

The man opened the door, motioning at us to enter. Cautiously, I stepped over the threshold, Av and Fiver behind me.

The door closed with a deafening bang, and the sound of the rushing water quieted to a constant trickling. A thin layer calmly flowed over the floor, tickling my toes.

I scanned the large room, desperately hoping to see

Cubby, but it was empty save for several Tunrar sniffing each other in a dark corner. The whole place was dark, with only little patches of natural light from the open windows. The walls were made up of vibrant stone—blues, reds, greens, and black.

Av had his neck cranked upwards to the immensely high ceiling; he was lost in the pictures that decorated it. He swayed a bit, and I steadied him. He grabbed the back of his head, and when he removed his hand I saw it was stained with blood.

Fiver hadn't noticed any of it. His eyes were on the Tunrar in the corner—dark, angry eyes that burned for what had been done to little Wasted. I quickly glanced at the large man, hoping he hadn't noticed, but he had. He was watching Fiver, his finger running along the edge of his spear.

A voice echoed through the room and a short, extremely melted woman entered from a dark corridor, escorted by the two Tunrar that had leaped on Fiver and Av. Her hair was in the same braid as the man's, wrapped around her neck.

The man spoke to her, and I thought I caught him saying "Ikkuma."

The woman's pink eyes lit up and her mouth hung open. On her forehead was the blue mark, just like the one I'd seen on Belphoebe's forehead. But Blaze, his had a line running through it. It was different. *I'm not anything…*

"Ikkuma boys?" she breathed.

I nodded.

"So young?" she said with a knotted brow. "So young. How you come here?"

"I'm here for my Brother," I told her in a voice that I hoped sounded something like Digger's leader voice.

122

"Brother?" she looked to the man, and he shrugged. She studied the three of us, and her eyes filled with pity. We were drenched to the bone; Fiver was bloodied and Av was swaying. She studied Av a moment, then shot the large man an angry look. Again, he shrugged.

Then she turned her attention to Fiver. While carefully looking him over, she briefly turned her head and spoke to me. "You swim?"

She spoke funny, and her accent was strange.

"Yeah," growled Fiver, answering before I could even open my mouth. "So give us what we came for."

"You know me?" she said, still staring at me.

"Gorpok Juga?" I asked.

She nodded. "How you know me?"

Blaze's warning turned over in my mind, short answers. "A friend," I said. "Please, my Brother? He's Ikkuman."

She shook her head. "Brother I no know."

"He's little," I said, stepping closer to her, my heart pounding. "And really skinny. He has blond, blond hair. He coughs a lot at night, and he's missing these three teeth." I shoved my fingers in my mouth to make sure she knew which ones I meant.

She spoke to the large man. She pointed to her hair, then her teeth, interpreting what I'd said for him. He was stroking the bald head of one of the Tunrar, and nodded. My stomach leaped.

"You know him?" I asked.

"No, no, no," she said. "I no know."

"Liar," growled Fiver.

Her pink eyes flashed to him and he shifted, looking down awkwardly.

Turning her attention back to me, she smiled.

"Ikkuma boys swim river." She smiled wider and let out a laugh. "Ikkuma boys swim river! Very brave boys!"

Av stumbled forward a moment and I grabbed him, he was in bad shape. She watched me warmly, and my body flooded with hope.

"I help you." She motioned to the corridor. "Come! Aju Krepin. He find brother if brother here."

This was it. Cubby was as good as mine.

She turned and walked into the dark corridor, a Tunrar following behind.

The large man nodded at me to follow and I hurried after her. Av struggled to do the same but tripped over his own feet and Fiver caught him before he fell.

"Av?" I asked.

He slurred something I didn't understand while Fiver inspected his head. Fiver held up his hand to me. It was stained crimson with Av's blood and I was stuck. Gorpok Juga was moving farther away, my chance to get Cubby back moving away with her, but Av needed help.

Fiver was staring at me and I felt myself hating him. What did he want me to do?

"Are you coming?" I demanded.

At that, Av struggled to follow me, forcing Fiver to help him along.

"Come, Ikkuma boys!" Gorpok Juga called.

The splash of the water under our feet echoed in the dark corridor and I could hear several Tunrar following beside us, keeping to the walls.

One of them slinked in close to me, hissing. I could feel its hot breath on my forearm and smell its stink.

Gorpok Juga whipped around at the sound of the hissing Tunrar.

She yelled something at it and then brought down a fist repeatedly on its shoulder. It let out a yelp so helpless and pitiful I couldn't believe it came from the Tunrar. Gorpok Juga was yelling at it, and the large man who'd been following behind us suddenly ran up, brandishing his large blade. I cried out as he came towards me, but he grabbed the Tunrar by the shoulder and sliced at its back with his sword.

The Tunrar backed away into the shadows, whimpering.

"Tunrar Goblins," said Gorpok Juga. "Impressive killers but must stay in place."

"What place?" I asked, trying to slow my pounding heartbeat.

"Shame," she said, rounding the corner and leading us outside onto a red marble walkway. The raging river poured through the railings and it took me a moment to figure out how to keep my balance. My leg hurt where the belt kept the gash together, fighting me as I tried to keep myself steady against the force of the water. Gorpok Juga didn't seem to be bothered. "Tunrar Goblins offend Beginning long time ago. Must forever pay, serve for forgiveness."

She stroked the head of the bald Tunrar at her side.

We came to another set of golden doors and Gorpok Juga pushed them open with ease.

"In here, Aju Krepin."

I looked back to make sure my Brothers were with me. Fiver was now practically carrying a drowsy Av across the walkway. He needed help, to rest. I wanted to tell him to stop, to tell Fiver to take Av back, but I knew Av wouldn't leave me.

"You come?" Gorpok Juga asked.

I nodded, swallowing my fear for Av, and walked through the door.

The room was bigger than the first, brighter and more colorful. The perfume of a thousand different types of flowers drenched the air. People sat in groups all over the place, the Beginners, all with hair like Gorpok Juga, the blue mark on all their foreheads. Statues, small and large, adorned the walls, the mark chiseled into all their faces.

In the center of the room stood a large altar raised above the floor, the only dry place in the Temple, I suspected.

Tunrar sat around it, lazily, while still more people sat all over it. On a large blue stone at the top sat a young man with a golden braid and draped in robes of lapis. He sat up when we entered and addressed Gorpok Juga, his deep, smooth voice echoing off the stone walls.

She answered him, the heads of all the people in the room turning to face us.

The young man nodded and spoke again.

"Aju Krepin welcomes Ikkuma boys," said Gorpok Juga.

I was so flustered. The man's softly tanned face was full of kindness, genuinely welcoming us, while dozens of his followers watched me with wary eyes.

The man spoke again.

"The Beginning brings you home," Gorpok Juga interpreted.

"Get on with it, Urgs!" Fiver yelled as Av drooped to his knees.

"Tell him I want my Brother," I said.

Gorpok Juga nodded and turned to Aju Krepin, interpreting with less force than I would have liked. He pointed to Av and spoke.

"Your friend is badly wounded," said Gorpok Juga.

"You can thank your disgusting Tunrar for that!" shouted Fiver.

Gorpok Juga didn't interpret that, and Krepin spoke again.

"Aju Krepin say, he prays Beginning keep him," said Juga. "Aju Krepin asks, do not all Ikkuma boys be much older when leave home?"

"Having your Little Brother stolen changes things!" I shouted.

Gorpok Juga regarded me a moment, then interpreted for Krepin. I was sure she wasn't telling him exactly what I'd said.

"You are certain brother is here?"

"Yes!" I shouted. "The Tunrar took him away! Tell him what I told you, tell him what Cubby looks like!"

"Aju Krepin want know how three young Ikkuma come to Beginners' High Temple?"

He was scratching his chin thoughtfully, patiently waiting for my response. I thought of Blaze, his mark, his fall into the Pit.

"A Brother," I said, hoping that would be enough.

"Who?"

I swallowed hard. "That's not important."

Gorpok Juga made no move to speak. From the look on Krepin's face, I could tell that he knew I didn't answer the question.

"Please." There was a swelling in my throat and my eyes became blurry with tears. They were ignoring me; it was like I hadn't said anything. "My Brother."

Krepin sat back lazily, his arm reaching out to one of the nearby people holding a silver bowl.

"His name is Cubby," I said, my voice breaking when I tried to say his name.

I watched a smile spread on Krepin's face, recognition there, as though he just liked something about the sound of it. And something else. Something I didn't like behind those eyes. Like he was pleased with himself that he was keeping Cubby from me.

"Cubby!" I said again. "You know who he is!"

He pulled out a handful of brightly colored petals and dabbed them lightly on his neck, more concerned with his own stink than with what I was telling him. He sat there, staring at me, rubbing the petals between his fingers.

"Gorpok Karlone!" His crisp voice rung out suddenly, slapping against the walls of the room and echoing back to me.

The heads of Krepin's followers turned and I followed their attention to the back corner of the room. Standing in the doorway was a tall, dark man, his spine curling at his shoulders giving him a hunched-over look. But the hunch didn't make him any less intimidating. He rubbed the back of his left hand, his gaze narrowed and focused on me.

The man raised his head to Krepin, who barked at him in words I couldn't understand. At Krepin's order, he left through the back doorway and Krepin turned his attention back to me.

"*Ha shu?*" he said.

My mouth trembled, unsure of what he had asked.

Gorpok Juga clasped her hands behind her back. "Who?"

"Nobody," I said, though I could feel the tension in the air like the heat coming off a fire. "What does it matter?"

Aju Krepin grinned and rubbed his stubble.

"Come on, Av," I heard Fiver say behind me. I turned and saw my best friend on his hands and knees, Fiver holding up his head and slapping his cheeks lightly.

"Av?" I hurried over and got down on the floor with him. His eyes were rolling backwards. "Av!" I smacked him. He focused on me a second.

128

"Wawksh," he slurred. "Eyesh an' wawksh."

"What?" He was such a mess, his eyes so far back that only the whites were showing. I looked at Fiver, who shook his head, frowning.

I heard a door open and Krepin speaking in a grand voice.

"Cubby is no more," said Gorpok Juga.

My heart stopped and my stomach dropped into my feet. The world went white, like I'd been struck by lightning. I couldn't breathe, I couldn't think. *Not Cubby*.

A line of children dressed in white, foreheads bearing the blue mark, were led by the man he called Gorpok Karlone to the front of Krepin's altar. Several Tunrar hissed at them, herding them after the hunched-over man.

The smallest, leading the line and clad in blue robes, was my Cubby.

"Urgle?" he said, his familiar raspy voice trembling.

A wave of relief rushed over me and my head felt dizzy.

"Urgle!" he cried out. Before he could run to me, a Tunrar leaped in front of him, hissing.

"*Linerk!*" Karlone bellowed at him. Cubby hung his head and stepped back in line with the other boys. I watched as Krepin smiled with satisfaction and that other thing. I could see it now, it was like pride, happy that my Brother obeyed him so quickly. His grin turned my stomach.

"Tell him I'm taking Cubby home!" I shouted at Gorpok Juga. "Now!"

"Krepin say, is no Cubby. Is Passage Linerk, servant of the Beginning."

"No!" said Cubby. "No! No! They said they'd kill me if I didn't do it!"

Karlone bellowed at Cubby again and several Tunrar began moving menacingly towards him.

I could see his little mouth trembling, his big green eyes begging me to help him.

Krepin turned to me, calmly saying words that I couldn't understand but knew I hated.

"Aju Krepin say," Gorpok Juga began, "Cubby was Tunrar sacrifice to Beginning. Krepin is love, gave Cubby choice. To give himself back to Beginning in death, or service. Cubby decide on service, become a Passage."

"He's coming home with me." My voice cracked as I struggled for the same kind of authority as Krepin.

"Aju Krepin say, Passage Linerk *is* home."

My pulse kicked up again, my stomach twisted and heaved. I had no idea what to do. I looked to Fiver. He was busy holding up Av, slapping his face, calling his name.

The room began to spin as my mind raced. I needed Blaze. Blaze would know what to do.

"*Ha shu,*" came the foreign words from Krepin again. He wasn't asking this time.

Cubby's eyes were turned to the floor, the ugly blue mark blaring at me like the numbing glare from the sun.

"*Ha shu!*" he shouted. He raised his right hand and Karlone seized Cubby by the scruff of the neck. Cubby cried out.

"Hey!" yelled Fiver.

"Don't touch him!" I took a step towards them but Juga stood in front of me.

The other boys cowered away from Cubby and Karlone, huddling together, knowing something I didn't.

Karlone threw Cubby to the ground; two of the Tunrar crouched over him, hissing and spitting with glee.

"Stop it!" I begged. "Leave him alone!"

"*Ha shu!*" Krepin shouted again.

"Maybe Krepin," said Juga, a glint in her eye as she pushed me back, "should give Beginning sacrifice after all?"

Karlone strode towards a brass stand with ornate staffs and blades resting within it. He pulled out a glinting silver edge and stormed back towards my Brother.

Cubby cried out, covering himself beneath the excited Tunrar. "Urgle!"

A tremor overtook my entire body, and from somewhere inside me I felt a powerful rumbling, as though the world around me was about to crumble to the ground. The Tunrar screamed and I closed my eyes tight.

Fiver cried out behind me. "Urgle!"

And then his name. It rose in my throat like a violent cough, and without a thought in my head I shrieked, "Blaze! The Brother's name was Blaze!"

When I opened my eyes, the heads of all the Beginners were swiveling from side to side, murmurs passing between them. But Krepin was still.

Karlone let the blade drop on the floor with a loud clang, and a smile oozed across Krepin's pristine face.

My breath came back to me and I gulped in air as I watched Karlone wave away the Tunrar. He lifted Cubby by the arm and threw him at the group of terrified boys, never taking his merciless eyes off me.

"Where is traitor Blaze?" said Juga. Her eyes were wild, looking at me like my head was about to pop off. They all were. Every face in the room was staring, like they were waiting for me to just burst into flames or something.

"I—I—I don't know," I stammered. I didn't.

"The thief come here?" Gorpok Juga pressed.

"Thief?"

"Blaze! He come here?"

I shifted on my feet, everybody in the room leaning with keen interest towards me.

"How long?" Juga growled.

"What?"

"How long he was here?"

"I—I don't know. He left just before we swam the river."

Gorpok Juga interpreted this to Aju Krepin, who barked commands, staring at me as he did so. Tunrar screamed and I cringed. Dozens of them climbed the walls, crawling out windows and running for doors. A hunt had begun.

Aju Krepin descended the altar, the people in the room murmuring low to one another as they stared at me.

I began to panic as he approached, the water at his feet parting wherever he stepped. It was just like Blaze's story, the gift of the twins, Ardigund and Belphoebe.

His icy-blue eyes locked onto mine, and I trembled. If it hadn't been scratched out, would Krepin's be the face above the girl in the Baublenotts?

He placed a hand on my arm. He spoke to me quietly.

"Aju Krepin give you Passage Linerk," translated Gorpok Juga. "After you help him."

"What?"

"Forget it!" yelled Fiver.

"What does he want?" I asked desperately.

Aju Krepin turned to Gorpok Juga and spoke quickly.

"He has many troubles. His Holy War on the blasphemers makes Aju Krepin no sleep."

I didn't understand. I needed Blaze to explain.

"The Belphebans raid supply lines to Aju Krepin's armies."

"I don't—I don't know what you mean," I told her.

"Aju Krepin plans big attack on blasphemers. Belphebans must not cause problems."

Hot tears rolled down my cheeks.

"I don't understand!" I cried. "What does he want me to do?"

"If Belpheban Head die, Belphebans must mourn until full moon. No more trouble from them for one month."

Aju Krepin's grip on my arm became tighter.

"You kill Belpheban Head."

My whole body was shaking. I'd never killed anything but Slag Cavies. "I—I can't kill anyone!"

"You are Ikkuma. If anyone want to kill Belphebans, it is Ikkuma boys."

"Who are these Belphebans?"

She tilted her head, surprised I didn't know. "They are you Mothers."

I could taste the bile in the back of my throat.

"You kill Belpheban Head, Aju Krepin give you Passage Linerk."

I remembered Blaze, his warning. One decision.

I was just Urgle. I was Useless. How could anything I did change anything?

"Why me?" I barely managed to squeak out.

Krepin squeezed my shoulders and smiled.

I looked at Cubby, tears streaming down his cheeks, the fresh blue mark on his forehead screaming at me. I would not abandon him here; there was only one choice.

"I will," I said, and nodded.

Aju Krepin took my face in his hands. Gently he pressed his forehead to mine, blessing me, his Ikkuma orphan assassin.

PART TWO

ONE

I can still remember the pain. The crumbling bits of rock of the Ikkuma Pit walls pressed hard against my naked back. I remember because I was mad, so mad, at my Big Brother.

"Time's come, Urgs," he'd said. "The little one's been dropped by the South Wall. I gotta go to make room."

He'd told me that morning, and by dinnertime he was gone. But not before showing me where to go. Scared and nervous, I went with him to the South Wall, and he pointed to the tree line, where Nikpartok peeked over the Ikkuma Pit.

"They left him there," Cheeks had said.

I was terrified. I'd only just turned seven and could barely throw a spear.

"No sense wasting time," he said, slapping me on the back. "Now get on up there and keep an eye on him."

Cheeks was anxious, eager to get going, to finally Leave. He'd been planning to go for months, but he couldn't. I wasn't ready yet. I was still useless, so he had to put off his Leaving Day longer than he wanted. And here I was again, holding him up.

"Don't be so useless, Urgle!" he'd said, pushing me up to the wall. "Get moving!"

So I did. I climbed up the South Wall, the highest I'd ever been, and stopped just before the top. I remembered looking out, the A-Frame just a brown pock on the black floor of my home and my Big Brother, Cheeks, barely visible as he made his way to the north . . . to his new life outside the Ikkuma Pit.

And then I heard it.

Just above me I could hear the cries of the little squirt, his raspy phlegm warble screeching for the monster of a woman that had abandoned him here. I risked a peek, even though my Big Brother had specifically told me not to.

"One night, Urgs" is what he'd said after he'd discovered the new arrival. "If he makes it through the night, he's all yours. If not, then he's not Ikkuma anyway. Don't let him know you're there. He'll cry all the more if he thinks someone's nearby."

I peeked anyway. I'd never listened to my Big Brother before, so what did it matter now? He'd abandoned me. I was the Big Brother—well, I would be—and I didn't have to listen to anybody.

A tiny soiled bundle of cloth fidgeted in the undergrowth of Nikpartok Forest. I'd never been that close to the tree line, and I remember how scared I was that some predator would come and gobble me up.

The crying stopped and the baby lay silent.

Was he dead? I didn't know. And the idea that I'd have to leave the safety of the Pit to find out made me nearly wet myself.

Then he howled. The baby screamed and cried, demanding somebody, anybody, pick him up.

But this was his test. The first night their Mothers abandoned them on the fringes of the Pit was a night they spent alone. If they survived, they were Ikkuma and adopted by their Big Brother. If not—I didn't really know.

The day drew on and I made myself comfortable, pressed up against the South Wall. My eyes grew heavy, and I slept to the sound of the baby's lonely cries.

By morning, I heard nothing. I awoke to silence and felt my heart stop. Was he dead? If the baby died, then I'd be no Big Brother.... But my Big Brother had left ... so I wouldn't be anyone's Little Brother. What would happen to me? I'd be all alone. Who knows how long it would take for another baby to be left for me?

Then I heard a snort—big animal, a predator coming to feast on the baby.

I held my breath and peeked over the top of the South Wall and saw the most massive beast I'd ever seen. My little imagination couldn't have dreamed up something so large. It stood on all fours, and its body was covered in a soft black fur. An Ashen Bear. It circled the baby, its black nose sniffing and probing.

I looked around for blood staining his snout, the ground, the blankets, but there was nothing. Then a giggle. The baby squealed with delight as the giant bear sniffed at his face. He'd survived the night at least. He was Ikkuma all right ... if the bear didn't kill him now. Then the bear reared back and sat against a tree, licking her lips and scratching her belly. The baby continued to giggle, and the bear let out a low sound that to me sounded like a growl.

"Please don't eat him," I whispered.

In that instant, her big, shiny eyes were on me. My heart stopped. How could I have opened my mouth?

The bear sniffed the baby again, then nuzzled him, like a Mother caring for her cub. She looked back to me, then waddled her giant form back into the cover of the trees until there was nothing left of her to see.

Trembling, I bolted from my hiding place and ran for the giggling baby.

Twigs snapped to my left, more to my right. The bear was out there. There could be more ... or something else, anything else. The forest was watching, ready to pounce, and the baby was inches from my outstretched fingers.

The ground slipped out from under me and I fell, scraping my palms and my knees. I lay with my face in the dirt, listening to the silence and begging my pounding heart to slow down.

A quiet cooing tickled my ears and I turned my face to see a pair of big green eyes looking back. His mouth was open in a wide, toothless smile, and his skinny fingers reached for me. He was mine.

I sat up and pulled him into my arms. He was so small and floppy I couldn't imagine how anyone could place him down in the middle of the wild. He was silent in my arms and rested his head against my chest. I hugged him close and my cheek brushed his fuzzy blond head. He was my Little Brother. And I would name him Cubby.

TWO

We'd been paddling furiously for what seemed like forever, fighting the current as we made our way from the Beginners' Temple. I sat in the front of the little vessel Gorpok Juga had given us—a tiny boat big enough for me, Av, and Fiver—and stared into the distance, wondering how I'd ever complete my task. "Kill Belpheban Head," Aju Krepin had said, "and you will get your Cubby back." But how? I didn't know anything about them—where I'd find them, how many there'd be, how I'd do it. I was lost in a world I knew nothing about, with no one to guide me.

"Urgle!" Fiver barked behind me. "Pull in over there, we got to stop."

I craned my neck round to argue, but when I looked behind me I saw his reason. Av was slumped still, his head collapsed into his chest, drool seeping down his chin. He was getting worse.

"We've got to find some fire moss!" Fiver yelled over the rush of the water. "That'll set him right."

I slapped the water with my paddle. "This isn't the Ikkuma Pit! Where are you going to find fire moss?"

I turned around and kept on paddling, fighting the water with all my anger. We wouldn't find fire moss in the Baublenotts. We had to keep going.

"Urgle! Look at him!" Fiver roared. "We're stopping."

I ignored him, pushing my arms to their limits, making up for Fiver's lack of paddling. Cubby was still with Krepin; I had to get him back.

"What is your plan here, huh?"

I didn't have one.

"You don't even know where you're going."

I'd find my way. I had to.

"Do you want to kill Av?"

My stomach flipped and my face burned. No, I didn't want that. Av was my Brother, my best friend. He needed help.

Fighting tears and trying to swallow my frustration, I nodded, and Fiver and I made our way to shore.

We climbed out onto the soft muddy banks of the Baublenotts, the swampy vegetation engulfing us.

"Help me here, Useless!" Fiver barked as he tried to haul Av's limp body from our rickety boat.

I grabbed Av's arm and the two of us heaved him out and onto the mud, leaning him against a tree. His eyes were glazed and his tongue hung limp in his open mouth, like it was swollen. This was my fault. This wouldn't have happened if he hadn't come here to help me.

I kneeled beside him and reached out to support his neck. "Av?" I whispered to him. "Can you hear me?"

His head wobbled a bit and I steadied him. "Oh, Av. I'm sorry."

A drop of blood slid down from his forehead, and he tried his best to sit up. That was how Av was, a fighter. I readjusted his shoulders against the tree, trying to make him more comfortable.

"Av, you're gonna get better," I told him. He had to. I couldn't do what I had to do without him. Av was the great hunter, the good Brother. "You just have to get better."

But how? Crow was so far away, and Fiver and I didn't know much about healing.

"All right," said Fiver, revealing a dagger hidden at his side. "Let's get looking for anything that looks like fire moss."

"You can't just give him something that looks like fire moss, it might not do the same thing!"

"Do you have any better ideas?"

"It could be poisonous!"

"He's dead meat anyway if he stays like this much longer."

There was nothing I could say to that. My stomach felt sick; it had felt this way for so long, ever since the Tunrar grabbed Cubby from the Ikkuma Pit, and it just kept getting worse. I couldn't remember what normal felt like.

The battle cry of an angry Tunrar sliced through the silence, followed by a chorus of others.

"Blaze," I breathed.

"What?"

My heart began pounding; the Tunrar screams were so close. "Krepin sent the Tunrar after him." Fiver stared at me blankly. "Listen to them shrieking. They've found him, Fiver! They've found Blaze!"

"Good. To the Mothers with Blaze. I hope they rip him apart."

"No, Fiver! Don't you see? Blaze knows this world, knows these people! He'll know how to find the Belphebans!"

Fiver grabbed me firmly by the back of my neck, his face

twisted in anger. "Forget about Blaze and the Belphebans, Useless! We've got to take care of Av."

I shoved him off me, laughing from the hope that surged through my body. "He can help Av! He'll know what plants are good medicine out here, he'll make him better!"

I didn't know that. I couldn't be sure of anything I was saying. All I knew was Blaze got me through the Baublenotts. Blaze got me to the Beginners' Temple. Blaze knew to ask for Gorpok Juga. If there was anyone who could get me, Fiver, and Av through the rest of this, it was Blaze.

"Urgle, you're losing—"

"What other choice do we have, Fiver?"

He looked away, tired of arguing or out of things to say, I wasn't sure. But he said nothing, staring only at Av.

"All right," he said finally. "We'll look for Blaze. But if those Tunrar have torn him limb from limb, I'm taking Av back to the Ikkuma Pit, got it?"

I nodded, knowing full well Fiver couldn't risk taking Av all the way back to the Ikkuma Pit alone. He was holding out for Blaze just as much as I was.

The Tunrar let out another shriek, and Fiver's head turned in the direction of the sound.

"Other side," he said.

My arms felt heavy and my shoulders slumped when I realized we'd have to cross the river yet again. I reached down to help Av up but Fiver smacked my head.

"Leave him," he told me. "Let him rest; we'll be back faster if we don't have to carry his weight."

I hesitated. Part of me knew Fiver was right, but when I looked at how helpless Av was now, leaving him alone in the Baublenotts seemed like a risky plan. Before I could argue, Fiver had already begun hauling the boat back into the water.

"Let's go, Useless."

"We'll be right back, Av," I said. He stayed slumped against the tree, giving no indication that he'd heard me.

Reluctantly, I ran after Fiver, leaping into the boat just as the current caught hold of it. We paddled hard, fighting our way across as we were pulled farther downriver. I glanced behind me and the shore was a mess of trees. I couldn't be sure where exactly we'd left Av; I could only hope Fiver knew.

The boat crashed into the opposite shore and Fiver leaped out, his body half in the pounding water.

"Help me!" he said as he heaved the boat ashore.

I lifted my legs over the side and slipped on the mud, landing hard on my stomach. Argh! Useless.

Blaze's belt slipped down my leg, and I readjusted, pulling it tighter than before. My leg began to throb at the wound.

Before I could help Fiver tie it up, he had the boat secured to a low branch and bolted off into the Baublenotts.

My leg still stinging, I got to my feet and followed. It had been a few minutes since we'd last heard the Tunrar scream, and I had no idea how Fiver knew where he was going—but he was going fast. He tore through the heavy undergrowth, sending branches whipping back into my face. I could barely keep up as he barreled on. Av had always told me what a great tracker Fiver was, much to my irritation, and as I tried desperately to keep up, I couldn't believe I was hoping Av was right.

As I plowed through a particularly thick, leafy bush, I emerged to find myself alone. Fiver was too far ahead, I hadn't kept up. Every second of thought was time poorly spent and I continued on, my feet flying, hoping I'd find him again.

WHAM!

My body slammed against what felt like a wall, my nose squished into my face, and I fell back onto the ground.

"Shh!" Fiver hissed.

He was like a tree. I'd nearly shattered my body when I ran into him, but he stood poised and silent, as unaffected by the impact as one of the Fire Mountains would have been.

I sat silently, my ears scanning through the chorus of birds, insects, water, and other sounds for any hint of Blaze and the Tunrar. I heard nothing.

Fiver took a few cautious steps forward and crouched to the ground. I joined him, wishing that just once I could see whatever a hunter's eyes were supposed to see in the mess of mud, sticks, and leaves.

I saw nothing.

Fiver could tell and he rolled his eyes, tracing for me the vague outline of a footprint. When he pointed it out, I could kind of see, but whether it belonged to Blaze, Tunrar, or something else I couldn't have said.

His finger guided my eyes to a path of minute destruction: a few snapped twigs, several gouges in the trunk of a nearby tree.

As I tried to process what I was looking at, Fiver took off again, sharply to the left, and I was left sitting in the dirt. I jumped to follow but I couldn't see him. I could only follow the swinging branches he'd left behind.

"Fiver!" I shouted, wanting him to slow down.

Nothing.

"Fi—" I stopped short when I heard the hacking. That

now-familiar, hideous phlegm sound, hissing through the throat of a Tunrar. It was coming from my right. As quietly as I could, I crept through the brush towards the noise and saw a clearing through the branches.

I moved in closer and there they were—a scrawny, snarling Tunrar and Blaze, backed up against a tree. I'd found him.

The sound that was hacked out of that gummy mouth flicked a switch in my brain, the image of my fight in Nikpartok and the giant Tunrar that had gouged my leg flashing across my mind. Holding on to that, I threw myself at its back in a flourish of seething hate.

I hadn't thought enough to do it quietly, and the angry roar I let out alerted the Tunrar quick enough for it to turn in time to throw me. My stomach crunched and my collarbone felt like it might snap as I was slammed into a nearby tree.

Blaze, unfazed by my presence and uninterested as to why I was there, spotted his opportunity to escape and made a run for the thick undergrowth surrounding the clearing. The Tunrar was faster and pulled him back, throwing him to the ground.

I found my breath and ignored the pain throbbing in my shoulder, flying at the creature for a second time, but before I reached him a heavy body crashed down on top of me—another Tunrar. It screamed its triumph and held me down. My shoulder was on fire with pain as its hand palmed the back of my head into the rotting leaves that littered the Baublenotts floor. I wriggled and thrashed but the Tunrar held firm. No matter how hard I tried to throw him, he stayed, without effort. I could hear Blaze grunting and growling as he struggled against the other, its hissing and shrieking goaded on by the monster that held me down.

Then came the distant cries of still more Tunrar, and beside me, a fresh set of knuckles stomped the floor. A third. He squawked his approval and threw leaves in the air, rejoicing in what his comrades had captured.

Then, interested in a closer look, he brought his face low and sniffed at my tears, that steamy rotten-meat breath burning my nose, that low growl rumbling in my ears. My eyes were wet and I fought the rising lump in my throat as I thought of Cubby, the evil blue that identified Beginners forever stamped into his forehead, forever a slave to Aju Krepin.

Just then, a heavy rock smashed into the head of the Tunrar that had arrived late, knocking him off balance. Under the weight, I couldn't see anything. Had it fallen from the sky? The one that held me down let out an angry scream and slammed my head into the ground harder as it tried to figure out where the assault had come from. The Tunrar on top of Blaze froze, while the injured one, obviously dazed, stumbled to face the direction the rock had come from too. The three were silent and stoic, watching the still vegetation. All that could be heard were Blaze's grunts as he tirelessly struggled against the immovable strength of the Tunrar.

Another rock, bigger than before, landed on the creature on top of me, knocking him slightly before it bounced off and landed on my angry shoulder. I cried out as my captor sprang off me and bolted in the direction the rock had come, but before he could disappear into the undergrowth, a familiar roar erupted from the silence and Fiver burst into the clearing, a log held over his head. With one tremendous swing he cracked open the face of the advancing Tunrar and it fell to the side, deader than mud.

The other two screamed and flew at him, but Fiver was

148

ready, screaming back with as much venom and predatory instinct as them. I jumped to my feet, and pain radiated through my shoulder and pulsed through my entire torso. I groaned, but I couldn't let it distract me. Fiver was strong, but he couldn't fight off two Tunrar alone.

Blaze was up now, searching frantically through the dead leaves, and I found myself hoping he hadn't lost his pistol.

I grabbed the rock that Fiver had thrown and without much of a plan ran at the Tunrar. I leaped onto its back, barely missing a swing from Fiver's log, and brought the rock down as hard as I could on the surprised Goblin's head.

Hardly flinching, it flung me off, and I was thrown to the ground. The two creatures tightened their circle on Fiver, dodging and ducking his every swing. Any second they would both pounce on him.

Blaze was still frantically kicking up leaves, looking for something, and I knew he'd dropped the pistol in the scramble. I started looking too, swiping aside the rotted shedding of the Baublenotts until a metallic glint caught my eye. I grabbed the pistol and tried awkwardly to point it at the Tunrar, unsure if I was holding it right. I'd seen Blaze do it once and I tried my best to copy what I'd seen.

"Hey!" I yelled.

The Tunrars' necks snapped back towards me, and, recognition widening their eyes, they hissed and spat, crouching low and squaring their shoulders as they braced for the lightning they'd clearly seen before.

"Urgle, don't!" Blaze ordered.

Don't my foot. I wanted this time-wasting fight over, and I was ending it now.

I stood shaking, pointing the gun towards the Tunrar

as I struggled to figure out how to make it go. With a squeeze of my finger the gun exploded, knocking me back. I heard Fiver cry out as my eyes shut from the noise and the pistol fell from my hands. The Tunrar screamed and danced, frightened and disoriented. I scrambled for the pistol but Blaze was there first. With a practiced hand, he took aim and shot at the first. The sound was deafening, and I jumped.

I waited for him to shoot at the second but he didn't, drawing his dagger.

"I'm out," he said.

"What?" Why wasn't he firing at the other one?

The Tunrar kept screaming, backing away slowly as Blaze advanced on it. This was a different scream. A howl, a high-pitched wail.

"Fiver!" he ordered.

Fiver was on the ground, clutching his thigh, his face tight with pain. He groaned and nodded, trying his best to shake off the sting. He reached for his log, unnoticed by the frightened Tunrar. It kept wailing, and Blaze was becoming panicked.

"He's calling for help! Fiver, now!"

With all his strength, Fiver brought down the log on the Tunrar's head and it fell limp to the ground.

The Baublenotts were silent again, and I shivered, noticing for the first time just how much colder the world had become.

"Nice aim, Useless," Fiver growled. He was pawing at his thigh, afraid to touch it but needing to see the damage. His trouser leg was ripped, like a knife had made a large slice across his thigh. I may have missed the Tunrar, but I'd managed to graze something, anyway.

"Fiver, I'm sorry."

"I'm fine," he growled.

"I didn't mean to, I thought—" My words were lost on my bleeding tongue when Blaze's fist connected with my jaw, forcing my teeth to bite down, and my eyes to see stars.

"Traitor!" he yelled.

Spitting out the coppery warmth, and stumbling over my swelling tongue, I tried to apologize. "Blaze, I'm sorry! They had Cubby right there, I almost—"

"I asked you for one thing!" he roared, grabbing my arm and shaking me so hard I thought he'd tear it off. "And you told him anyway!"

"They were gonna kill Cubby if I didn't!"

With a glare full of poison he released me and I felt a hot shame creeping up my neck.

"I'm sorry, Blaze! I didn't know he'd—"

He stopped listening and walked away, disappearing into the Baublenotts. I looked to Fiver, who was nursing his bleeding leg. "Go after him!" he barked.

I ran after Blaze and found him not far ahead, slicing through the thick vegetation of the Baublenotts.

"Blaze, wait!" I begged. "I need your help."

"Get away from me, Urgle."

"Just stop a minute, will you!"

"I helped you get to the Temple, now you're on your own. You gave me up to the Beginners. I've got to get the hell out of here. You're the last person in the world I want to help."

There wasn't a lot I could say to that. He was right. He'd told me not to mention his name, and as soon as Krepin had asked, I gave it up. Out of ideas, I tried a new approach. "Where will you go?"

"Far away from here. Three Tunrar found me, dozens more are on the way. You heard that thing howling; they'll be flocking here any minute."

I thought of Av, slumped alone by the tree, groups of Tunrar descending on him.

"Blaze, I need your help."

He said nothing and trudged forward, doing his best to ignore me.

"Blaze, Av's hurt, really bad. He could die and we don't know what plants are what out here. And now Fiver's hurt too; we need your knowledge if we're going to survive this."

He kept going.

"I'm asking you as a Brother!"

"Go back to the Pit, Urgle," he said as though he couldn't have cared less.

"I can't!" Desperate to make him help me, I grabbed him by the arm and yanked him around. "They'll give me Cubby if I find the Belphebans."

His eyebrow rose. He'd heard me. "The Belphebans? What for?"

"I don't know. They're interfering with some, some big fight the Beginners are having."

"The Holy War."

"Yes! And he said, if I kill the Belpheban Head, he'll give me Cubby."

At that, Blaze burst out laughing, a maniacal laugh, unlike any I'd heard from him before.

"Krepin's sending *you*?"

"Yes! And I'm going with or without you, but if you help me, I'll have a better chance."

He caught his breath and wiped his watering eyes. "Urgle, do you even know who the Belphebans are?"

"Our Mothers."

Blaze nodded, his laughter spent. "They told you that much, huh?"

He flicked his hair out of his eyes and leaned back against the nearest tree, letting the air rush into his nose. I watched his chest rise and fall, his nostrils flare, and I wanted so much to ask him everything, to get him to put an answer to every question swimming around in my head. But he was just so mad at me, I wasn't sure I should push my luck. I had to know more, though. "It's like your story," I said, hoping he wouldn't tell me to shut it. "About the twins. That girl's name, it was Belphoebe, right?"

He stayed leaning against the tree; his eyes appeared closed as they watched me under his heavy lids. "That's right," he said. But he didn't just say it. His voice went up at the end, like he was asking me something, to go on working it out maybe.

"So the Mothers, they got something to do with that girl?"

"They're her daughters."

I swallowed, trying to moisten my throat as it dried up on me. The Mothers had always been nothing but faceless monsters, creatures that existed only to abandon me and my Brothers and cause evil outside the Pit. But that face, the face of Belphoebe I had seen on the rock, there was a kindness there, a beauty even, playing on her smile. She was their history, part of their story. I remembered her eyes, the shadows cast by the fire making them look alive. She was a part of mine.

"And Krepin," I started. Blaze's nose wrinkled. He hacked up some throat juice and spat. I didn't know if I should say it, I'd been so scared, so worried about Cubby, my mind might not have been working right. But still, I had to know. If I really did see it, Blaze would know. "The water, he could, I don't know, when he came up to me in the Temple, he moved it, right out of his way. It was like what you said about the gifts."

Blaze snorted and spat again, smashing the splatter into the Baublenotts with his foot.

"It was like your story."

Blaze nodded.

"Is he—Aju Krepin, I mean—is it like the Belphebans? Is he Ardigund?"

Blaze laughed, but it was empty, malicious. "He'd sure like to be." Blaze kept digging his foot into the ground, the spot where his spit had landed growing into a muddy hole. His eyes didn't notice. He was watching something in his mind again. "Ardigund lived thousands of years ago, Urgle. Krepin's just one in a long line of his successors."

"Successors?"

Blaze shook his head and his foot stopped moving. "Never mind. He's not Ardigund, no matter how hard he tries to be."

My stomach felt sloshy. The way Blaze talked about Krepin, it reminded me of things I'd say about a Brother I wasn't happy with, like Digger, or Fiver.

"You know him, don't you?" I asked.

He nodded.

I felt my teeth floating in the back of my head and I bit down, trying to keep them steady. He'd remember if I asked it, remember it was me who gave him up to Krepin. But I had to know.

"Blaze," I said quietly, "what did you do to make him so mad?"

Blaze grinned, his icy-blue eyes glinting with pride. "I took away his secret."

I couldn't understand that but when I opened my mouth to ask him more, he stood up and ran his fingers through his hair. "The Belphebans don't stay in one place long. Not easy to track down, even for Ikkuma."

He was done answering questions.

"They told me I'd find them somewhere. . . ." I racked my brain, trying to remember what Gorpok Juga's last instructions were to me: last seen in Manoa Pass. "Near the Manoa Pass."

"If that's what the Beginners think, then that's the last place they'll be," Blaze told me.

My stomach sank and my whole body was heavy. I had no idea where the Belphebans were, no idea how to help Av, and no idea how I'd get Cubby back if I didn't complete my mission.

"Sable Root," Blaze said. "That should help your friend. Orange Blossom. Four petals. Size of your fingernail."

"Wait!" I couldn't lose him. There was no other way to get my Little Brother back. "That's all?"

He sighed and rubbed his neck. "I've helped you enough, Urgle. I have my own problems." He certainly did. Whatever secret he'd taken from Krepin, it was clear Krepin was going to do his best to get it back. If Blaze left me now, I didn't think I'd ever know what it was. Blaze stood facing me for the longest time, the two of us silent as he thought. I watched his mind struggle to decide whether to help me or not, his brow furrowed, his eyes roaming over the miserable swampland of the Baublenotts.

"Head north along the river," he said finally. "Towards the mountains."

"Is that where the Belphebans are?"

The distant scream of a new group of Tunrar echoed through the trees. "No. But you should come to a roadway. Follow it west, to Fendar Sticks. If anyone knows where the Belphebans are camped, it'll be the gentlemen of Fendar Sticks."

He shrugged off his outermost skin. He handed it to me for the second time. "You'll need this."

And that was it. He turned and started on his way, and I didn't know whether to celebrate or cry. He'd told me exactly what I needed to know, even though he didn't have to. I stood a chance of getting Cubby back. But I was going on alone, without Blaze, without my guide. There was nothing I could say to make him stay. He had to run. The Tunrar could find him at any moment. If they caught up to him again, he'd face them on his own. I watched him pick out a long stick and plunge it into the pool nearest to him. If they caught him, it would be because of me. It would be because I'd betrayed him.

THREE

It took us longer than expected to get back to Av, Fiver's leg slowing him down, though he was still pretty quick, considering the size of his gash—longer than mine had been. Sticky Willow would have set him right, but I didn't know if there was anything like that around here. Didn't matter if there was, though, 'cause whenever I mentioned it, he just kept on growling that he was fine.

"You have to treat it, somehow," I told him, feeling worse by the minute. I started undoing the belt that covered my own wound, but he stopped me.

"Leave it alone, Urgle," he growled. "Let's just get back to Av."

He limped ahead and I hated myself for each labored step. He was hurt because of me. And so was Av.

Av was exactly the same way we'd left him: his chin slumped into his chest, drool staining his clothes, his back against the same tree. He hadn't moved in all the time we'd been gone.

As my heart suddenly accelerated and my brain feared

the worst, Fiver gave him a gentle kick to the foot. Av managed a low groan.

"Well," said Fiver, shrugging, "he's not dead yet."

I swallowed the panic that had made its way to my throat and nodded.

I opened my sweaty clenched fist and unveiled the crushed orange petals of what Fiver and I had, after much debate, decided was the Sable Root Blaze had told me about. We measured with our fingernails as best we could, but we weren't sure if it was the blossom that was supposed to be that size, or the entire plant.

Blaze's hide hung heavy over my shoulder. I kneeled down beside Av and draped it over him, hoping the warmth of it might help him feel better.

Fiver, with a face contorted by pain, carefully took a seat beside Av and began studying the damage I'd inflicted on his thigh.

"Well, Useless?" he said. "Give it to him."

A new swell of panic rushed through me as I looked at the wilted little plant. "How?" I asked.

"I dunno, just—jam it in his mouth."

Wrong. I'd seen Crow work with plants and herbs a dozen times, and never had I seen him just shove a flower in someone's mouth. There was a lot of prep work: picking, peeling, squishing, mixing, boiling, frying—even fire moss needed to be boiled in a tea before it could help someone's pain.

"Maybe we should boil it," I said finally.

Somewhere in the distance, the screams of an army of Tunrar rang out, not far.

"We don't have time, Urgle. Just give it to him."

I began to sweat again as I remembered something Crow told me a long time ago. I was young, still just a Little Brother myself, and Cheeks had banished me from target practice because I accidently hit him in the leg with a way-ward spear. I was told to sit with Crow and his Big Brother while everyone kept practicing. Crow was crushing a bunch of roots, I remembered the black juice staining his hands.

"Always gotta crush Wheezy Weed, before you boil it," he said.

Confused by the amount of work and grossed out by the mess, I asked him, "Why can't they just eat it as it is?"

Crow's jaw dropped and he looked at me very fright-ened. "No! No! Just eating Wheezy Weed could kill some-body! Don't you know how strong it is?"

Now I looked at the little flower in my hand, my palm flecked with small orange stains from squeezing it so tight. It might be too dangerous to give it to Av just the way it was, but time was running out.

Av lay there against the base of the tree, still and silent.

"Come on, Useless," said Fiver, grabbing Av's mouth in his hand and forcing his jaw open.

The Tunrar screamed. Closer.

"It could be dangerous," I said.

"What in the Mother isn't dangerous in this forsaken world?" Fiver growled as the screaming grew louder, and constant. "Just do it!"

Without a thought, I shoved the flower, the stem, its leaves and roots into Av's mouth and clamped closed his jaw.

"Chew it!" I yelled over the chorus of hideous screams and wails that were closing in.

Av just stayed the way he was, completely out of it and unable to do anything.

Fiver growled and shoved me out of the way, grabbing Av's face. He fished out the plant and ripped off the pedals before stuffing it into his own mouth.

"What are you doing!" I yelled.

Fiver ignored me and chomped on the flower. He spat it out chewed to a pulp and forced the regurgitated petals into Av's mouth. Av swallowed.

Then Fiver chewed up the stem and handed me the root. Thrilled to see it working, I chewed as quick as I could, spat it out, and forced it down Av's throat.

Just as he swallowed the last bit of Sable Root, a Tunrar rushed out of the undergrowth and ran at Fiver.

I reached for the paddle from our boat and bashed it in the face before it had the chance to pounce.

Fiver looked up at me from his spot on the ground. "Not bad, Useless."

I reached for him and he took my hand. I hoisted Fiver to his feet and together we grabbed Av's limp body and flung him into the boat as we saw shadows leaping in the treetops, more Tunrar descending from the sky.

"Get us out of here!" Fiver yelled as he did his best to heave his throbbing leg over the side of the boat and join Av.

I pushed the boat with all my might away from shore and jumped in. Grabbing an oar and thrusting it into the angry river, I paddled hard and fast, my limbs heavier than I'd ever felt them, dead and unwilling to move. My body was exhausted, but I kept plunging my paddle into the torrent.

The Tunrar screamed, unwilling to brave the waters and running along the shore, following us, tripping over each other as they hissed and roared and protested at our unfair advantage.

"Now what?" shouted Fiver from the front of the boat.

"We go up the river."

"You know where the Belphebans are?"

I shook my head. "A town: Fendar Sticks."

FOUR

By the time we saw the mountains that Blaze had promised we'd find, my arms were fighting against me, refusing to obey, and I could barely keep paddling. Not only that, but my skin was stinging, like burning, but I couldn't stop shivering. My teeth were chattering and no matter how I tried to keep my blood flowing, my body grew numb the further we pushed on. No wonder Blaze had given me his outermost skin. Av lay on the floor of the boat, Blaze's heavy brown hide draped over his motionless body. I inched my frozen toes under the thick cloth and felt Av's warm shoulder at their tips.

"Look, Urgs!" shouted Fiver, pointing to the shores of the river. The river had become narrower, the shores so close that if the Tunrar had kept following, they could have jumped in. The water was shallower too, the raging torrent just a gentle flow. And at the edges of the banks were crystals clinging to the surface of the water, crusting to everything from rocks to earth.

I barely acknowledged Fiver's discovery and wondered if the roadway would ever appear. I had to get out of this boat, had to find warmth, if only for a second.

In that moment, something in the distance obstructed the river. I could see it was a low bridge that connected to a rocky pathway.

"The road!" Fiver cheered, and we both cracked our frozen cheeks into smiles.

I angled the boat just so and it drifted to the shore, gently scraping along the bedrock to a stop.

Fiver and I both shivered as we forced our bodies out of the little craft and onto the shore. Fiver stumbled, and he winced, grabbing at his injured leg.

"Do you need me to—?"

"It's fine," he snapped. Fiver's eyes were wide when he looked at me and I felt a surge of fear.

"What?"

"Fire. Your insides are on fire, Useless."

He was right. I could see light clouds emerging from below my nose, and when I looked at Fiver, there were clouds coming from his mouth. Our warm breath danced on the chilled air and disappeared before our eyes. Fiver cupped his mouth to catch it, his cheeks a frozen red, his nose a perfect circle of blush.

"Your lips are blue," he said, and I realized his were too. This was a wretched way to be. How any creature could survive this, I didn't know, and as I glanced around at the barren landscape, white-peaked mountains, rocks and dirt, and patches of white dust stretching into forever, I suspected they couldn't.

We heard a groan and Av's head was wobbling. My heart swelled with relief, almost bursting with excitement. He was moving.

"The Sable Root!" I said. "It's working!"

I rushed to Av, who was clutching his arms to his chest,

his whole body shaking beneath Blaze's hide. His lips were blue, even bluer than Fiver's, and his eyes were still rolling, but he was moving. Under his own strength, he was moving. He responded to my touch and weakly tried to struggle out of the boat with my support.

As we held Av up, I couldn't help but notice this was the closest I'd been to Fiver or even Av. We were clinging to each other, desperately trying to absorb each other's warmth, Fiver draping Blaze's hide around the three of us. It wasn't as effective as I'd hoped.

"Now what?" said Fiver, his voice swallowed by the enormous empty space that surrounded us, swallowed by the windy quiet, by the cold.

"Walk, I guess," was all I could say, "till we get to Fendar Sticks."

So we did. Fiver and I started forward and Av tried to follow; he still hadn't said anything much more than a groan, and his weak effort to walk on his own was almost a complete failure. Fiver caught him before he fell to his knees and I took up the other side.

"How you doing, Av?" asked Fiver.

Av groaned and tried to lift his head, but it barely moved an inch and flopped back down. He was still drooling.

I wiped it away with the back of my hand, drying the wet on my Larmy skin. "You can do it, Av, the Sable Root's already started to work."

He tried again, but his head fell limp. I wrapped my arm around his waist and leaned his head on my shoulder.

I was waiting for an argument from Fiver, another fight that we couldn't keep going like this, but he didn't say anything. He just sighed and slung Av's arm around his neck and the three of us tried pathetically to move as one.

It was a jumbled, jostled mess. Fiver was having a hard time with his leg and I nearly lost hold of Av's mostly limp form multiple times, but we pressed on. The ground was hard and numbing on our feet, burning in its own way. It was like walking on hot coals, but there was no heat to be found anywhere. As night closed in, the air became colder and the wind picked up speed.

I couldn't feel my naked toes, and my fingers were almost gone too. My nose was running, but I barely noticed, and my cheeks felt like someone had been slapping them over and over again.

"I'm so cold," Fiver whispered.

I nodded silently, but there was nothing to be said. The only option was to keep going. I had to save Cubby and this was the only way.

Until Av started shaking. Without warning, his whole body convulsed and what little strength he had slipped out of him and he fell to the ground.

"Av!" I shouted.

He was writhing, shaking, the whites of his eyes showing, and a gurgling choking sound escaped his throat.

"Come on, Av," said Fiver, crouching down and taking Av in his arms.

A bubbly foam, a familiar orange tint, oozed out of his mouth.

"The Sable Root!" I screamed. "Fiver, we've poisoned him!"

"Come on, Av," Fiver said, ignoring me and rocking Av back and forth as his body trembled and shook. "Hold on." He turned to me. "Urgle, how much farther?"

I didn't know. Blaze had just said to follow the road.

Av couldn't die here, not like this. I'd never forgive myself.

With no thought in my head, and no hope in my heart, I screamed into the night, "Help! Help us!"

Who I was calling for, I couldn't say. Blaze? A desperate dream that maybe somehow he'd be nearby and hear my cries. Rawley, the First Brother? A hope that he'd watch over us. Whatever my reason, my heart couldn't handle losing Av. Not when I'd given him the Sable Root, not when it was all my fault.

"Help!" I screamed again and again as Fiver rocked him back and forth.

And then a faint rumble echoed in the distance, a small light not far down the road. Someone was coming.

"Help us!" I shrieked and waved my arms with all my might. "Please! Someone help!"

From nowhere, a rickety wooden cart, pulled by a large Sibble Cow like I'd seen in Abish Village, slowed to a halt, and a deformed, bent, melted person leaped down from a saddle placed neatly on the creature's back.

The man called out to me in yet another tongue I couldn't comprehend and I just kept screaming for help. I rushed to him and grabbed his arm, pulling him to come and get Av, to come and save him. The man was ancient and couldn't stand straight, his body bent forward, long white hair poking out from under his hat. He followed me to where Fiver held Av and worry flooded his face. He said words, more words I couldn't understand, and pointed to his cart. He motioned to Av, then to the cart, and immediately Fiver and I sprang into action. I didn't know who this man was or where he had come from, but Av needed help. It was trust him or let my friend die.

I grabbed hold of Av's legs, while Fiver grabbed him under his arms, and we shuffled him over to the cart. The giant beast whinnied and snorted, shifting his weight and jostling the cart about. Just when I thought it wouldn't let us climb aboard, the old man held the creature's face in his hands and whispered a quiet "Shh."

The animal stood still long enough for me to climb aboard. I reached out to Fiver, who handed me Av, and the two of us worked to haul him onto the rickety cart. He wasn't thrashing about anymore, but his eyes were closed and the orange foam still oozed from his mouth. His lips were blue and he was so still that I worried it was too late.

"Is he dead?" I whispered.

Fiver shook his head and the two of us took a seat. I held Av's head in my lap and wiped the orange from his chin. "It'll be all right, Av," I told him. But I wasn't so sure.

The old man shouted something to us: "*Eh no ki atah yay Fendah.*"

The last word hit me like a punch to the face. "Did you say Fendar?"

He didn't say anything more and reached for the saddle high atop the beast's back, and I doubted the old man's bent frame could handle the climb, but with a single push off the ground he hoisted himself atop the creature with relative ease. His body was working a thousand times better than any of ours. With a kick of his heels the animal reared and took off into the night. Towards Fendar Sticks? I didn't know. But he'd said Fendar, I was sure of it. I pressed my lips together and hoped to Rawley I'd heard the old man right.

The cart swayed and bounced as the animal sped down the road and we were knocked about violently. My head slammed against the side more than once.

I kept my hand near Av's mouth, needing to feel him breathing at all times, dreading the moment it might stop.

The rugged landscape rushed by, the giant mountains and rock formations only shadows in the darkness. The mountains were monstrous, much bigger than the Fire Mountains back home. I'd never known anything could grow to be so big. The towering peaks watched silently as we hurried, like stone guardians urging us on. An endless landscape of rock and ice.

The moon was the only light until we reached a large town. It glowed like a fire in the darkness, and the smell of it teamed with life—like animals and warm clothing, a hundred kinds of food cooking away, and smoke. The old man slowed his animal companion as we passed onto the village roads.

A group of men, no, not men. As we got closer I could see they were boys, barely older than Digger. They were all dressed the same, dark clothes with padded shoulders that made them look thicker than they really were. They waved at the old man and he stopped.

The shortest of the boys, red pocks clustered all over his chin, barked at the man in a voice that sounded too deep for him. "Ah lu ette a hi Fendah Steex?"

I sat up. "Fendar Sticks?"

At the sound of my voice, the short one nodded to two of his friends and they hurried around the back of the cart. Their eyes went wide when they saw me and Fiver.

The boys started shouting, nothing I could understand, and they grabbed Fiver by the shoulders and hauled him out of the cart.

"Hey!" They ignored me, throwing Fiver to the ground, and I knew Fiver wouldn't be happy about it. I don't know what we did, just the sight of us seemed to have angered them. I lifted Av as gently as I could and laid him down, hurrying to help Fiver, who was scrambling to his feet and ready for a fight.

"Fiver, stop!" I told him. One of the boys grabbed me by the scruff of the neck and threw me to the ground at Fiver's feet, my palms ripping open on the dirt road.

The boy standing over me had a pistol pointed at my face, the other pointing one at Fiver. I nearly jumped when I saw what had been threaded onto the breast of their uniform above the heart—the mark. I squinted when I saw it, seeing the color was different. The mark was white, and just like Blaze, a line ran through the whole of it.

The old man was talking quickly, and the short one listened, an eyebrow cocked and lips pursed, his entire face drenched in suspicion.

"Please," I said. "My friend, he's sick."

I pointed at the cart, but the two boys kept their pistols held at us.

The short one strode over and grabbed Fiver by the neck, moving aside his collar and inspecting the skin. He let out a grunt. Then he bent down and grabbed me, his pointy fingers jabbing into my throat as he pulled aside my Larmy hide to have a look at my neck.

He released me, and I reached up to rub out the sting from his rough hands. Were they looking for a mark like Blaze's?

The short leader mumbled something and the two boys dropped their pistols at their sides. He moved towards the cart and looked at Av lying motionless.

"*A fin do hai*," he said to the old man, motioning for us to move on. The old man tipped his hat and waved at us to climb aboard.

I hurried over but Fiver was still facing the two boys, his fists clenched at his sides.

"Fiver," I said. "Come on!"

He stayed there, glaring at them, and I knew all he wanted was to teach them a lesson, to show them he was stronger, but there wasn't time.

"Fiver!" I grabbed him by the shoulder. "Av needs us, let's go."

Reluctantly he followed, and the two of us jumped aboard as the cart jerked forward, rumbling farther into town.

The brick-paved streets were lit by yellow torches, and lights from the windows of the stone buildings glowed with a warmth I could practically feel as the light hit my face.

But there were marks on this town, signs that something had come through here. The roofs on the darker houses looked eaten, like flame had chewed them into almost nothing. Some of the doors and windows were supported with beams of wood that you could tell hadn't always been there, and almost everything was scarred with the black bites that only fire leaves behind.

The old man yelled and hollered at shadowed people walking through the streets, growling at them to make way as he hurried as best he could. My heart swelled with thanks and a part of me wondered if the man had been a Brother once upon a time. Who else could be so helpful to us but one of our own?

The cart stopped and the man leaped off his beast and waddled up to a large stone dwelling, the golden glow from its windows giving us just enough light to see by. Through the windows I could see people: men and women dancing and drinking, coming and going through a black open door. Hidden slightly to the right was a red door. The old man banged on the red door and then disappeared inside.

Av was still unconscious and Fiver and I waited nervously to see if the man would return for us.

The door stayed closed and I worried my mind had prematurely thanked the melted old man.

Just before my mind had the chance to slip into complete panic, the door burst open and our rescuer emerged with a second old man who was perfectly circular from the fat that filled out all of his angles. The two rushed over to the back of the cart and our escort pointed at Av while speaking quickly in his own language to the round man.

The fat man's eyes narrowed when he looked at Av and he reached in and grabbed his wrist. The concentration on his face was one I'd seen before and suddenly, more than ever, I began to ache for home. Then he nodded and barked commands at us that neither Fiver nor I understood before he waddled back towards the house.

Our bent friend smiled and motioned for us to come out and follow the pudgy waddler.

"What's happening?" said Fiver.

"I think the fat man is their Crow."

Fiver's eyes lit up with comprehension and the two of us hurried to carry Av into the house, hoping this man could heal Av the way our own talented Brother would have been able to.

We struggled to the red door, which the round man held open as our bent friend mounted his Sibble Cow and drove off without a goodbye. When I got in the door the only thing to see was an incline of steps stretching up to the second level. My chest deflated as I realized I'd have to carry him all the way up there, when a frantic wailing sounded from somewhere inside the building. Fiver and I hesitated and my stomach leaped into my throat. What on earth could make that kind of noise?

Then we saw her. An old, melted woman, of similar build and roundness to the healer, came rushing down the steps towards the door. She was wringing her hands and motioning for us to hurry inside. I couldn't tell if she was crying, but she was kicking up such a fuss that it was overwhelming me as I tried to keep my strength long enough to get Av up to the top of the dwelling.

The healer man seemed to be just as overwhelmed and shooed her back, yelling over her wails and grumbling.

The spherical couple scurried ahead of us, leading us up the stairs to a small room with a soft, cushy bed. Without needing to be told, we dropped Av carefully onto the bed and stood back, gasping for breath, to let the healer help him. He barked some orders at the old woman, who nodded and hurried away.

With fat, meaty fingers, he opened Av's right eye, then his left. Then he turned Av's head and inspected the back where the Tunrar had slammed it into the ground. Av's dark hair was crusted and matted with the dried blood, and at the sight of it my throat felt like it was closing up. The old man shook his head and made a *tsk-tsk* noise with his mouth.

Then, with his sausage fingers, he wiped the drool from Av's mouth and smelled it. He shook his head and looked at me and Fiver, speaking quickly in a deep gruff voice and waving the finger at us. He wasn't yelling, but he was serious and urgent. I held up my hands and shook my head, hoping he'd know I didn't understand.

Fiver held out his hand and inside were a couple of the Sable Root plants that we'd kept in case we needed to give Av more. The old healer took a look and nodded thoughtfully.

He rifled through a cluttered shelf and pulled out a jar. He opened the lid and took out some dried flowers, holding them out to us. The flowers were orange and a similar size, but there was no doubt they were different from the one we'd given Av.

Just then, the woman returned, a basin of steaming water and a large cloth cradled in her pudgy arms.

The old man motioned to a small wooden table and she placed the basin down. The old man threw the petals into a cup and dunked it in the steaming water. With some kind of tool, he squished the flower and the water turned orange. The old man blew on it, then tilted Av's head back, forcing it down his throat.

Burning guilt filled my stomach. This was my fault. I'd picked the wrong flower.

The old couple spoke to each other, her face withered with concern, his knotted with concentration. She flitted something sounding like a question, and he grumbled a long answer. As he spoke her concern melted and she smiled and nodded. Then with glistening eyes she looked at Fiver, who shifted awkwardly and refused to make eye contact.

I watched as she looked him up and down, gasping when she saw his leg. Her chubby hands reached out for Fiver's gash and he jumped back, nearly knocking over the table with the water.

"Hrmrah?" said the old man.

She went on, pointing to Fiver's leg and covering her mouth in despair.

Fiver pressed his back against the wall and scooted over to stand behind me.

The old man squinted, trying to get a look at Fiver's leg from where he sat. "Bah!" he grumbled, and then began listing things on his fingers for the old woman.

She nodded at everything he said, her head bobbing up and down. Then the old man waved her off and she scurried over, shoving me out of her way. She grabbed Fiver by the arm.

Fiver yanked away and backed himself into the corner, like a frightened Slag Cavy. I'd never seen Fiver look so small, so helpless.

"Shh, shh, shh, shh," she said. She reached up and grabbed his face in her pudgy hands and cooed. Then she took hold of his wrist and dragged him past me.

"Urgle?" he said as she pulled him out the door.

I took a step to go after him, but Av groaned and I stopped.

"Urguth," Av said, and I crouched down beside his bed, taking his hand.

"Wawksh an' eyesh," he said. It was the second time he'd said that.

"Av?" I tried. "I'm here."

He groaned at the sound of my voice and after that he was quiet.

"Oh, Av, I'm so sorry."

The old man was cleaning the wound on his head, and he smiled when he saw the worry on my face. The melting that had pulled down his skin seemed to bunch together when he did, round lines bunching around his eyes and his mouth. It made the smile look better than a regular one somehow, like it took a lot of work to lift up all that skin, so if he was going to smile, it had to mean something for the effort.

He patted Av on the shoulder and nodded, then he patted me.

"Can you fix him?" I asked.

He reached out and tapped me twice on the nose. "Boop, boop," he said, grinning.

A roar from Fiver exploded somewhere outside the room and there was a bang and a crash. The old man looked to the door, then back at me. He nodded for me to go.

I got up but paused in the doorway, looking back at Av and the old man working to save him.

"You really think you can?"

The old man grinned and tapped his nose twice.

I'd seen Crow work on a patient enough times to know that if the healer can grin, it must be a good sign.

I let out a long breath that I must've been holding for a while, and left the old man to his work.

I followed the sound of Fiver's growling into another room, where stone and wood adorned the walls and the furniture. A fire trapped within a little stove warmed the room, and candles lit it up with a soft glow.

"Argh! Mother seeker!" Fiver screamed.

The little old woman had him seated in a plush, cushy chair woven of colorful fabrics. She was huddled over his leg, threading a needle through the gash.

"Urgle," Fiver said, "she's crazy! Get her off me!"

"Oh, pshaw," said the woman, smacking his other knee.

I took a step closer and saw the pistol wound, which

was halfway closed by the thread she'd used to bring the skin together. It was clean and healthy.

"Hey," I said, surprised. "She's fixing you!"

"I don't care!" he yelled, grimacing. "Just make her stop!"

She looked up from his leg and said something to me, a lined smile lighting her face. She waved her hand over to a tray sitting on a stand beside the fire; several glass bottles filled with a dark brown liquid were arranged in a tidy circle.

I walked over and looked back.

"Dah, dah," she said, pointing to the tallest bottle.

I picked it up and she nodded, so I handed it to her. She bit off the lid and passed the bottle to Fiver.

"Now what?" he moaned. "Poison?"

"Kasi she," she said, and made a drinking motion with her hand.

He smelled the liquid and let out a cough. "By Rawley, that's awful!" he said, then handed it back without taking any.

She laughed and cut the thread, giving Fiver another pat on the knee before she stood and hurried over to the stove.

His gash was fully closed, the skin around it healthy save for a black thread keeping it together. I'd never seen a wound closed with anything but Sticky Willow. But she'd closed it her own way and closed it nice. I could just imagine Crow's face when we told him.

"How's Av?" Fiver asked, putting the bottle on the floor.

I wiggled my toes, feeling the warmth seeping into them. I felt relief wrap around me with the heat from the fire. If the old man was as skilled as his woman, then Av was in good hands.

"I think he's going to be all right," I said.

Fiver nodded and inspected his leg, his fingers prodding at her work.

"Ah, ah, ah!" she yelled at him, waving a finger, and he stopped immediately. She laughed and grabbed him by the chin, planting a kiss on his cheek. At first I thought he might hit her, but instead he just rubbed his face where her lips had touched him, his eyes wide and confused.

Then the old woman hurried over and grabbed my face—her strength surprising for such a tiny old thing—and kissed me too, pressing her wet old lips hard against my cheek. She was so warm, her hand on mine and her lips pressed against my cheek, that I was surprised when I realized I'd welcomed the touch of a woman, those dark and evil creatures that had caused so many nightmares.

Her eyes fell on the belt I'd tied around my thigh, and without warning she pulled it down, revealing the gash from the Tunrar. It was black and swollen, puss seeping out of the sides.

She gasped and rushed back to the stand with all the bottles. She pulled out one with what looked like water, and scurried back to me, dunking half of it on my leg.

It stung and I jumped, but she grabbed my arms to keep me still. Then she tore away the belt altogether and tied it with new, clean dressings.

"*Tu lay*," she said with a satisfied grin, pleased with the work she'd done.

At a long scuffed wooden table at the other side of the room there were two cups and two bowls laid out. The old woman went over to it, chattering on even though I was certain she was aware we didn't speak her language. She pulled out two chairs, one in front of each place setting, and motioned for us to sit.

I looked at Fiver, who looked at me. We both weren't sure what to do, but she laughed a hearty chortle and smiled so warmly that I couldn't help but smile back. Fiver was the first to move. Getting to his feet, he accepted the seat at the table, all the while eyeing her like she was an Ashen Bear waiting to attack. I joined him, the savory smells basting the air making my stomach grumble.

I stared at the empty bowl in front of me and breathed in the aroma of whatever was cooking on top of the stove. My stomach practically roared from hunger. I was ravenous and warm, and unexpectedly at ease.

The old woman waddled over with a large pot and giant spoon and filled our bowls to the top with a beautiful chunky, meaty slop. It smelled like everything my stomach had ever wanted, and I lifted the bowl to my mouth without a second to lose.

The woman screamed and I nearly dropped the bowl. Had I offended her somehow? But she laughed when she saw the look on my face and waved her mouth, miming that the food was still hot.

Relieved, I blew on the mixture with all my might, and in moments I was face deep in chunks of vegetables, meats, and other soft, mushy, savory bites I couldn't identify, all of it swimming in a thick gravy.

Fiver was snarling, snorting as he shoved the meal into his mouth with just as much ferocity as me.

She chuckled a jolly laugh and patted our heads, filling our cups with a warm, fragrant tea.

She took a seat beside Fiver and prattled on as we ate and drank. I found myself enjoying the sound of her clucking chatter, not minding that I couldn't understand a word. Fiver kept one eye on her at all times, and I could see the

178

struggle in his brain as he tried to decide what to think. This was the first woman he'd met, after Gorpok Juga, and anyway, Juga was sort of easier to accept. She was more like what we'd expect of a woman, I guess. Melty, sure, but evil enough. This smiley old lady, filling our bellies and warming our toes, and fixing Fiver's leg, was something else altogether. She was something hard not to like.

Finally she got up from the table and wrapped a colorful blanket around her shoulders, waving and bowing as though she were preparing to leave.

Fiver stood up as she headed for the doorway that led to the steps we'd climbed when we'd first come in. "Where's she going?" he asked as she waddled out the door, surprising me with the demand in his voice.

I shrugged.

That wasn't a good enough answer for Fiver. He rushed after her and peeked down the hall of steps. Not wanting to be left out, I jumped from my chair and rushed to join him.

As we watched, the old woman jiggled and wobbled as she made her way carefully down to the red door, but she didn't go through it. Instead, to her right, there was another door I hadn't noticed when we had first walked in. She opened it and light, music, and laughter spilled into the hall. Then, as she disappeared inside and closed the door behind her, there was silence.

"Let's go," said Fiver.

"What?" I wasn't so sure. "We can't leave Av."

"He's bedridden and the room she went in is just down there."

I felt my eyebrow rise; Fiver had always taken zero interest in anybody but himself, and Wasted maybe, but this old woman certainly had his attention. He noticed my suspicious look and moved his eyes to his feet, embarrassed. His unease made me soften, and part of me wanted to let him go after her. But I felt bad leaving Av behind when he was sick and couldn't join us.

I looked back to my bowl, which was still streaked with gravy. "I still have some food left," I said.

Fiver rolled his eyes and looked at the table: his bowl was streaked too. He sighed and flopped into his chair again. I picked up my bowl and slid my finger along the sides, licking up the salty greasiness.

"She did an all right job with this leg." Fiver was massaging the skin around his wound. "Maybe even better than Crow."

That was the kind of thing Fiver would have beaten the living flame out of a Brother for saying.

He caught me watching him out of the corner of his eye and quickly put his leg back down on the floor, then lifted his bowl to his face and took a big slurp. "So how far to these Belphebans of yours?"

I sucked on my thumb, trying to put off telling him that I didn't really know. I shrugged.

"Urgle," said Fiver, "what did Blaze say?"

I cleared my throat. "He said they're somewhere around here."

"Somewhere where?"

I slid my tongue along the edge of the bowl, trying to get every last trace of food. He hadn't said where. Just that people in Fendar Sticks would know. I shifted in my seat. How was I supposed to ask if I didn't speak the language?

Fiver didn't seem to care that I didn't answer; his eyes were on the door, his knuckles rapping against the table as he impatiently cleaned out his bowl with the fingers of his other hand.

"Now can we go downstairs?" asked Fiver as soon as he'd licked them clean.

I bit the inside of my cheek. "Fine. But just quick, all right?"

FIVE

The two of us made a break for the steps, barreling down until we reached the right-hand door. Fiver turned the knob and it opened to a huge, busy room. A sour, pungent smell assailed our noses, and music and voices filled our ears.

There were people everywhere, men and women, old and young, drinking and dancing or just sitting and talking.

A group of men sitting at a table to the right of the door stared blankly at us, a frothy foam dripping from their beards and their mugs raised mid-sip. They wore the same clothing as the boys back in town, the mark on all their chests.

I hesitated, thinking they'd come at us the way the first ones had. Fiver must have been thinking the same thing, because he shoved past me, standing up straight and staring down the table, daring them to try and grab him again.

The now-familiar wail of our old lady sang out, and we saw her standing behind a long bar. For a moment I was worried she'd be cross that we followed, but even with her hands on her hips she still had a smile on her face.

I looked back to the group of men, but they'd already

forgotten us, laughing amongst themselves and chugging from their mugs.

The old woman threw up her hands with a hearty laugh and motioned for us to sit at a booth near the window.

Fiver quickly limped to the booth and sat down. I followed, bouncing on the soft red cushion of the seat in front of him.

In an instant, the plump lady was standing in front of the table with two fine-looking goblets in her hand. They were filled to the brim with a red liquid. I took a long, happy sniff and my nose wrinkled at the sour, earthy smell. Like fermented Baublenotts.

The old woman erupted with laughter at the look on my face and motioned for me to drink.

Fiver needed no invitation. He'd already knocked back the entire glass.

"Oh! Hoh!" cried the old lady, and laughed again, pinching Fiver's cheek.

He glowed under the praise and blushed when she hugged his head close to her.

She said something that sounded happy and then patted my head, and I watched as she made her way back behind the bar.

Fiver watched too, his feet swinging beneath him.

"What?" he said, when he caught me watching again.

"Nothing," I said. "You just look . . ."

Fiver's glow was gone and his stare bored into me, daring me to say what I was thinking.

"Nothing," I said, biting back a grin and looking away. Whatever had caused the change in Fiver, I knew I preferred him this way.

Men slouched on stools and propped their heads on their

hands in front of the old lady as she gobbled and gabbed. They also didn't seem to mind. Every other one seemed to be wearing the cloth with the mark on it.

"What's it they're trying to keep out, do you think?" said Fiver.

"What?"

He nodded at the group of men sitting by the door where we'd come in.

"Keep out?" I asked.

"Seemed that way to me, back there with those scrawny Cavy farts. I thought they were going to tell us to turn back."

He was right. It was like the Shibotsa back at Abish Village. Blaze told us it was to keep out the Beginning's fight. The Holy War, he called it. A knot twisted in my stomach as I thought of the short boy looking at my neck, the same spot where Blaze had his mark. Something told me Beginners were not wanted here.

Fiver kicked me.

"What?"

"I said, what do you think they were looking for?"

I shrugged, not wanting to tell him what was going through my head. It didn't matter anyway. What mattered was getting Cubby back. What mattered was finding the Belphebans. But how? Blaze said the men of Fendar Sticks would know, but what good was that? I didn't speak the language. My entire body felt heavy, exhausted by the whole situation. We were in the middle of a world we didn't understand.

You wouldn't know it to look at Fiver. He'd lost interest in our conversation, enjoying another refill of the sour drink and reclining lazily in his seat. I wished I could relax like that, but as long as Cubby was with Krepin, I couldn't. My gut was twisting, telling me to get up, to get moving. But with Av upstairs and injured, there was no going anywhere. Not for the moment.

My eyes wandered as I took a small sip of the sour drink and it warmed my throat all the way down to my stomach. Beside the bar sat a group of men, each playing a different instrument. In the Ikkuma Pit we had music. Drums and shakers, simple things completely unlike this. Two of the instruments I especially liked. They held one end with a hand, the other under their chin, and slid a stringed stick back and forth to make a melody that had nearly everyone on their feet. I found my foot tapping to the sound.

A glass shattered in the far corner behind Fiver where a group of people were dancing. A woman, young and tall, dark hair cut to her chin, had fallen to the floor. She was laughing obnoxiously as a burly man chuckled and helped her to her feet. Another woman, just as tall and youthful, blond locks tied back from her face, stomped up to the fallen girl and shoved the man away. She helped the woman to her feet and scolded her for being so clumsy.

A man with a nasal voice and dark beard stumbled across to our table and sniggered as he forced his way in beside Fiver. He was dressed in the clothes with the mark too. The mark was everywhere in this town, but what did that mean? What was the Beginning to them?

The man's eyes twinkled with mischief and Fiver angled himself away, shunning the intruder with his shoulder. Even from across the table I could smell the man, as though he'd bathed in the red drink our old lady friend had brought for us. He kept putting his hand out, holding it just above the floor as he spoke, then rubbing his thick beard and scratching Fiver's chin fluff. He was either pointing out that we were short or we were young. I couldn't be sure which.

"Ah?" he said, his finger pointed to me, a gap-toothed smile spread across his hairy face. "Ah huh?"

I shrugged and shook my head, the best I could communicate that I didn't understand him. He was strange, like he wasn't right in the head, but still, he was a man of Fendar Sticks.

I sat up in my seat, swallowing my nerves, and decided to take a chance.

"Belphebans?" I asked him.

His mischievous grin faded and his eyes flashed with disbelief.

"No!" he said. Then he looked to Fiver and began inspecting his clothes, tugging and pulling at Fiver's filthy Larmy skins. "No! No! No!" He erupted with laughter. "Ikkuma?"

I looked to Fiver, who was more irritated now that the man had touched his clothing.

"Ikkuma!" he roared, clapping his hands and laughing hysterically. I began to feel really hot, immediately regretting saying anything. Many heads turned and pairs of eyes now watched us with curiosity as the man continued to make a spectacle. Most were sniggering, bemused grins across their faces, while others seemed annoyed at the disturbance. But the woman who'd helped her fallen friend, the blonde, had stopped dancing, and I noticed she was watching us differently. She wasn't annoyed or amused. She looked frightened.

Fiver caught my stare and turned around to see what I was looking at. We watched as the woman rushed over to her stumbling friend, seizing her by the arm and whispering in her ear.

It was then that our generous host arrived, squawking

and scolding our rude guest. He laughed and raised his mug to her but she swatted it from his hand and grabbed him by the ear. Groaning with pain, the man got up and ran away, and she cooed and fussed over Fiver and me, refilling Fiver's empty glass, much to his pleasure.

He grinned a lazy grin but I was starting to feel uneasy.

"We should probably get back to Av," I said.

Fiver wasn't listening.

"S'not bad, eh?" said Fiver.

"What's not?"

"The Mother."

My eyes shot open. "The what?"

He waved his goblet sluggishly towards the bar. "The woman, the old lady."

"You said, 'the Mother.'"

Fiver's eyes shot open the same way mine had, his posture suddenly rigid. "No, I didn't."

"Yes, you did."

"I did not."

I sighed, sitting back in my seat. I didn't want to fight. "I'm going to go check on Av."

Fiver pounded a lazy fist on the table. "You're right. Let's go."

He picked up his goblet and then tilted it back and back, guzzling down his full glass.

I glanced around the room, waiting for him to finish.

The two women were still conspiring, the blond one tugging at her stumbly friend's arm and ushering her to the door. The stumbly friend had gained her balance, mostly by hanging on to the blonde, and her razor eyes were focused on me.

"Guess we found your ladies, eh?" Fiver said, and let out

an obnoxious burp. His eyes were looking puffy, like he was tired but . . . happy to be.

"What do you mean?"

"They're Belpheban." He was so confident, so final, I almost laughed at how quickly he'd jumped to that conclusion.

"What makes you think that?"

He wiped his mouth with the back of his hand and looked at me like I was stupid. "Who else would look at us like they'd seen a ghost? Like their past has just caught up with them?"

"You can't tell that from a look," I protested. But he was right; they couldn't keep the horror off their faces. I looked away.

THWAM!

A hand slammed down on our table and the woman who had fallen, her cropped dark hair draped over her face in greasy strands, eyes smeared with black, was hunched over our table, glaring at me and Fiver.

"What do you want here, ah?" she hissed.

My heart stopped. She spoke Ikkuman. She had a strange but lovely accent, much different than Gorpok Juga's, and she spoke it better, less broken and stunted.

Fiver stood up slowly and returned the woman's vicious stare. "That's none of your business," he growled.

"Farka," her friend barked from the entrance, ready to leave, while some man pawed and pulled at her. She ignored him and called to her friend. "Farka! We're leaving!"

"You do not belong here," she said, scowling in Fiver's face. "You leave Fendar Sticks, and you leave now"—she turned to make sure I got the burn from her hateful glare— "little boys."

A crash and a loud bang caught our attention and we looked to the front entrance, where the other woman now had her foot on the touchy man's throat, pinning him to the floor, where he was groaning and grabbing his head. She held his angry friends at bay with a dagger pointed in their direction.

"Farka!" she shouted again. "Now!"

Farka gave us one last glare, the upper corner of her lip twitching before she stumbled to follow her friend, our old lady screaming and scolding after them.

"Believe me now?" Fiver said.

I didn't answer. I jumped to my feet and rushed out after them, Fiver right behind me.

The air hit me like a slap in the face, frigid and icy. Up ahead, we saw Farka and her friend hurrying into the shadows, fleeing the lights of the street lamps.

"Come on," I said to Fiver as I hurried to follow. I heard him groan before he started running.

The shadows of the mountains and darkness of the surrounding rocks made it nearly impossible to see.

Soon I couldn't hear them anymore, but I crept along, keeping low and close to the rocky slopes.

I looked behind me and could see Fiver's silhouette. He'd stopped moving and was standing still, taking a moment to warm up, I figured.

I crept along and tried to see through the shadows, rocks and boulders tricking me into thinking the Belphebans were just ahead.

Suddenly Fiver grabbed my arm.

"Let's go back," he said.

"What? We'll lose them!"

"They know we're following them," he whispered.

"What?"

"They're watching us."

"How can you tell?"

He smacked me on the back of the head. "Learn to know when you're being stalked, Useless. By Rawley!"

With that, he turned back towards the town and I felt embarrassed and deflated all at once. I'd come all this way and I was still nothing but useless.

That night, our generous host and her helpful healer put Fiver and me into warm beds with clean clothes not made of skins but something else entirely, like some of the fabrics that Blaze had worn. They were light and warm against my skin, and I slept better than I had since I'd left the Ikkuma Pit. I didn't have nightmares, I didn't even dream, I just slept.

When I opened my eyes to the cozy room we'd been left to sleep in, I felt a twinge of guilt in my stomach. I'd forgotten Cubby, only for a little while, but I still had. I worried that if I didn't get him back, I might forget him altogether.

A sharp pain shot through the tip of my ear as someone flicked it. Annoyed, I turned over and saw Av, a wide grin across his face. He was standing on his own, like nothing had happened at all.

"Av!" I shouted, and grabbed him for a hug.

"Whoa!" he laughed, pushing me away. "Take it easy, Urgle."

I let go, relieved to see him alive and healthy.

"How are you feeling?" said Fiver, his face still buried in a big fluffy pillow.

He shrugged and rubbed his head. "Bit of a headache, but I'm all right."

Fiver rolled onto his back and grabbed his face. "Me too."

Av raised an eyebrow. "What did I miss?"

"We found them!" I said. I could hardly wait to tell him about our night in Fendar Sticks, about our run-in with the Belphebans and his near-death experience.

"Found who?"

Fiver groaned and covered his ears with the pillow. I'd forgotten how long Av had been out of it. There was so much he didn't know.

The door flew open and in rushed the round old lady, chirping and chatting, flinging off the blankets that covered Fiver to check his leg. He growled, but stopped as soon as she waved a savory plate of puffy cakes in front of his nose.

"First we eat," said Fiver, following the old woman.

I nodded. "Then we get Cubby back."

SIX

Our new friend, the old lady, wept as we prepared to leave, and the healer man rolled his eyes at her the more she carried on. I didn't really understand it. We'd only just met, but the way she hugged us and squeezed our cheeks so frequently, you'd think she'd known us forever. We'd come across so many strangers outside the Pit, and none of them seemed to like us. But the old lady, she treated us nice. I was sorry to say bye, though not as much as Fiver, who hugged her goodbye and held on long and tight. Av's mouth fell open and I just shrugged. It was too hard to explain. Fiver might have hated the Mothers, we all did, but if he could have had one, I knew he would have hoped for this one. She held out three pairs of thick foot coverings, which I suspected she'd made herself. They were warm and fuzzy on my aching feet. The old healer shook our hands and gave us each a heavy tunic and a colorful woven blanket that I was grateful for. He patted Av on the back, his farewell speech completely lost on our ears but his good wishes accepted with gratitude.

We set off by midday carrying a large pack filled with

baked goods, meats, and bottles of the red liquid, supplied by the kind old woman. Thanks to her, hunger was one less thing we'd have to worry about. We followed on the same path Fiver and I had stalked Farka and her friend along the night before, trying our best to find their trail through the rocky slopes. I tried to pretend I knew what I was looking for, but mostly I was counting on Av and Fiver to point the way.

The slopes of the giant mountains were steep and jagged, but my feet were well protected by my new foot coverings. It was strange to walk in them. My feet had been naked my entire life, and swaddled in this thick fabric they were starting to sweat.

"How did he look?" Av asked. He listened quietly as we walked and Fiver and I filled him in on all the things he couldn't remember, which was everything after we swam the river. "Was he"—Av watched me as he spoke, trying to read the answer on my face—"hurt?"

I didn't say anything. When I saw Cubby, he looked healthy enough—no bruises or limps. He looked better than we did. But he had the mark.

"He didn't look hurt," said Fiver for me. "Scared, though."

I swallowed, the image of him cowering beneath the Tunrar forcing a lump in my throat.

Av nodded. "That's good."

There was something on his face, something he wasn't saying. "Why do you ask?" I said.

He stopped, planting his foot in a notch in the slope. "I just—" He turned and looked at Fiver. "Nothing, I was just wondering . . ."

He was hiding something.

"Av, what is it?"

He looked to me and shook his head, silently asking me not to make him say. I couldn't do that. There were no secrets. Not now. Not when it came to Cubby.

"Tell me," I said.

"I just had a dream, all right?"

"You mean like . . ." I looked at Fiver, realizing now why Av didn't want to say. "You mean like your usual one?"

He shook his head.

"Dream?" said Fiver. "What dream?"

Av sighed and wiggled his foot deeper into the notch. "When I was sick, I kept having the same dream, over and over."

"About Cubby?" I said.

He nodded. "And other things."

"You saw him hurt?" I asked, needing to know more.

He shook his head. "Not hurt. I saw him. Smiling like usual. But . . . when I saw him, I felt sore. Like this really bad ache. I get the same thing with the dream about my—my other dream. I get these feelings. But this time it was different. It was . . . stronger."

"What does that mean?"

"I'll tell you what it means," said Fiver. "Means he hurt his head really bad."

"Yeah." Av shrugged, rubbing his chin. "My head's just not right."

My stomach felt hot, the juices inside raging. What if Cubby was hurt? What if Krepin did something to him?

Av kicked at the notch in the slope, then reached for another above his head and tried to hoist himself up, but his strength seemed to give out and he fell back into me.

I held him by the arm to keep him steady.

"Av, you all right?"

He nodded. "Fine. Just a little dizzy all of a sudden."

Fiver threw down our pack from the old lady. "She put something in here for you," he said. He fished out a small glass bottle of the brown liquid he'd tasted the night before. "Tastes awful, but it's for pain, I think."

Wincing from the ache, Av reached for the bottle and took a sniff. *"Ewf."* He took a deep breath and knocked the drink back, his face turning almost green as he swallowed. He coughed and sputtered and took a seat beside Fiver. "By Rawley, that's foul stuff."

Fiver smiled and handed him a piece of some kind of dried meat. "Here, takes the taste out of your mouth."

He handed a piece to me, then set to work opening a bottle of the red liquid I didn't much care for. I bent the piece of rubbery meat back and forth in my hand, my stomach too unsettled to take a bite.

"How are you going to do it?" asked Av. He was looking at me.

"Do what?"

"You know, kill her."

My body went rigid. Fiver let out a laugh. I hadn't thought about it. It hadn't really hit me that I'd have to take a life until he asked. How would I do it?

"You really think it's going to be Useless who does it?" said Fiver.

"What do you mean?" I said.

Fiver shook his head. "Look, they sent you, so if you want to give it a shot, fine. But let's not pretend you're not going to muck it up and need me and Av to jump in and help you."

My cheeks went hot.

"Why did they send you?" Av scratched his nose and waited for me to answer.

"What?"

"Why did this Krepin man send you?"

"Because," I said, "I'd do anything for Cubby, and he knew it."

Av shook his head. "That's why you agreed to do it. But if this is so important to him, why send *you*? He doesn't even know you."

"Doesn't know I'm useless, you mean?" Since when did Av agree with Fiver? "Who cares why he did it! The point is I have to do it if I want Cubby back—nothing else matters!"

"Don't get angry, Urgle," said Av. "I'm just saying it sounds like there's more to it. Why would he send a boy he doesn't know?"

My ears felt like they were on fire and my cheeks and neck flushed. Only Krepin knew the answer to that. This was his game after all, his rules. How was I supposed to win it?

The three of us sat quietly, eating and drinking, all of us lost in our own web of thoughts. I was glad for the quiet, glad to not be answering any more questions. Questions, questions, questions. There were so many, and all the time. But in the quiet, I remembered there was really only one thing to think about: Cubby. Nothing else mattered.

"Think the Tunrar have caught up with Blaze by now?" Av asked, breaking the silence.

I didn't say anything. I didn't know, and I didn't want to think about it. If they did catch him, it would be because of me.

"I hope so," he said to himself.

I looked at him, surprised. "No, you don't."

"Why not?" said Av, annoyed that I was defending him. "He killed Digger."

I tore off a piece of meat with my teeth. There wasn't much I could say to that.

"And he would have killed me if it hadn't been for the old healer man."

"What?"

Av wiped his chin on his shoulder. "He told you what plant to look for, didn't he?"

"Av"—my face went hot—"it was our fault, I'm so sorry."

"Our fault?" said Fiver.

"We picked the wrong plant. The healer man gave you the right one. It looked like ours, but different. We made the mistake."

"Right," said Av. "Just a bad coincidence, then."

"You think Blaze knew we'd pick the wrong one?" asked Fiver.

Av looked down at the piece in his fingers and spoke quietly: "Don't you?"

"No," I said. Av looked up, his jaw tight as he chewed. "I just—there's no reason for him to do that."

"Do what?" said Av. "Kill me? Like he killed Digger."

"Digger was suffering!"

"So was I."

"He's one of us!" I shouted.

I couldn't look Av in the eye. I knew he'd think I was choosing sides. I kicked at the ground. "Why would he hurt one of his own? He took us to the Temple, even though the Beginners were looking for him."

I glanced up to see Fiver shrug, not much caring either way. But Av was staring at me.

"'Cause he's a thief, right?" he said. "He admitted it, didn't he?"

I nodded. Stole a secret.

"Blaze is gone," said Fiver. "What's it matter now?"

"Doesn't matter to *me*," said Av.

I looked away and forced myself to swallow the meat that I'd chewed to a pulp between my teeth. Blaze was gone, why did it matter? Because I couldn't believe it. Blaze helped me. He told me what I needed to know. Why would he help me and then hurt Av? He was a Brother. Brothers take care of each other. It was me who made the mistake. Not Blaze. But I couldn't convince Av of that, not now. He was too mad at Blaze, too sad about Digger to hear about any of the good things Blaze had done for us. I could only hope that with Blaze gone, Av would start acting more like himself.

"How do you feel?" I asked him, hoping he wasn't going to be mad at me the rest of the day.

He rubbed his head and sighed. "All right. That stuff isn't tasty but I guess it really works." He stood up and tossed me his last piece of dried meat. "We should get moving."

I nodded. The dried piece of meat said we were all right.

After a few hours of uphill hiking, we came to a blockage of fallen boulders, sharp inclines on either side. The only way out was to turn back or climb around. Fiver and Av scoured the slopes but I couldn't tell what they were looking for.

"Well?" I asked. "What do you see?"

Fiver laughed.

"There's not a lot to see out here, Urgs," said Av. "We're mostly guessing at this point."

"What?" That was not what I wanted to hear. I didn't need guesses. I needed to know. I needed to know exactly how to find the Belphebans. Fiver and Av were supposed to be the best hunters in the Ikkuma Pit. How could they be guessing?

"We're used to Nikpartok," said Fiver. "Baublenotts was sort of the same terrain, but this is a lot trickier. There's too much rock."

"Why didn't you tell me this last night!" I was furious. "We had them then! We could have followed them then!"

"They knew we were following them. They—"

"I saw this too," interrupted Av.

"Saw what?" said Fiver.

Av kicked at the pebbles by his feet. "All of this." His eyes flicked to me. "Rocks and ice."

At first I didn't know what he meant, but his eyes bore into mine. And then I remembered, his groggy voice spitting out nonsense. *Wawksh and eyesh.*

"Rocks and ice?" I said.

He nodded.

"Wh—" I tried, not sure what to say. "What does that mean? Does that mean you dreamed we would be here?"

He shook his head and looked away, touching his wound where the old man had fixed him up.

"Does that mean—" I felt a sour sting at the back of my throat. "That thing about Cubby. You said he was hurt. Does that mean he's hurt?"

"By Rawley, Urgle!" snapped Fiver. "It was just a lousy dream. Quit making yourself crazy. He said the kid was smiling!"

"He's right, Urgle," said Av, tying the lace on his foot covering. "He was smiling."

I stared at him, wanting him to explain himself, wanting him to say what exactly he'd dreamed. But he was done talking about it. His dreams had a way of scaring him, and he wouldn't face them until he was ready. But if he really did see this, then his dreams were starting to scare me too.

"I say we go up this way," he said finally, pointing up a sharp slope to our left that looked like an awful climb.

"Are you kidding?" argued Fiver. "Up and over this rock pile is the easiest way."

"Unless you don't want to be followed." Av shrugged.

Fiver thought a moment and nodded. "All right, we'll go your way."

This was not the conclusive decision I'd been hoping for.

With a heavy heart and all the tension I thought I'd lost the night before suddenly weighing down my shoulders again, I followed Av and Fiver up the steep incline.

It wasn't as bad a climb as I'd feared. In fact, it was less difficult than climbing the walls of the Ikkuma Pit, and we reached the rocky shelf we were aiming for with relative ease.

Once we were up, there was little guesswork to be done. The shelf only extended in one direction, into a cave in the wall of the mountain, so we had no choice but to venture in. I wasn't too thrilled about heading into a dark, unexplored cave, but the light was easy to see and I knew how long we'd have to walk before we came out on the other side. Not too far.

As we made our way through the dark tunnel, more doubts and concerns crept into my mind. Av said he saw this. How? How could he see what hadn't happened? Could he see what was happening to Cubby? What would happen? Did he see us finding the Belphebans? A new wave of sick rushed over me at the thought. If we did find the Belphebans, which at this point was looking less and less likely, what then? How exactly was I going to kill their leader? How would I even know who she was? The more uncertainty I built around my task, the more I had to ask myself Av's question. Why send me?

Then there was screaming. I tensed and readied for a brawl with the Tunrar, but the sound was different. Melodic and human, voices instead of animal shrieks. They were angry. The light from the tunnel exit was gone, and a figure stood in its place. Fiver readied his fists and Av unsheathed his dagger, the two of them poised for battle. Her legs were long and lean, her shoulders delicate but squared away, as she stood planted in front of us. She gripped a bo staff that, from the way she was standing, we could assume she knew how to use, and well.

Leaping down from above her dropped another equally leggy woman, whirling her sling at her side.

I wished I had some kind of weapon on me, like a pistol.

More screams sounded behind us and my back muscles tightened when I realized they might have pistols of their own.

Behind us came another woman, her hair a mess of wild curls. Her giant-bladed ax glinted when she brandished it above her head, catching the natural light. She advanced on us slowly, her face as hard and cold as the rock walls that trapped us.

"Well," said Fiver, "looks like we found them."

Behind her, still more were coming: blades and slings, spears and other weapons I didn't recognize but that I knew would hurt me pretty bad if given the chance.

"We're trapped," I said.

"Get behind me," said Fiver.

Fiver rolled and held up his club, which only brought on a chorus of cackling laughter from the advancing banshees. Apparently, Belphebans didn't scare as easily as Tunrar.

Fiver swung at the ax-wielder, who dodged out of his way. He lost his balance when his swing didn't connect and she threw him up against the wall of the cave, pinning his arms and chest behind the staff of her ax. Av flew at her, but one of her friends, a metal chain attached to two heavy balls gripped firmly in her hand, was on top of him, easily holding his arms behind his back. She quickly tied them together with the chain. I was the only one left.

My feet shifted from side to side as I danced moronically, trying to decide which way to flee, both exits blocked.

"Where will you run, little boy?" crowed a familiar voice. Farka approached from the back, a long blade held in her left hand. She smirked as she watched me bounce and tremble.

"Run, run, run," she mocked as her friends cackled around us.

"Bring them," commanded the woman with the bo staff from the mouth of the cave.

Farka grabbed me by the scruff of the neck, and the three of us were dragged outside.

There were about eleven of them, their clothes a mishmash of different heavy fabrics wrapped tightly against their bodies to protect from the cold. The cloth clung to their figures and I couldn't help but notice their swollen chests, their round hips. Their hair was long and wild, and they were all relatively young and healthy, not melty or rounded like the Abish women or our generous old lady. They were beautiful, every one of them, and I felt awkward and small under their scrutinizing stares.

We were brought before the one with the bo staff. She was shorter than the rest of them, but muscular and regal. She had a look of detached interest, as though this were less exciting for her than it was for the others.

"You said there were two," she said, her smoky-smooth voice commanding silence from her companions.

Farka spoke up, gripping my neck tighter. "There were. These are them, I'm sure of it."

"Elome?"

Farka's friend from the night before emerged from the crowd and looked over me and Fiver, then nodded. "Those are the same boys."

The shorter woman grunted and looked directly at me. "Ikkuma?" she asked.

I glared at her, silence the only weapon I had left.

Farka shook me hard and I growled under my breath.

"Speak! Little boy." The last words were sneered at me through tight teeth, and I saw that she was loving every second of my anger.

"You are Ikkuma, are you not?" the short woman asked, her tone commanding me to answer.

I nodded.

"Yes!" Farka barked at me.

"Yes!" I shot back. "We are from the Ikkuma Pit."

Murmurs erupted from the crowd of warrior women and the shorter one's disinterest suddenly melted away.

"You are quite young, are you not? To have traveled so far from your home?"

I didn't know what to say. They'd caught me before I could finish my task, caught me before I could rescue Cubby. I stewed silently and stared at the ground, refusing to meet her eyes.

"We seek our Mothers," Av blurted out.

My body radiated with embarrassment and I opened my mouth to argue. The very idea that we had traveled all this way to find our Mothers, that we were, by definition, Mother seekers, those spineless Brothers who needed to know the woman that abandoned them, to find her and beg her to keep him, was offensive. I would never. We would never.

But Av was smart. There was no better reason to give them.

Fiver, obviously just as offended at the thought of being a Mother seeker, opened his mouth to protest, but I cut him off as quick as I could. "That's right!" I shouted. "We seek answers! We've come to face our Mothers!"

Farka let out a frustrated groan in my ear and threw me to the ground.

"Never mind why they are here, Serin!" she shouted at the short woman. "They tell us lies! No Ikkuma this young has ever come to us. It is a ruse! Let us kill them here and now. What if they are spies for the enemies?"

Well, Farka may have been a nasty piece of work, but she was sharp. I had to give her that.

Serin looked down at me, her lips tight while she thought. I could tell our story hadn't convinced her.

"Serin!" said another woman, older, her hair silver and tied back tightly from her face. "I suggest you take them to her Sacred Innocence. Let her decide the right course of action."

Serin considered this a moment, but Farka was thirsty for our blood.

"No!" she said. "No more delays. Just finish them now. You can't bring them back to camp."

Serin sighed. "Her Holiness will be able to judge them better than I."

"You cannot bring them into the camp when so many suffer from the Guilt. Whether the Sacred Innocence condemns them or not, our plagued sisters will be tortured by their presence!"

"Enough, Farka," Serin ordered.

Yes, I thought, *enough, Farka.*

Serin nodded to the women holding Av and Fiver. "Bring them."

We walked for ages, every step a struggle as we tried to move in sync with the wretched wenches who held to us tightly. I tripped a few times, and Farka was always quick to kick me and shout at me to get up. It was clear she was not the Belpheban Head, but with each kick to my side I wished she was.

In the distance, a group of several white figures approached, their hands held out in welcome.

Serin laughed when she saw them. "I take it our Sacred Innocent has seen our special guests."

The woman in the center, her garb significantly different from the warriors that had captured us—long, flowing white fabrics, a scarf wrapped round her head—smiled and bowed.

"Her Holiness was worried for your task this morning, dear Serin. She has sent us to comfort you."

Serin smiled and took the woman's hand in hers. "I am comforted," she said, and bowed.

"Visitors from the Ikkuma Pit," the woman called to us. "She is waiting for you."

Who *she* was, I had no idea. I figured if I asked I'd get a bruise from Farka.

The woman in white turned and began walking towards an encampment; tents and crates peeked out from behind rocks and boulders.

Farka and the other two forced the three of us forward, dragging us to follow the white-garbed woman and her companions.

The woman turned and scowled at Farka. "That won't

be necessary, Sisters. The boys are capable of walking on their own."

The women holding Av and Fiver let them go without hesitation, but Farka held on to the back of my neck a moment—I could feel her wanting to argue.

The woman in white narrowed her eyes, and Farka scoffed, releasing me and pushing me away from her.

"Follow me, gentlemen, I will take you to her," the woman in white called.

We did. What else could we do? Though, whoever *she* was made me feel a bit uneasy. Just saying *she* was not giving us a lot of information. *She* was not a name, or a face, or an idea. I gulped because that last part wasn't really true. *She* was an idea. *She* was an idea I'd had since I was left at the walls of the Ikkuma Pit. A sick thought crept into my mind, the thought that *she* might be the she I'd hated my whole life. I shook my head, trying to get rid of it. *She* could have been anybody.

The woman in white led us towards the encampment, and as we approached, more Belphebans emerged to meet us. I suddenly understood why Farka thought this was a bad idea, and I was surprised to find myself agreeing with her. The women of the Belpheban camp behaved in two ways: half crowed and hollered at us to leave, throwing things and jeering. "She isn't here!" they mocked. "Go back to the garbage dump she left you to rot in!"

The other half were trying not to cry, or were crying in hysterics. They tried to get close to us, tears streaming down their faces, our guide calming them and gently turning them away.

"Is that my Benedon?" one wailed.

"My boy! My baby boy!" cried another.

"No, no, Sisters. They are not yours!" our guide assured them.

"Forgive me, my son! Forgive me!"

They were reaching for us, clawing at us, wailing and jeering, pulling and pushing, and I grabbed on to Av, more frightened than I had been in Abish Village. I tried not to look at the faces flashing by me, terrified I'd recognize one, the one female face I might know, a distant memory made real, the *she* I was afraid of, the face of my own wretched Mother.

I'd been so focused on doing what Krepin wanted, on getting Cubby back, that I hadn't even thought that I could be marching right into the den of that monster. She could be here. She could have been any one of them. And would she recognize me if she saw me? Had she seen me already? Would she come for me? The urge to run buzzed in my legs and I thought about making a break for it, hiding in the mountains. I never thought I'd face her, and here I was, facing her a hundred times over with every Mother who wept and reached for me.

I closed my eyes trying to get ahold of my pounding heart. If she was here, I told myself, if I had to face my Mother, I'd face her for Cubby.

Our guide ushered us into a grand cave, the Belphebans stopping at the mouth as though an invisible force prevented them from following us inside.

I was shaken up, trembling. I was so frightened but I'd managed to make it through the crowd. Av kept looking back nervously, making sure the women weren't following. Fiver clutched to the bag of supplies from the kind old Fendar Sticks lady, his eyes distant and unfocused.

"Forgive them," said the woman in white. "They tend

207

to behave that way whenever a son returns for answers, though I can't say we've ever received three at once."

So it was true. When some of the Brothers left on their Leaving Day, they went searching for their Mothers. I suddenly felt embarrassed, ashamed that any of the Brothers who left could have come here on such a pathetic search. Though I suppose technically, we were the same as them now.

"How many have you seen?" asked Av.

"Oh, dozens. As long as there have been Belphebans, their sons have come to find them."

"Do you ambush them too?" growled Fiver.

The woman in white sighed heavily. "These are tense times, child. You must understand that."

We didn't really, but we were getting a better idea every day. I thought of the damage we'd seen in Fendar Sticks, the boys with their pistols stopping us on the road. Somehow, the Beginners' Holy War was a force bigger than I could have imagined.

"Where are we going?" asked Av.

"To the dwelling of our High Priestess," said the woman in white. "The Sacred Innocent."

The cave tunnel opened up into a large cavern; the ceiling stretched so high, and white crystals bigger than the A-Frame hung down from above and protruded from the walls. Rows of women dressed in white were singing softly and sat with their foreheads on the floor. They didn't acknowledge us, absorbed in their music.

We approached a group of crystals in the center of the cavern, a nest of white pillows and blankets at its base, and standing in the middle was a small contorted figure—a girl. Her eyes were closed, her arm stretched towards the ceiling, her spine bent so far back her head was nearly upside down. Her right foot stood rigid and sturdy on the floor, while the left curled upwards to cradle her head.

Fiver snorted as he tried not to laugh, while I tried to keep my mouth from dropping open. Was this what we were in for? Would they torture us by twisting our bodies so badly that we'd tell them everything? About the Beginners? About my mission?

I was knocked in the shoulder as Av took a step back. His nostrils flared as his chest rose and fell quickly between panicked breaths. Did he dream this? Did he know what they'd do to us?

The woman in white bent on one knee before the contorted girl and addressed her: "On you all my happiness, Holiness."

The girl's eyes shot open and, without difficulty, she righted herself until she was standing before us like a normal person. She smiled, her cheeks betraying perfect dimples and shining with a radiant blush. Her lips were full, and she kept them pressed together while her dark eyes twinkled as she took us all in.

I stopped breathing, the face that had smiled at me in the Baublenotts suddenly alive in front of me. Belphoebe, the sister of Ardigund, alive.

"Mine for you," she said to the woman in white. Her dark hair was veiled by a white scarf draped around her head, and across her forehead she wore a silver band. When she looked at me, my body flushed and I felt my cheeks burning. My stomach was leaping and I looked to the floor before she could tell I was having some kind of nervous fit. I'd never felt anything like this before. She had my head spinning. Blaze said Belphoebe lived thousands of years ago, it couldn't have been her. But the dimples were the same; the kindness was just the same.

"These are the boys from the Ikkuma Pit we were told had been seen in Fendar Sticks," the woman in white explained.

I mustered enough strength to look back at the girl again, but when I did I saw that her big brown eyes were all for Av, her warm smile devoted to him. She had forgotten about me. He shifted awkwardly and cleared his throat, but she kept drinking him in with her gaze, her eyes welling with tears.

Of course he was all she could see. He was Av. The best hunter in the Ikkuma Pit. Av the Selfless, who helped his best friend without concern for himself. Av the Fearless, who knocked out full-grown men. Av the Strong, whose body never weakened even after it had been poisoned.

He stood there, taller than me, taller than Fiver, smooth olive skin and slender limbs defined with practiced muscle. Where else could she look?

The girl moved closer to him and he backed away.

"May I?" she asked him, holding her hands up by his face.

Av looked at me nervously, but I turned away, suddenly jealous.

With no other options, Av nodded and she placed her hands on either side of his head and closed her eyes. She stayed like that a moment, and tears began to fall down her face.

She released him and wiped her cheeks.

I thought of the Abish fortune-teller, and for one terrifying moment I thought this girl had seen our future, seen us kill the Belpheban Head, like the Abish girl had seen danger in my hand. And then a worse thought came to me. What if she was the Belpheban Head?

I looked to Fiver, who was equally frightened, and we watched the girl as she wiped her eyes.

A tremor of doubt fluttered in my stomach. Maybe Fiver was right, maybe I wasn't capable of doing what I had to do.

Then the girl burst into a gracious laugh and threw her arms around Av.

The woman in white gently touched the girl on the shoulder. "My lady?" she said quietly.

"Forgive me, forgive me," the girl managed to say, smiling through the tears. "I'm just so happy you have come." She grabbed Av's hand in hers and looked to me and Fiver. "Please come! We have so much to discuss!"

"But, Your Holiness," said the woman in white. "Serin, and the others. They are waiting for your judgment."

The girl checked her level of excitement and composed herself all of a sudden, radiating a nobility and authority similar to Serin's. "Tell them I have seen inside the boys and they are pure in their intentions. We will welcome them with open hearts."

At that, she pulled Av towards her nest of pillows and motioned excitedly for me and Fiver to follow.

Fiver let out a sigh of relief, thrilled to discover the Sacred Innocent's special gifts were lacking. Me, on the other hand—I was still shaking. I should have been happy. The girl had saved us from a Belpheban execution, but she'd done it for Av. I thought she was the most perfect thing I had ever seen, and she didn't care what happened to me.

SEVEN

"You must forgive Serin," said the girl when we sat down on the plush white cushions. "She has much to worry about."

Fiver and Av nodded if only to be agreeable, both of them avoiding her eyes, both of them still unsure how to handle themselves around a girl. Me, I couldn't keep my eyes off her. Or Av. Her gaze was devoted to him, drinking in every curve of his good-looking face. She'd barely even glanced at Fiver.

Or me.

"As the head of our sisterhood," the girl went on, "she is charged with protecting her sisters. It is no easy task."

My ears perked up. So the Belpheban Head was Serin! I took a deep breath. I think if you asked anybody, they'd bet two Larmy legs on Serin coming out of this unharmed, and me deader than mud.

A woman dressed in white came with glasses of some kind of creamy milk and the girl went on: "Since the attack of the Beginners' forces on our old camp only last month, she has had to be extra careful. They came for her, you see."

At that she stole a glance at me and I got a sick feeling. Did she know what we were up to after all?

"The Beginners want her dead."

"Why would they want that?" I said, trying to sound as innocent as I could.

"Because she's been helping the Resistance."

"The what?" said Fiver.

The girl smiled and hugged her knees. "The armies who oppose Krepin and his war against the blasphemers. It is lovely that the Pit keeps you so protected from all this war ugliness."

Not protected enough, I thought, my heart aching for Cubby.

"Holiness," said Av. "We only want—"

The girl laughed and grabbed his hand, "Oh, no, no, you must call me Lussit. That is my name."

Lussit. It couldn't have been more perfect if I had chosen it myself.

"Lussit," Av corrected himself. "We only want—"

"I know what you want."

All three of us jumped at this confession. Had she seen it all over me? Seen what Krepin wanted me to do to Serin? My insides withered. Had she seen how I thought about her? About her smile? About her eyes? I felt a hot rush spreading across my cheeks and I glanced towards the cave entrance, wondering if we would have time to make a run for it.

The girl sighed as she watched our faces. "I know what you have come for. I also know why."

"You read Av's thoughts?" said Fiver.

The girl nodded. "In a sense. I come from a long line of Sacred Innocents. The Belphebans have had one for thousands of years, all the way back to our founding Mother. Her gifts are in the blood, you see. My blood. Since I was born, I've been able to lay a hand on another's skin and see into their hearts, like she could." She pressed her hands to her chest. "The mind is a muddy place; people tell too many lies up there, especially to themselves. The heart, though, that's where you find a person's truth. You find what they love, what they hate, what they want, what they long for." She looked at me. "You have lost someone special?"

I nodded, a lump rising in my throat.

"And for him you want to do something bad, something bad to Serin?"

None of us said anything. The girl nodded, our silence admission enough.

"Because of *them*, yes?"

Them. Them. I was suddenly so angry, furious that one group of people could cause so much hurt and pain to so many others. And here I was, ready to hurt another on *their* orders. I was Krepin's slave so long as he had Cubby. Did that make me a *them*?

"Who are they?" I begged her, desperate for answers, to understand this disgusting world outside the Ikkuma Pit.

She reached out and held my hand in hers. It was warm and soft, and I felt goose bumps race up my arm, my sadness and anger fading.

"The Beginners are a religion. Their followers can be found all over, which is why they are so powerful."

"I don't know what that means," I confessed.

She sighed and let go of my hand, leaning back against a pillow. "The Beginners all believe in a life force. They call that force the Beginning. Everything started somewhere, at the Beginning. One day, they believe, life will end, circling back to that Beginning. So they give themselves to it, mind, body, and soul, so that the Beginning will keep them safe."

My finger scratched at the pillow I was sitting on, embarrassed to say I still didn't know what she meant, afraid she'd think I was stupid.

Fiver was less self-conscious. "Sounds like a bunch of Larmy dung."

"Does it?" she asked him. "Suppose I asked you where Rawley came from, what would you tell me?"

I was taken by surprise. The Mothers weren't supposed to care about Ikkuma. How much did she know about us? How much did all the Belphebans know, about their sons and their lives alone in the Ikkuma Pit?

"His Mother," said Fiver, without batting an eye.

"And his Mother? Where did she come from?"

Fiver looked to me, but I didn't know the answer to that.

"And the Pit?" Lussit went on. "How did that come to be?"

Fiver began to scowl, but Lussit didn't seem to mind.

"It got there somehow," she said. "If you asked a Beginner, they'd tell you it was the Beginning that did it."

"And you?" I asked. "What would you say?"

She smiled warmly. "My own Sisters and I have our faith. I am charged with protecting that faith, guiding it every day. If you asked me, I'd say it was the Essences."

She sat up, pulling her foot into her lap. "It's silly, though, really. Belphebans, Beginners, Ikkuma, we're all coming from the same basic place."

"I doubt that," said Fiver.

But I was interested. "The same place? How?"

She stared at me a moment, obviously deciding whether she wanted to tell me. Then she leaned forward. "I suppose they don't tell the story of the Sacred Six where you come from?"

Av gave me a sideways glance but I was already leaning towards her, nodding. Blaze had told us about Belphoebe, about Ardigund. "The twins?"

She smiled. "The twin sons of rock and ice, the twin sons of diamond and sand, the twins of water, one boy and one girl."

"Belphoebe and Ardigund," I said.

"You do know the story?" she asked.

Fiver nodded. "Sort of. Just a little." I watched him wriggle in his seat, making himself more comfortable, ready to absorb what Blaze hadn't finished. The storyteller knew a good one when it came his way.

"Could you tell us?" I asked.

She laughed. "Anyone can tell you! It's the oldest story there is. Though I suppose there are different ways of telling it. I only really know the version passed down by our Sisters."

It didn't matter. I just wanted her to tell me something, tell me anything, to help me understand.

This Account of the Sacred Six was first told by Belphoebe to her daughters, and passed down orally through the generations.

Long ago, when the lands were dark with death and madness, the People who believed in the Essence of all things were fractured, forced apart by the landscape that divided them, fighting over what was truth and what was fiction. To bring balance, peace, and wisdom, the powers of the Essence surged, and from its flesh bore six children: brothers Amid and Azul, born of rock and ice; brothers Keely and Hines, born of diamond and sand; and out of water and mud came one boy and one girl, the twins Ardigund and Belphoebe.

The Six Sacred Innocents were brought together by the peoples of the lands. They grew up together as six, a family of divine wisdom, beauty, and strength. Amid and Azul were the masters of mountains, Keely and Hines the shepherds of the earth. Belphoebe connected with the waters, but where she found strength, her brother Ardigund found only weakness. Jealous of Amid, Azul, Keely, and Hines, Ardigund blamed his sister. "Had you been my brother, like Azul to Amid, Hines to Keely," he often told her, "I would have strength to rival the others."

When the boys became men, so too did Belphoebe become a woman. Each of the four brothers tried desperately to win the beautiful girl's affection. But for Ardigund, there was no woman, no Sacred Innocent to share his children. Infuriated that no other female had been born for him, he forbade the others from pursuing Belphoebe.

Unbeknownst to Ardigund, Belphoebe had already given her heart to Amid, one of the twins of rock and ice, and before the new year she found herself with child. When he discovered his sister's secret, Ardigund vowed to take the baby for his own. "Where my sister has made me weak, her son shall make me whole, and restore me to the strength for which I was destined." Ardigund snuck into Amid's chambers and put a poison into his cup. Weighted with grief, Azul confronted Ardigund, who insisted he played no part in Amid's death. That night, Azul met the same fate as his brother.

Afraid for Belphoebe's life and the pure Innocent growing in her belly, Keely and Hines whisked her away, hiding in the mountains of Amid and Azul's birth. But Belphoebe knew her brother's heart, knew Ardigund would come for them and kill *her dear friends to have the child for his own. So under cover of darkness, she left the twins of diamond and sand.*

When Ardigund found Keely and Hines, he tortured them, hoping to uncover the whereabouts of his nephew, hoping to find his successor. The twins of sand and diamond died without ever giving up Belphoebe.

With four other Sacred Innocents dead and one in hiding, Ardigund was free to lead the people in his own design, warping the image of the Essences into a force he named the Beginning. Ardigund appointed a legion of devoted followers he dubbed Gorpoks to help him control the people and placed himself above them as the first of the Ajus, the high ruler. But even with all his power, he still had the desire for more, and continued his search for the child born to his sister.

Fiver and I sat in awed silence, waiting for Lussit to go on. Her cheeks flushed and she looked down at her hands. I had been so wrapped up in her story that I hadn't noticed she'd been holding Av's hand the whole time. I looked at Av, his throat rising up and down as he swallowed hard, his entire body tense. I wasn't sure he'd heard anything she'd been saying, too uncomfortable with his hand in hers.

"Well?" asked Fiver. "Did Ardigund find her?"

Lussit didn't answer.

"He didn't," I said. Her big dark eyes flashed to me. "Because that's why you're all here," I told her. "You're her descendants."

She nodded.

"What about the baby?" asked Fiver.

Lussit let go of Av's hand and fiddled with the scarf around her head. "Of course, that's just how we tell it. If you asked a Beginner, I'm sure they'd tell you something else altogether."

"Like what?" I asked.

"The way they tell it, Ardigund is a hero."

I sat up, disgusted. "How can that be?"

"According to *them*, Amid kidnapped Belphoebe and she did not love him. According to *them*, Ardigund was only trying to save his poor sister."

"So . . ." Fiver looked to me, his brow knotted. "How do you know whose telling is the right one?"

"We can't know," she said, "not without proof."

"Proof of what?" he asked.

"Who Ardigund was. Was he a jealous killer? Or a dutiful brother?"

After meeting Krepin, I knew whose version I believed.

And now Krepin was in control.

"And Krepin?" I asked. "What does he want?"

"What the Aju before him wanted," she sighed, "and the Aju before him, on and on and on, right back to Aju Ardigund himself: more followers, more power, more control. The Ajus before him always hated anyone who didn't follow them, but Krepin took that hate beyond anything before. He wages war on the 'blasphemers,' people who don't believe in the Beginning, to try to scare them, enslave them into following him. People have a choice: join the Beginners or die."

Without thinking, I put my head in my hands and drowned in the flood of thoughts and fears that were taking solid shape in my mind. My poor Cubby. All alone with Krepin. All alone with the leader of the Beginners. And what about us? Lussit knew why we were here. She'd never let us get away with killing Serin, who'd be watching us at all times anyway. I didn't know which path to take. It was all coming to a head, and it was all impossible. I decided then that the only option left was to storm the Beginners' High Temple on my own and break Cubby out, or die trying.

I felt that heavenly touch wrap around my wrist, and she said, "You're very brave, Urgle."

I moved my hands from my face and saw her smiling that gentle smile.

"You're all very, very brave. . . . That's why I'm going to help you."

"What?" My brain almost shut down.

"Why would you do that?" asked Fiver, just as confused.

She grabbed Av's head gently in her hands and kissed his cheek. "Because," she said, smiling, "Av is my Brother."

EIGHT

Before our brains had a moment to remember to breathe and Lussit could offer us a bit more information about how she had come to this conclusion, we were interrupted by the woman in white.

"Holiness," she said, cutting through the silent stranglehold Lussit's words held on us. "Serin would like a word."

Behind the woman in white stood Serin and several other women: the silver-haired woman from the ambush, and a couple of other older ones. Lussit sighed and then produced that gentle smile that seemed to be made of pure love. She nodded and Serin stepped forward.

"On you all my happiness, Sacred Innocent."

"Mine for you," said Lussit.

Av was staring at the ground, his eyes wild and his nostrils flaring as he forced himself to take deep breaths. His jaw was tight and he didn't blink.

He was more than just surprised.

He believed her.

"Many sisters have asked to meet with our guests."

I looked to the older women behind Serin, their faces

drenched in hope and wearing similar smiles to Lussit's, the love smile. Their eyes wandered from me to Av to Fiver, their hands held over their hearts. They looked so warm and kind, but their smiles were slightly different from Lussit's. The smiles on these women's faces were special, not the everyday smile they gave all the time, but reserved especially for us. You could tell they didn't always smile like this. But Lussit, it was like she knew no other way.

"Holiness," Serin said, "I have collected the Potentials and they have invited myself and the Ikkuma boys to share the evening meal."

Lussit bit her lip and looked to Av, but he was still just staring, just breathing—well, trying to, anyway. Her eyes moved to me, but I was no help. I felt myself getting warm, my forehead starting to sweat. The sound of *Potentials* made me nervous.

"You must go with them," she said quietly out the side of her mouth. "I am not in charge, Serin is, so there's nothing I can do to stop this from happening."

"Potentials for what?" Fiver whispered.

"Your Mothers."

My heart began to race and I felt myself getting dizzy. I couldn't face that woman, never. Whoever she was, I wanted her to remain faceless, an evil shadow of the past that I was lucky to escape. She was an unfeeling monster. The kindness and warmth on these women's faces were emotions my Mother would not be capable of conveying. I couldn't face her. I wouldn't face her.

I began to back away, my feet tripping over themselves, and Fiver grabbed me before I could fall backwards.

"We have to, Urgs," Fiver whispered to me. "That's why they think we're here."

He was right but I didn't want him to be.

I heard a sharp intake of breath, and saw Av's eyes come up from the floor as he composed himself. If Av could get himself together after what Lussit had dropped on him, then I could too. I was here for Cubby. I had to do it for him.

Lussit held out her arms to her sisters. "What a generous and loving offer. I release them to your tender care." She turned to the three of us, and said in a grand, ceremonious voice for everyone to hear: "I will pray you find the answers that you seek. May love fill your hearts." With that, she bowed to us and gestured to Serin and the "Potentials."

I knew this was what I had to do, but as I looked at their slightly wrinkled, teary eyes, their hopeful smiles, my feet refused to move. Av nudged me forward and I couldn't help but resist it. I guessed Av just wanted to go through the motions and not think about his mother. He didn't even ask Lussit to tell him who it was. She was his sister, after all; she could have told him and he wouldn't have had to go through any of this. That was when Fiver decided to intervene and he smacked me on the head. I snapped out of it and fell in line, following Av and Fiver to the group of waiting women.

Serin was the only one not smiling. She was still cold and icy, still unsure of us. "Do you remember Tanuk?" she asked, pointing to the silver-haired woman from the ambush. Her face was tender, a happy smile with sad eyes. She'd been the one to suggest we go to Lussit, and really, she'd saved our lives. The three of us nodded and Serin continued. "We will share her hearth tonight."

Without another word, Serin began to head for the cave opening, and the three of us were quick to follow, too frightened to be left behind with these gushing, weepy Potentials.

As we approached the mouth of the cave, light from the outside hurt my eyes. I looked back, hoping to catch a last view of Lussit, but whatever view I might have had was blocked by the following Potentials.

Outside, the camp was alive with all kinds of women, different shapes and sizes. A scattered group of withered old things was waiting by the entrance, their heads pressed to the floor, singing and praying, while more seemed to be waiting to see us. Old faces and younger ones, girls as small as the Abish fortune-teller giggled in groups and whispered as we passed. Two girls, closer to our age, I guessed, fought each other with bo staffs and sticks. They were growling and viciously battling. My jaw nearly fell open when the smaller one flipped over the taller one, taking out her feet with a single swipe as she landed. The taller girl fell on her back and roared with frustration.

I looked to Av, who wasn't paying attention, his mind a million miles away from where we were, occupied by a million questions for Lussit, no doubt. But Fiver—he was grinning. It was a big stupid, gawking grin and I hoped way down in my soul that I hadn't looked like that when I first saw Lussit.

"Our girls learn young," said Serin when she noticed us watching. "And they learn fast. It's important to be well versed in combat when you are a Belpheban."

"And if they don't?" asked Fiver.

"I'm sorry?"

"If they don't learn fast, what happens?" I didn't like the tone in his voice. He was challenging her and she knew it. "You throw them away like you do all the boys?"

I held my breath and waited for Serin's response, but she

224

said nothing. She simply looked at him with a bit of what I could only identify as pity.

All of a sudden one of the Potentials ran out of the cave and burst into a full-blown wail as she rushed at Fiver. "Benedon! My Benedon!" she cried. "I had to! I just had to! It was the only way to keep you safe!"

Before she could wrap her bony arms around him, Fiver threw her thin, frail body and the woman went flying backwards into the waiting arms of the other Potentials.

In an instant, Serin had him firmly in her grip, his arms pinned behind his back, her bo staff holding up his chin.

"Sisters," she said to the Potentials, who were busy quieting the crazy woman, wiping her tears and smoothing her hair. "Our visitors have had an exhausting day. Let them rest over a nourishing meal before we reunite them with their Mothers."

"She's not my Mother!" Fiver growled.

"No, I doubt she is," agreed Serin. Then, turning back to the sobbing woman: "Amala, Benedon was born over twenty years ago. These boys are too young to be your Benedon."

The woman fell to her knees, lost in grief, while Serin let go of Fiver and pressed on to our destination.

"What in the name of Rawley is wrong with these women?" Fiver said.

Serin turned to look at him, stunned at his reaction. "The same thing as you, little Fiver. Heartache for what they lost."

"Then maybe they shouldn't have chosen to chuck us in the first place," Fiver grumbled under his breath.

Serin stepped up to him, pity gone. "Chosen? What choice is it you think we Belphebans have?" That suspicious look was back on her face. I didn't like it. "Tell me something, Ikkuma boy. What made you so sure our dear Amala was not your Mother?"

He couldn't be. He wasn't. He said nothing, shrugged, and kept scowling at the ground, but the damage had been done. It wasn't that Fiver knew the Amala woman wasn't his Mother; it was that Fiver didn't want to know. He didn't want to know who his Mother was as much as I didn't. But we had to pretend we did want to know . . . and we were failing . . . and Serin was noticing.

"Pity for the timing," she said, backing away, an obvious restraint in her posture. She didn't want to come down on us just yet. "Amala would have been a wonderful Mother to have. You would have been lucky if she were."

Still, Fiver kept his mouth shut and the group, minus Amala, continued on towards Tanuk's home, a dwelling of low walls of stacked stones and mud with an orange canopy draped over the top. Serin stopped at the opening and Tanuk pulled aside the curtain, ushering us inside.

It was modest, even simpler than the A-Frame. Nothing but blankets and pillows and a corner devoted to dishes and pots and a few bags of grain, as though they didn't want to make themselves comfortable. I guessed that was the point. Blaze said they moved a lot.

A little girl, younger than Cubby, with curly golden hair and dimpled cheeks, giggled when we entered and ran to an older girl with the same golden hair, a stunning picture of beauty were it not for the monstrous swollen gut she was resting her threading on. I stared; the belly wasn't fat, it was round, swollen, like someone had filled her full of air. It looked sore, though she seemed comfortable enough.

"My youngest daughter," said Tanuk, and the round-bellied woman nodded and smiled.

Fiver was staring too, almost frightened by the look of her.

"The baby will be here any day."

The girl placed a hand on her stomach and rubbed. "I'd hoped for today, but she doesn't seem to want to come out!"

Out? I looked back to Fiver, who'd gone pale in the face. Out of her stomach?

Serin watched the confusion on our faces and a wry smile spread across her lips. "Not much learned about the birds and the bees in the Ikkuma Pit, is there?"

"A bee did that?" said Fiver, incredulous.

Serin threw back her head and let out a cackle, and I noticed the rest of the women had started to giggle.

"Don't tease them," said Tanuk, smiling. "Come now, boys, let that be a lesson for another day." She ushered us away and picked up the little girl. "My granddaughter, Pepper."

We nodded politely and the little girl giggled.

"Please sit, let us eat."

We looked around, unsure of what to do. Serin and the other Potentials sat easily enough, plopping themselves down on the pillows and blankets, forming a perfect circle. The three of us did the same and sat in awkward silence while Tanuk dispensed bowls to each of us filled with some goopy, sloppy mush that smelled like feet.

Then, the night got worse. As I tried to choke down the bland, salty slush, each of the Potentials trotted out a bunch of keepsakes from when their sons had been born, sons they hoped might be us. They handed their bundles to us one by one—swaddling clothes, dusty and ragged blankets, wooden toys and rattles—and asked if any of it looked familiar. It didn't. Even if these items had once belonged to me, I was just a baby. How could they expect me to remember? I

227

shook my head no, over and over as the next Potential passed me her trinkets. Av and Fiver did the same and I wondered why Lussit was putting us through all this. She could spare Av all of this and just tell him who their mother was. Maybe she didn't want the others to know they were related. Perhaps she was trying to save Av by not telling him.

Every look of disappointment from my headshake should have made me happy, I should have taken delight in inflicting misery on these awful women, but instead I found myself feeling sorry for them. "The Guilt," Farka had called it, and each of the Potentials was covered in it. They'd spent a lifetime regretting letting go of their baby boys.

"No," sighed Av as he handed back a fuzzy pink blanket to Tanuk. "I'm sorry, I don't."

His hand rubbed his forehead and I didn't know if it was his injury or the Sister thing that was making his head hurt.

Tanuk nodded and folded the little blanket on her lap.

Tanuk had been the easiest Potential to deal with. She wasn't as crushed as the rest of them when we said no, and she didn't watch us like all her life's hopes depended on one of us being her son. She simply accepted what we said and her posture stayed straight. She didn't slump, she didn't frown. She just watched us patiently, fingering the blue pendant around her neck, and treated us with all the respect and hospitality she could. Tanuk had a quiet strength about her, a dignity that I had to admire. If I had recognized her fuzzy blanket, it may not have been the worst thing.

I watched as her hand dropped from the object on her neck. It was a tube, kind of, a tube I'd seen before, only much smaller. "What is that?" I said without thinking.

"What? My Abish shroud?" She looked at the blue stone object dangling from her neck and smiled.

"Abish shroud?"

She slid the object off her neck and handed it to me. "A tricky little contraption invented by the Abish to keep secret things safe."

I turned it over in my fingers. It was identical to Blaze's flint box, though smaller. The stone was so bright and smooth.

"Secret things," I repeated.

"It keeps my treasures for me," Tanuk said, and winked. She reached over and twisted the top to the left, then the bottom to the right. She pressed each end between her index fingers and with a click the little blue tube opened, a frayed old cloth poking out.

She pulled out the cloth and unraveled it to reveal a little black footprint pressed into the fibers.

"My boy's," she said, smiling sadly.

The foot was small enough to fit in the palm of my hand, little toes no bigger than a seed.

I nodded awkwardly, not sure what to say, and handed it back.

"Has anyone ever found the son they were looking for?" Av was talking to Serin and she smiled as she swallowed her food.

"Of course. There have been many."

"So . . . a lot of us come back, then?" Av looked disappointed, as though every Big Brother had been nothing but a Mother seeker all along.

"A few. Not often, but indeed there have been some. I can't remember the last one that came. What was it?" She looked to her Sisters and asked, "Four years ago?"

"Four," agreed Tanuk, clicking the stone tube closed and hanging it around her neck, hiding her treasure once more.

"Four," came the familiar, snake-like voice of Farka as she threw aside the curtain and stormed into the room.

"Farka," said Serin, nodding in a rather cold greeting.

I tensed when she looked at me. She made my whole body cold and stiff, she made me feel like a Slag Cavy, caught in the hunter's eye.

"Boys," said Tanuk, handing Farka a full bowl of her salty slop. "This is my eldest, Farka."

Poor Tanuk. Stuck raising a monster like Farka. No wonder she sought her son. Any child would be better than Farka. I shuddered at the thought that she could be my Sister, but I doubted it. She was sharp and strong, a good hunter. We had nothing in common.

"Yes, many have returned and reunited with their Mothers," said Serin. "Most don't ever find their Mothers, of course."

"Sad when that happens," said Tanuk.

"What's sad about it?" spat Farka. "They aren't supposed to be here."

"Quiet, Farka," snapped her Mother.

Farka simmered in the corner and no one moved to make room for her in the circle. She sat, scooping up the slop with her fingers and glaring at the three of us as she ate.

"And they just leave?" I asked, doing my best to ignore the burn from her stare.

Serin nodded.

"So . . . where do they go?"

Serin just shrugged but Tanuk smiled and patted my leg. "Bigger things, my dear," she said. "Many of them have even joined the Resistance against the Beginning."

"Well," said a woman cradling her lost son's rattle, "if only to follow the first."

Tanuk nodded and smiled. "Yes, you boys are stronger

than you know. Not long ago, one of you nearly took down the entire Beginning order." She turned her smile to me and squeezed my shoulder. "You're so much like him. . . ."

I couldn't help but think of my Big Brother, Cheeks. We'd been nothing alike and everyone back home was quick to point that out. No matter how much Cheeks tried to pass on what he knew to me, I never seemed to pick it up. No one back home would have ever said I reminded them of Cheeks.

"What did he do?" I asked.

"Tragic story, really," Tanuk sighed. "He came here. He'd just had his Leaving Day. I'd say he was a couple years older than you boys now."

Av and I nodded, and I hoped Farka wouldn't comment on how young we were again. Tanuk continued. "Anyway, he never did find his Mother, poor thing. But he did find love. He fell hard and fast for one of our young Sisters, and it wasn't long before the two fled from us."

"How come?"

"They wanted to be married. That's something a Belpheban just does not do."

"Why not?" asked Fiver.

Tanuk let a breath escape her nostrils. "Love is little better than a curse for our kind. Ever since the time of Belphoebe, any Belphebans who find love quickly find misery and destruction."

I remembered the rock twin, Amid, murdered for his love of Belphoebe.

"And so it was for our Sister in this case. Since the Belphebans do not allow marriage, the two went looking for a people who would. Unfortunately, all they found were the Beginners."

"Stupid girl," hissed the woman with the rattle.

"They were quickly wed and embraced by their society, marking them with the brand that marks all Beginners." Tanuk pointed at her neck where it joins to the shoulder. Just where Blaze's had been. "The mark of Ardigund. And the two lovers, so skilled and so smart—they were descendants of Belphebans, after all—climbed the ranks of the Beginning order rather quickly, too quickly. Both became the pride of Krepin's armies. Our Sister, she was utterly seduced by the teachings of the Beginning, and the words of Aju Krepin."

My stomach twisted at the sound of the name, the memory of his icy eyes flashing across my mind.

"But the boy, he remained skeptical . . . especially when their baby came."

I felt Av shift beside me and I knew he'd been just as startled as me. The idea of a Brother with a baby was not one that had entered our heads before, and it was a shocking thought.

"Every lesson preached by the Beginning made him worry more and more, and he didn't like the Aju's strange interest in his child. The Aju kept the new family very close."

"Why?"

Tanuk looked at me, surprise on her face, and I felt my cheeks get hot.

"Because," she told me, "the baby was Ikkuman and Belpheban."

Av's brow was knotted, and he looked to me but I was just as confused.

"Why should that matter?" I asked.

"My dear boy, the Sacred Six! The baby was a pure son

of Belphoebe. Krepin believed some nonsense that he could somehow restore the powers of Ardigund."

I could still see the water in my mind, the way it moved away from his feet as he walked towards me, like the water itself was afraid to be too close to him. How much power did the man have?

A popping noise brought my attention to Av, who was nervously cracking his knuckles beside me.

Fiver was mesmerized. "So what happened?"

"Well, naturally the young Ikkuma was very disturbed by the Aju's attention. But the Mother, she was devoted, mind, body, and soul, and so he stayed, if only to keep her happy. When Krepin eyed the couple's son to become the next of the Ajus, the Ikkuma boy refused to hand his child over."

"How come?" asked Av.

"Because it meant the child would be Krepin's. The couple would lose the baby forever."

There was a bad taste on my tongue, and I didn't think it was the food.

"The Beginners mark all their leaders with a mark to the forehead; it is a huge honor among their people. But when Krepin went to place it on the forehead of his child, the Ikkuma boy refused. Naturally, Krepin was furious, and so he set his Gorpoks upon the young parents. His loyal priests surrounded the couple's modest home, barring them from leaving, and recited the incantations from the ancient teachings of the Ajus. Day and night, Krepin's Gorpoks spoke words of poison, invading their dreams, until the two found themselves on the edge of madness. Their minds had gone queer from the assault of the Ajus, and the girl found herself believing that her son belonged to Krepin.

"The Ikkuma begged his wife to run away with him but she wouldn't hear of it. She'd fallen under the spell of Krepin's Gorpoks, honored that her baby had been chosen, poor brainwashed girl she was. One night, while the Ikkuma slept, the Gorpoks' whispers overcame his wife and she took the child, disappearing into the night. She followed the voices to Krepin."

"Did Krepin take the baby?" asked Fiver. He was hanging on Tanuk's every word.

She shook her head and breathed a heavy sigh. "It was the river that took the baby in the end, and the Mother. When they tried to cross to the High Temple, they were swept away and lost over the falls. You can imagine her husband was furious and grieving. He wanted to destroy Krepin, but storming the Beginners' High Temple and wringing the devil's neck wasn't the most practical solution."

Why in the name of Rawley not? I thought. Krepin had certainly earned it.

"So he did the one thing that could hurt Krepin the most. He stayed."

The three of us raised an eyebrow. This was not the violent revenge we were quietly hoping for.

"He stayed and climbed the ranks of Krepin's armies, pouring his efforts into the Holy War, proving himself as a soldier. When Krepin planned to attack the city of Norale Heights, it was time for the grieving father to take his revenge. Norale Heights is a city of millions. To take them by surprise would devastate Norale and choke the surrounding lands with Krepin's power . . . if they were surprised."

Tanuk gave a mischievous smile and Farka scoffed. "Get on with it, Mum."

"They weren't surprised?" asked Fiver, barely containing his excitement.

"Certainly not. Not after our hero turned over every detail of the attack to the armies of Norale Heights. They were ready for Krepin's troops, and the result was devastating to Krepin's efforts. His army was destroyed and he was forced to retreat to the Baublenotts to rebuild his forces. The Beginners' Holy War has suffered ever since, and the Resistance has had the chance to double in size."

"Did Krepin ever find out who ratted on him?"

"He did," Tanuk said, nodding. "He imprisoned the boy in the bowels of that hideous High Temple, and scratched out his mark so he would be known to all Beginners as a traitor. Krepin left him to die down there. But his soldiers who loved him for the warrior he was snuck into the High Temple and secretly freed him. Furious, Krepin ordered his Tunrar to devote themselves to hunting the man down, demanding his capture."

"Have they caught him?" Av asked.

"Not to this day, at least that I know of anyway. It's been so long since we've heard news of Blaze."

My stomach leaped into my throat and Fiver began to choke on his own spit.

Serin smacked him on the back to dislodge the surprise that had caught in his throat, while Tanuk gripped my wrist and looked at me, concerned.

"Dear boy, are you all right? You look ghostly pale."

All I could manage was a weak nod as my mind reeled from all the images connecting in my mind. I heard his mumbling that first night, echoing in my memory: *Not my baby, end to the Beginning.* The mark on his neck, different from Cubby's, a line running through the whole of it. It marked him as a traitor.

"That mark," I said, my voice faltering, "the one the men in Fendar Sticks wore . . ."

"It's the symbol for the entire Resistance," said Tanuk proudly. "To mark their allegiance with our brave Ikkuma boy."

I leaned forward, doubled over, as I realized the magnitude of what I'd done, of what Blaze had done, of what he'd risked by helping me.

I felt Tanuk's hand on my back. "Child, are you ill?"

"He's fine," assured Av. "All this traveling has finally caught up with him, I think." He laughed nervously but Tanuk didn't look convinced. Me, I was too devastated to care about putting in a good performance. I'd sold Blaze out to the world's biggest villain. Blaze, the hero of the Resistance, nearly destroyed by the Ikkuma boy whom history would name Useless.

NINE

After Tanuk had brought out a large gourd filled to the brim with what they called squash wine, and Serin had helped herself to three mugs full, she was more than willing to let us head back to Lussit.

"Certainly, certainly!" she slurred as she held out her mug to Tanuk for a refill. "Off to bed with you, boys. Try again in the morning, eh? Plenty more sad Mothers where these wenches came from!"

Tanuk smacked her playfully and they both broke into a fit of laughter. Whatever was in it, that squash wine made the stone-cold Serin a much happier person.

The three of us walked towards Lussit's cave in silence, trying to sort out our thoughts and fight sleep at the same time. Dawn would come soon, and my mission was nowhere close to being complete.

"Blaze," said Fiver. "I can't believe it."

"I should have never given his name in the Temple," I said, desperately trying to hold off the guilt that threatened to topple over the stack of worries and concerns I'd built up since we left the Pit.

"All right," said Fiver, stopping in his tracks. "Here's what we do: see that outcrop of rocks down a bit from Tanuk's? We camp out there for now and when Serin leaves we take her by surprise and finish this. We get out of this place tonight."

"Are you insane?" I whispered. "Keep your voice down, someone could hear you."

"There's no one around! Let's quit dragging our heels and do what we came here to do."

I shook my head and tried to think of something to say. What were we here to do? After Tanuk's story, I was more frightened of Krepin than ever. The thought of doing what he wanted me to do, of killing Serin, of killing anyone, was making me sick to my stomach. My whole body shivered as the feel of driving a dagger through her chest crept into my mind.

"We can't go yet," whispered Av. His eyes were puffy again, hollow and tired from too much stress. "I have to know if this Sister thing is true."

"It's not," said Fiver.

"I think it is." He was so quiet, I could barely hear him, like he hadn't wanted to admit it out loud.

"Why?"

He heaved a heavy sigh, like he knew we wouldn't understand. He shrugged. "When she held my arm, I just . . . I knew before she told me."

"What do you mean, Av?" I asked.

He stopped, his eyes unfocused, too many thoughts flying around in his head. "It was like . . . like the rocks and ice." He sighed again, as if no one was with him. "It felt like the dream about my Mother."

On instinct, I glanced quickly at Fiver. Av only ever

talked about his dream to me, the dream about his Mother. It was our secret and I'd promised I'd never tell anyone. Fiver would have been the last person I'd ever let know about it. He'd make sure the whole Pit thought Av was a Mother seeker as soon as he found out.

"I'm starting to think I wasn't seeing my Mother," he said.

"Your what?" said Fiver.

"I think . . ." His eyes met mine and they were wet. He was exhausted, overwhelmed, and I put my hand on the back of his neck and squeezed.

"You think what?"

"I think I was seeing Lussit."

Fiver scoffed and kicked the dirt. I believed him, though, after everything he'd said, about his dreams, I had to believe him. A part of me felt that twinge of jealousy, a dark, evil part of me hating that Av, special and talented as he was, might also have some gift in the way his Sister did.

"Av's right," I said, wishing away the swelling and red- ness around Av's exhausted eyes. Av wouldn't sleep until he knew the truth about her. "We can't do it yet."

"Ah, come on, Urgs!" growled Fiver, doing his best to keep his voice down. "Whatever happened to 'No time to eat! No time to rest!' Remember Cubby? Huh? Remember him?"

A familiar lump began to swell in my throat. Of course I remembered Cubby.

"I can't save Wasted now. He's gone. But if I could"—he bit his bottom lip, fighting through the pain of saying his Little Brother's name—"I'd slit Serin's throat right here right now and get back to him as fast as possible. That's what Krepin wants you to do. That's what you have to do."

"What Krepin wants . . . ," I repeated.

"Yes!" said Fiver. "What he wants, you have to do!"

"Weren't you listening, Fiver? What makes you think a man like that is going to keep his word?"

"Yeah, I was listening. It was epic. Like Rawley battles his Mother. It's big. Get it? It's so much bigger than us, Urgle. What's one little boy to a man like Krepin? Why wouldn't he keep his word?"

I didn't know. Tanuk's story was changing so much of what I thought.

"Urgle," said Fiver, "what other choice do you think there is?"

I let the cold air fill my lungs until it hurt, and nodded. There was no other choice.

"What about me?" said Av.

"What about you?" Fiver grabbed him by the shoulders and shook him gently until Av looked up from the ground. "You don't know for sure. I know what you said, but let's get serious. There's no way *she* knows for sure, and even if she is . . . you were fine without a Sister before. You'll be fine after."

Av, who looked unconvinced, nodded sadly. We were here for one reason: Cubby. Nothing else mattered.

"We'll do it tonight," I agreed. "Back to Krepin by morning."

"Bad luck, little boys," said Farka's serpentine voice from somewhere in the shadows.

Before I had a second to register the direction of the voice, she swung a blade at my feet and I jumped back, stumbling to the ground.

Her foot sailed over me and she kicked Fiver in the throat.

Saved by his speed, Av ducked and rolled just in time to miss another swipe of her blade, which sparkled menacingly in the moonlight.

Farka screamed in frustration, and I heard interested voices stirring from nearby hearths. It wouldn't take long for them to come out and catch a glimpse of the commotion. This was it: us or Farka. Cubby or Farka.

I sprang to my feet and saw the shadows: a tall leggy Farka moving to take out Av. He dodged her blade, but not the swift leg that followed, and her foot connected with his chest, throwing him to the ground.

"Ikkuma spies!" she hissed as she brought down her blade to finish Av. He rolled and she missed, but only just.

Fiver coughed and gasped on the ground, completely immobilized while the voices rose around us.

Farka growled and kicked Av, knocking him down before he could get up.

We couldn't be caught.

I threw myself onto Farka, grabbing a fistful of her hair and wrenching her whole head back.

She roared and reached back to claw me, her long nails digging into my cheeks.

Av seized the moment and threw a punch to her stomach, winding her, but she struggled all the more. Another punch from Av, and she only got angrier, flipping me over her back and throwing me into him.

The ground connected with my chin as I slammed into it, and I was dazed.

Av groaned from the pain, but we couldn't slow down now. I shook away the stars and as Farka raised her sword, I tackled her, throwing all of my weight into her gut. The two of us went down and she lost her grip on her weapon. Av was ready, and scrambled to grab it.

He grabbed my hand and pulled me to my feet, keeping Farka on the ground by the tip of her sword.

"You know how to use that, little boys?" she whispered, amusement oozing through every syllable.

Av growled and pulled back, preparing to thrust the blade straight through her, but with a swift move from her feet, so fast my eyes could barely register it as movement, she grabbed the blade between her feet and wrenched it from Av's grip, throwing it into the air and catching it in her left hand.

It was all so easy to see now, her flourish of skilled movement lit by the soft glow of flames all around us.

"Enough!" shouted Serin.

"Spies, Serin!" screeched Farka.

Serin, Tanuk, and the Potentials, plus a host of other faces, surrounded us, all of them angry and stern.

"I told you they were spies!"

Serin stepped in beside Farka and stared at me, Fiver, and Av long and hard. Not even the squash wine could make her smile now.

"Krepin sent them to kill you!" Farka went on. "I heard them, every word! They are assassins for the Beginning!"

There was a chorus of gasps and murmurs from the crowd of onlookers.

"She's lying!" I yelled, but Serin's tight jaw showed who she believed. She'd had a hard time trusting us since the start—she was smart.

She took the blade that Farka was keeping threateningly close to our hearts, and raised it to my throat. "What have you come for, Ikkuma boy?"

"My Mother," I said through gritted teeth.

Her eyes searched mine for a long silent moment until finally she dropped the sword and I let out a breath.

"Tie them up, take them to the top of Sammerson Peak."

242

In an instant, the crowd moved in, seizing me, Av, and poor Fiver, who was still coughing, sputtering, and rubbing his neck as he tried to get his breath back.

We were in trouble.

"Tomorrow," Serin announced, staring at the three of us with that cold detachment I had seen right after the ambush. "They die in the morning."

TEN

They tied us together, hands behind our backs, on one long
wooden stake driven into the rocks. They left Elome, Farka's
friend from Fendar Sticks, standing guard a few yards away.
The hike had been long to get to the top of Sammerson Peak,
and even longer thanks to the assortment of angry jeers and
wads of spit hurled in our direction. Younger girls had run
from their hearths to join the mob that took us up the hill,
running up occasionally to kick our shins, then cackle and
disappear into the crowds. My shins were still throbbing as
I sat there, in the freezing cold, my back against the stake,
my head hung low, and not a sound but the wind through
the mountains and the breath of my Brothers.

Fiver was grunting, pulling and tugging at the ropes,
but it was no use. They'd tied them tight and we weren't
going anywhere. This was it. I wasn't mad. I wasn't sad. I
was out of feelings. And I think, deep down, some quiet,
hopeless part of me knew it would end up like this—Cubby
lost to the Beginners forever, me dead in the wilderness
somewhere.

That's what everyone must have thought. Useless. I'd proved that time and time again, and finally, just before I died, I'd make absolutely sure that "useless" was the legacy I left behind.

"Just stop it, Fiver," I told him. "It's over."

"What?"

"Just stop squirming!" I was shouting, there was no controlling it. "It's over! I failed! Just stop trying to escape, 'cause it's over!"

Fiver stared at me, a little stunned, and I couldn't look at him anymore. I couldn't look at Av either. I just wanted to be alone.

Suddenly Fiver slammed his head into my face, and my eyes welled with tears when his forehead connected with my nose.

The pain was like an explosion, radiating from my nose and out to my entire body as I felt a hot river of blood flood down into my mouth.

"Mother seeker!" I yelled.

"Feel better?" Fiver growled.

"What in the name of Rawley was that for?"

"For sounding like an idiot," he spat. "You're just feeling sorry for yourself, so I thought I'd give you something else to feel for a little while. Just feel your nose now, don't you?"

I said nothing, wrinkling my nose to try and stop the bleeding.

"I didn't come all this way, following your useless face through all this trouble," he went on, "just to wind up skewered by a bunch of she-monsters."

"What do you want me to do, Fiver?" I shouted.

"I want you to remember what you are."

What I was. A failure. The reason Cubby was lost.

"Useless, I know." My head hung so low the words were said more to my chest than anybody.

"You're Ikkuma," Fiver growled. "A Big Brother."

I tasted the salty metallic sting of my blood and spat. I wished he'd stop talking, stop reaching for hope where there was none. I wanted him to give up, like I'd given up. I wanted to shut down my brain, to stop the images of Cubby that kept pushing their way to the front of my mind. I just wanted everything to stop.

"Yeah," I muttered, "Big Brother to a scroungee."

Before I knew where it came from, pain jolted my shin and I cried out, realizing Fiver had slammed his heel into my leg.

"Don't call him that," he growled.

"Me?" I shouted. "You're the one who calls him that! You've always called him that! I know what you think of me, Fiver, and Cubby!"

"*You* don't call him that."

I turned my head away to keep from screaming at him. I didn't want to waste my breath. All my life, Fiver thought I was a bad Big Brother, and now I knew he was right. What was left to fight about?

He let out a sigh. "Do you remember Bones?"

I did. But I couldn't remember Fiver ever talking about him. I kept my face turned away, but I was listening. Fiver never talked about his Big Brother.

"What about Boo? You remember him?"

I'd never heard that name before. I looked at him, confused, and saw that Av was just as unfamiliar with the name.

"No? What about Chance? Know him?"

No. I didn't.

"Keeper? Newbie?"

I stared at him blankly. What were these names? Where were they coming from?

"No," he said, nodding. "You know Fiver, though. Lucky number five." He looked away, away from me, from Av. His eyes were on his lap. "I'm number five. And that's no thanks to Bones."

"What are you saying, Fiver?" asked Av.

"They're dead," he said. "Boo, Chance. Keeper and Newbie, one after the other. He just didn't care, Bones. He never cared about anyone but himself. He lost one Little Brother, he got a new one, lost another, got a new one. Like trading in throwing daggers, he just didn't give a flying Cavy fart, and you know why?"

I shook my head, too surprised to say anything.

"Because he was selfish. Then he got me. Number five. I took care of myself, though. I'm alive because of me."

I barely remembered Bones; he was older, so much older than Cheeks was. I only remembered I was scared of him. He was so big and loud, and if you got too close he'd launch you into the air by your wrists and call it a baby bomb.

And I remembered Fiver. Alone. He was always alone in those days, our Little Brother days.

"You think Bones would lift a finger for me if I had been taken?" He shook his head, answering his own question. "Cubby's alive because of you, Urgs. You're not like Bones."

I swallowed a lump that was rising in my throat, the memory of that lonely, curly-haired little boy teaching himself how to use a sling suddenly making sense to me.

"You're a good Brother, Useless," he said. "A bit lousy with a spear, sure, but good . . . and not just to Cubby."

247

I looked up, surprised.

"You're the one who never stopped moving," he told me. "Remember? Anyone else would have given up, called it quits right there in the Baublenotts. I wanted to. You wouldn't let us. You kept going."

I didn't believe him, wouldn't let myself. I couldn't have got this far without him, without Av. It was them carrying *me*. But as I looked at Fiver's stern face, his dark eyes ordering me not to argue, I couldn't help but wonder how far they'd get, how far any of us would have got, on our own.

"Someone's coming," whispered Av.

Fiver shut up and we both listened to the night air. Just a cold midnight breeze rustled in my ear, nothing more.

"I don't hear anything," said Fiver.

"She's there."

There was a crunching in the distance, the distinct sound of foot on earth. Someone was coming.

Elome stood up from where she'd been sharpening a knife as a figure came into view. There was mumbling as they spoke, and then finally Elome made her way back down the slope.

"Lussit?" Av said.

My stomach did a cartwheel that it might be her, and I thanked Rawley for letting me see her one last time.

Sure enough, it was Lussit, hurrying over to us with her head turning back to make sure Elome had gone. Her body was wrapped in a thick knitted blanket. She looked around warily, making sure there was no one else nearby, then crouched down to hug Av.

"My Brother!" she whispered. "My friends! When they told me what had happened I tried my best to hurry to you, but they wouldn't leave me alone. The camp's on full alert.

They are terrified there could be more of you nearby. How could this happen?"

"Never mind," said Av. "What did you say to Elome?"

With slender fingers she undid the knot binding Av's feet. "I told her I had come to use my gifts to uncover secrets from the prisoners. I asked her to go and bring my ladies to assist me."

"What will happen when they find out we're gone?"

She smirked, a devilish grin, and I felt a flutter in my stomach. "They'll assume the Ikkuma boys got the better of the defenseless Holy Child, don't you think?"

Her eyes flashed to me and her mouth opened in horror when she noticed the blood pouring from my nose. "Urgle! What did they do to you?"

"I'm fine," I assured her. She held my face in her freezing hands; they were like ice from her long climb.

"He's fine," said Fiver. "He deserved it."

Lussit, confused, accepted what Fiver had said and left me alone to fiddle with the ropes that bound us together.

"Give me one moment," she said, sliding a knife out from under her blanket.

Av started to squirm, his face lined with worry. "If they find out you helped us?"

"It doesn't matter," she said. "I've been without my Brother for too long. Let them be angry." She made a cut and the ropes around my wrists loosened.

Within seconds the three of us were free.

"All right," laughed Fiver, jumping to his feet and wiping the dirt from his arse, "we make one quick stop, surprise Serin while she's sleeping, and boom! We're off to the Baublenotts!"

"I can't let you do that," said Lussit. My heart sank. Of

course she couldn't. Serin was her leader, and she was a good one. I didn't want to kill her. But Cubby.

"Sorry, girly," said Fiver. "But what else did you think we were going to do if you let us go?"

"Go back to the Beginners," she said. "I know why they want Serin; they've been hunting her since this war began. But they'll be just as happy to accept me."

My voice caught in my throat. "What?"

"What better prize for Aju Krepin than the Sacred Innocent of the Belphebans? I am just another Belpheban but I am their spiritual leader. Although I cannot command the same control as Serin, Krepin would be overjoyed to have me as his own."

"No," said Av. "We aren't getting you involved in this, you're in enough trouble just for helping us."

"Exactly, and what's a little more?" She was grinning ear to ear. She was excited, and small wonder. I suspected she'd spent her whole life praying and contorting, meditating and advising. But we couldn't let her sacrifice herself like that for us . . . could we?

"I appreciate your concern for my safety, Brother, but you really don't have another choice." She placed her hands on Av's shoulders and spoke in a voice with such maturity and authority that I couldn't imagine anyone telling her no. "They'll notice I'm gone sooner rather than later, and the longer we stand here arguing, the closer they come to finding out you're free."

"We can't just hand you over to that maniac!" Av protested.

She smiled. "My Sisters will come for me. Besides, I'm not afraid of Krepin."

"Then you're foolish," he snapped.

She did sound foolish. "What if we . . ." I trailed off, not sure if the poorly thought-out plan that had just sprung into my head would be enough to end the debate. "What if we just say we're handing her over, and then don't?"

"Urgle, what?" Av was giving me an impatient glare. He knew I'd given this about as much thought as a tree.

"If I show up to the doors of the Temple with Lussit, they are bound to let me in, right?"

Fiver nodded, eager to get a plan under way, while Av just kept watching me skeptically and Lussit smiled with a grin that was all for me and my jumbled, stuttered words.

"And I promise Krepin Lussit in exchange for Cubby. Meanwhile, you and Fiver are waiting on the river with the boat. Remember the bridge we had to walk on? With the rushing water? Wait beside there. Then, once Krepin releases Cubby, all the three of us have to do is run for the bridge and take off in the boat."

"All you have to do, eh?" said Av.

"Works for me!" said Fiver, ready to take off running.

"Me too!" Lussit grinned and linked her arm in mine.

"Wait!" growled Av as Fiver and Lussit led the way down the mountain, Lussit's frozen hands firmly pulling me along by the wrist and making my head rush with a fog of excitement. "This isn't even a plan!"

"It's all we've got!" laughed Fiver.

He was right. It wasn't much of a plan. In fact, it was a bad plan, and with Lussit's hands on my wrist I knew I'd be afraid to bring her into the Temple with me, let alone offer her as a condolence prize to Krepin.

ELEVEN

We made our way back through Fendar Sticks easily enough, though Fiver and Av were adamant about complete silence until we hit the road that led to the river. The streets of the town were silent too, the warm glow of the indoor lights completely gone while the villagers slept. It was only us that moved through the shadows. . . . We hoped it was only us, anyway.

We made it to the road without so much as a hiccup and it seemed the Belphebans hadn't noticed Lussit's disappearance.

"This was stupid," said Av once we were, he decided, a safe distance from the ears of the sleeping villagers.

"Oh come on, Av," said Fiver, a new spring to his step and a renewed energy flowing through him. "Your Sister is trying to do you a favor. Be grateful."

"Watch your mouth, Fiver," snapped Av. He knew Fiver was only making fun of him. Fiver didn't believe they were related any more than he was related to a Tunrar.

"Av, really, I think Urgle's plan will work," said Lussit, reaching for his shoulder.

He shrugged her away violently. "It's not a plan! It won't work, and if you were my Sister you'd be smart enough to see what an idiotic idea this whole thing is!"

She stepped back and I waited for her to get angry, to yell back at him, but she didn't. Her eyes just got sad, and her mouth trembled as she decided what to say.

"Of course I'm y-your S-Sister," she stuttered. "I felt it, you must have felt it. Did you feel it?"

He looked away from her and muttered, "I don't know what you're talking about."

"You do!" she said, tears beginning to fall down her cheeks. "We come from a long line of Sacred Ones, and they all had the same gift you do. My Mother and her Sister, their Mother and her Sister, on and on since the start of everything! It's always two, we come in pairs. And you and I are a pair. You know that."

Av said nothing, trying to avoid looking at her tear-stained face. Whether he had felt this connection she was talking about or not, I didn't care. I just wanted him to say whatever it was she wanted him to so that she would stop looking so upset.

My eyes went from the one to the other, and I started to notice the resemblance between their faces. Her brow was knotted just like his, her glossy eyes the same shape and color. If she'd cared what I thought, I would have told her I knew it.

He took a while, choosing his words carefully, and I could tell from the way he was grinding his teeth that she was right, he had felt it. He was just as certain they were twins as she was.

"I just wish you hadn't come," he managed, and her face lit up.

Thank you, Av.

"Oh, Av, don't worry about me. Everything will be all right, I—"

"I'm not worried *about* you!" he shouted. "I'm worried about what happens if the Belphebans catch us *with* you!"

He stormed away from her, walking as briskly as he could, Fiver trotting alongside him.

I moved to follow, but Lussit just stayed where she stood, swallowing hard. I could tell she was doing her best not to cry. The tears gave her away.

"You coming?" I asked.

She looked at me, her big dark eyes exposing every ounce of hurt Av had inflicted on her, and I wanted to punch him. I wanted to pin him down and make him apologize, take it all back. She nodded and wiped her eyes, then hurried to my side. We walked together silently, her head hanging down but looking up every so often at Av and Fiver marching ahead.

"He didn't mean it," I said, desperate to make her happy. "He's not good with this kind of thing."

"This kind of thing?" she asked.

I wished she hadn't asked that because I really didn't know what I'd meant. Girl kind of thing? Surprise Sisters kind of thing?

"Surprises," I said. "You took him by surprise is all."

"I ruined your mission?"

"What?" How she came to that conclusion I had no idea. "You saved it. The three of us owe you our lives. Av just said all that 'cause he really does care about you. I promise; I'm his best friend, I can tell. I think it's just freaking him out a little bit. But it only freaks him out because of how much he cares."

She said nothing.

"Better?"

She looked up at me and smiled. "Yes, better." And she slipped her arm through mine.

We walked that way awhile, not speaking, just linked, and I felt like I could walk that way forever.

"What about your Brother?" she said, finally. "How old is he?"

"Six."

"What is his name?"

"Cubby." I thought of him then, if he could've been there with me, met Lussit. He would have loved her instantly.

"He has a very good Big Brother."

I bit my lip because it wasn't true. "There are a lot of people who would disagree with you. . . ."

"What do you mean?"

I shrugged, not sure I wanted to get into the whole thing, not sure I wanted to talk about how I was a miserable Big Brother to Cubby, always annoyed, always snapping at him. I couldn't teach him anything because I wasn't good at anything, so I took it out on him. Truth was, Cubby had rotten luck getting stuck with me. Before I knew it, I'd told all this to Lussit, who listened attentively. When I was done, I felt that lump, that annoying, painful swell in the back of my throat that so often crept up on me these last four days.

She rubbed my arm gently, her hand making the skin instantly warm in the frigid night air. She got on her tiptoes and kissed me on the cheek. "Cubby is very lucky to have someone who cares about him as much as you do."

She gave me that smile that was all love and kindness and then looked ahead, continuing with the journey.

I walked with her, arm in arm, but my brain was still

255

back at the moment she kissed me. I wasn't sure what I did right—if anything I thought she'd be appalled and run away, but she hadn't. She'd kissed me.

"Mother seeker!" Fiver bellowed up ahead.

I could hear the quiet trickle of water, and I could make out the bridge, just a shadow in the distance. We'd reached the river.

"Boat's gone," announced Av. "Water must have carried it."

Av was right. We hadn't tied it to anything.

"So we walk?" I said.

"And fast," said Fiver. "Those Belphebans will be hot on our trail come first light."

Lussit nodded. We were running out of time.

Av took off at a quick jog down the bank of the river and me, Fiver, and Lussit silently followed. We were in for a long night, but we had to put as much distance between us and an angry Serin as possible.

Too late.

I watched a dagger sail out of nowhere, just barely missing Fiver's head and slamming into a nearby tree.

"Already?" screamed Fiver, who didn't stop running. None of us stopped, we just ran faster.

Lussit was lagging behind so I grabbed her hand and pulled her along. She was trying, but her top speed was a lot slower than ours.

Another dagger whizzed by. This one I could hear as it flew past my right ear.

I veered to the left, dragging Lussit with me. Fiver and Av kept running ahead. I didn't know where they were going, I didn't know where we were going, but we had to go. I ran as fast as I could with Lussit slowing me down. Neither of us was a particularly good runner and I realized we were the easiest people in the world to track. Lussit was squealing every time a branch flew back in her face, or she had a momentary loss of balance, while I was snapping every brittle twig that came under my foot. We were loud and destructive. They'd follow us easily.

I stopped.

"What are you doing?" she gasped between labored breaths.

There was a thick mossy trunk just beside us, vines and undergrowth weaving around its base.

"Get in there!" I whispered, and gently pushed her in that direction. She was quick to follow my instructions and we forced our way into the shelter of the leaves and vegetation.

It was a tight space, and we sat, her hands on my lap and her frightened breath hot on my ear. She smelled like spices and water, and I began to worry that she'd notice my stink. We sat as quietly as we could, waiting with thumping hearts, and I promised myself I'd do whatever I could to keep her safe from whatever came for us.

There was the sound of snapping twigs nearby, just one or two. Then nothing. Silence. It could have easily been an animal, but a cold chill ran up my spine and I had a feeling, a feeling like Fiver must have felt that night in Fendar Sticks. We were being watched.

Just then, I was yanked by the throat and pulled with a mighty force from my hiding spot. Lussit let out a scream and I was thrown to the ground, my face in the dirt.

"You thought you could escape, little boy?" Farka. She circled around me, snarling and seething.

I moved to get up but she kicked me in the stomach and I collapsed, gasping for breath and wincing from the pain.

"Farka, please," cried Lussit. "Let him go!"

"But, Sacred Innocent!" Farka said. "I've come to save you! They are in league with the Beginners."

"No, they aren't," pleaded Lussit. "I don't need you to save me, Farka. They are our friends."

I got ahold of myself again and moved to get up. Farka was waiting for it and she pelted me in the groin. I bit down and my whole body lit up from the pain.

"My lady! They were plotting to kill Serin!"

She kicked me again.

"Farka!" boomed Lussit in that commanding voice she hid so well when we were talking on the road. "I am guided by the ethereal light, and I know what I am doing. You will leave these boys alone."

Farka stared at Lussit, dumbfounded and confused. That was when Fiver bodychecked her.

He flew in from the shadows and sent Farka to the ground, landing on top of her. She screamed and roared as she struggled underneath him, and then Av arrived, taking the opportunity to grab her sword.

"Careful," I sputtered as Fiver finally crawled off her, "we've been here before."

"Fiver, get something to bind her."

Fiver nodded and rushed into the bushes, emerging moments later with an armful of thick vines.

He hurried to tie up Farka, but as soon as he grabbed her arm she flipped him over her head. He landed with a thud and a growl, but Farka didn't try anything more. Av had the blade firmly pressed against her neck.

Fiver wrapped the vines tightly round her chest and arms, wrapping and threading all the way to her wrists.

"How many more of you are there?" Av demanded.

Farka smiled defiantly.

"Tell me!" he barked.

Still Farka said nothing. Lussit took a hesitant step forward and placed her shaking hand on the top of Farka's head.

"She's alone," Lussit said.

"There are many coming," Farka hissed.

"There aren't," Lussit countered. "She's all alone. She must have been following us since we left the camp."

Av nodded.

"Wait!" protested Fiver. "How do we know she's alone for sure?"

Av looked at Lussit, then glared at Farka before he took a long, frustrated breath. "She's alone."

"Av!" barked Fiver. "Lussit can't know that!"

"She's alone!" said Av, officially ending the conversation.

I cleared my throat to break the awkward silence. "So what do we do with Farka?"

Av and Fiver said nothing. There was really only one option.

"We take her with us," said Lussit.

"Excuse me, Holiness," laughed Fiver. "But there's definitely a more convenient way to deal with this. Av, kill her."

Farka began to laugh and Av held the blade to her neck.

"Av, please," begged Lussit.

"Get up," he ordered Farka.

With a sour scowl, she got to her feet, arms secure behind her back.

"Move."

"I don't believe this," grumbled Fiver.

Farka took a couple of lazy steps towards Av, then spat in his face before she stumbled back towards the river. Av followed, blade pointed firmly at Farka. Lussit walked beside him, and I looked to Fiver, who stood with his arms crossed, glowering at the sibling pair.

I shrugged and smiled before I fell in line.

"What are you smiling about, Useless?"

I wasn't sure. Maybe it was the fact that we'd dodged death for the third time that night. Maybe it was the defeated scowl on Farka's face. Or maybe it was because Av had let Lussit have her way. Mostly, though, I think it was because we were closer. We were so much closer to rescuing Cubby; I was so much closer to having him back.

TWELVE

By the time morning light peeked through the treetops, we were deep in the Baublenotts, following the river and hacking through thick vegetation. I was exhausted, but the sound of the thundering water invigorated me. We were getting close to the Falls of the Faithful.

The sound of rushing water didn't have the same impact on Lussit, and she stumbled a few paces behind us, dark circles forming under her eyes.

"We should rest a minute," said Av, noticing Lussit at the same time I did.

Normally I would have argued, but I was feeling just as tired as Lussit looked and I knew it was better to face Krepin with a bit of rest behind me.

Fiver grunted his approval and hunkered down against a tree for a quick nap.

"Come on, Lussit," I called to her. "We'll rest here."

Av kept Farka's blade on Farka, and he escorted her to a seat on a rotting log.

"Here, Urgs," he said, shoving the sword at me.

"Me?"

"Yeah, you." He glared at me, still mad that I let Lussit come with us. "Just keep pointing it at her; I'm going to try and rest."

He was miserable, tired, and in a bad mood. The last few days had been a lot for Av. He'd survived a vicious head injury and poison, and he was now dealing with the fact that he had a sister. And Goobs. He had to be missing his Little Brother, worrying about him alone in the Ikkuma Pit.

I accepted the blade and my hand trembled a bit when I pointed it at Farka. She chuckled bitterly to herself. Av sat down beside Fiver to get in as much sleep as he could for the moment.

"Is it because of me?" asked Lussit. She'd caught up and was standing awkwardly, as though waiting for an invitation to join us.

"What?"

"Did we stop because of me?" She looked so worried, so disappointed in herself.

I shrugged. "I think we're all pretty tired."

I yawned—it started off as just for show, but once I thought about yawning, I was yawning for real, my lack of sleep suddenly catching up with me. I leaned against the trunk of a nearby tree and slid to the ground, careful not to take the blade off Farka, who was watching me like a hungry Tunrar.

Lussit came and sat down in front of me, fiddling with a twig between her fingers. I waited for her to say something, but she didn't.

"You should try to sleep," I told her.

She nodded and then crawled up to the tree trunk and sat next to me.

"Did that hurt?" she asked, pointing to my right leg.

I lifted my leg into my lap and traced the bubbly scar on my ankle with my finger. "I was a baby, I don't remember."

She stared at it a moment, her brow crinkled as she tried to understand. When I looked at it through her eyes, I could see how it would seem like a weird thing to do. But that's how it had always been in the Pit, how it always would be. And my mark, I kind of liked it. It reminded me of home.

"Did it hurt Cubby?" she asked.

I shrugged, not wanting to talk about it. The memory was too painful. I remembered his little body squirming in my skinny, tiny arms the night he was welcomed into the A-Frame. When I burned his leg he screamed so loud I was worried his bright red face would explode, but he calmed down quickly while the rest of our Brothers laughed and cheered and congratulated me on having a new Little Brother. I remembered looking at him, so quiet and calm nuzzling my chest, and I felt my eyes getting wet.

My silence didn't bother Lussit. She accepted my shrug as a satisfactory answer and leaned her head against my shoulder. She was asleep in seconds, her arm linked in mine.

"You've bewitched her," hissed Farka. "Somehow, you little boys have fiddled with her brain, that's why she trusts you."

I checked Lussit but she didn't seem to have heard Farka. She stayed resting on my arm, her perfect round cheeks wearing a sleepy grin.

"You'd better know what you're doing, Ikkuma boy."

I glared at Farka, trying to return the same hate and disdain she'd been giving me since we'd met. It didn't affect her and her lips crept into a satisfied smirk. I didn't know what I was doing and she knew it.

"Shh. Can you listen?" She looked up to the treetops and

I listened. Far away, I could hear the faint sound of Tunrar screaming and howling as the new day dawned. "Many hungry Tunrar wait for you, little boy. Tell me, when the time comes, how will you protect our Sacred Innocent?"

I kept quiet, hoping my grim expression would shut her up. I looked at Lussit, still happily asleep on my arm, and all at once I felt sick. I didn't know how to protect her from Krepin, or the Tunrar, and I wondered if Av was right. Maybe we shouldn't have let her come. But without her, I'd have nothing to offer the waiting Aju Krepin.

"Or will you cast her aside when you have what you want?"

The words struck a nerve inside me, and before I could stop myself I said, "You're one to talk about casting things aside—monster."

"Monster?" she hissed.

She was offended and I'd done it. My chest swelled with a new confidence and anger. I wanted to hurt her, infuriate her. So I would.

"You're the stuff of nightmares," I spat. "Boys wake in the night screaming because they've seen one of you when they close their eyes."

At that, the piercing sting of her glare was gone, replaced by confusion, and I felt the power of our little discussion shift.

"You tell me, Farka. How many baby boys have you thrown away and forgotten?"

Her face softened suddenly; her hard eyes were round and wet and she looked away from me, her sagging shoulders reminding me of all the Potentials. She held it in a different way than Tanuk, but still, it was there, like a stink she tried to cover with all her anger and hardness. I swallowed hard. It was the Guilt.

"That's what you think we do," she said quietly, "just . . . throw you away."

I shifted in my seat—this was not the reaction I had been going for. I nodded, trying not to seem surprised by her sadness.

"Can't you see?" She leaned forward, her eyes boring into me. "It is to save you."

I sat there, stunned and confused, and she shook her head. "From Ardigund."

The first Aju.

"What about him?" I asked, careful not to sound too interested.

"Ever since the Beginning rose to power, it has hunted the sons of Belphoebe."

"Ardigund never found her baby," I snapped, remembering Lussit's story. Fiver asked about the baby and she—I watched Lussit sleeping quietly—she never answered him.

"He couldn't," she said. "We hid you much too well."

My entire body felt strained, like a pressure was about to take me over and crush all my bones to pulp. "Hid who?"

"You," she said. "All of you. The Ikkuma Pit is a dangerous place. Barren, hot, no man can survive in its belly. What Aju could believe a baby would survive down there? But the fires of the Ikkuma Pit kept you, all of you."

Nothing can survive down here but us.

"Since the time of Belphoebe, when she laid her son down on its ashen floor and prayed its fires burn only for him."

I felt dizzy. Belphoebe's baby. The First Brother. "Rawley," I breathed.

Everything went silent—the Baublenotts froze at the mention of his name. All that was left was a ringing, a deafening alarm resonating in my own ears.

"Can't you see?" said Farka. "The Beginning wants you for its own."

"Why?" My arm began to tremble and I hoped it wouldn't wake Lussit. "Why would they want us?"

"Because with you"—her body was leaning forward, her right shoulder dropped as her eyes became wet—"Ardigund believed his powers would be restored."

"We don't have any powers."

Farka's head tilted as she looked at me. "Rawley was Ardigund's blood," she breathed. "The blood of the Belphebans, yes. But also, the blood of the Beginning."

My heart stopped dead and every hair on my skin stood on end as my own veins suddenly felt like they were pumping tar.

"It is Ikkuma blood," she told me. "Your blood."

I tried to think, tried to make my brain refuse to believe it, tried to think of anything but opening up my own skin and letting any trace of the Beginning flow out of my body.

Blaze's son. Krepin lost him to the falls.

Oh, Cubby.

I closed my eyes tight, digging my knuckles into them, my nose burning and my throat caught on a violent scream. My Cubby. He couldn't do what Krepin wanted him to do. He was just Cubby. My Cubby. Could Krepin really believe he'd restore Ardigund's powers?

The other boys in the Temple, they were in white, but Krepin had Cubby dressed in blue. He was different, singled out, it was right there in front of my face. I'd seen Krepin's eyes, the way they lit up when I said Cubby's name. I

266

thought of the new one he'd given my Little Brother, Linerk, the way he looked at the little boy from the Ikkuma Pit—not with menace. There had been pride.

No. Please. Not Cubby.

I opened my eyes, and the world was blurry; I had to steady myself on my hands and knees to make the spinning stop. My throat burned with bile.

Krepin was never going to give Cubby back. He was going to use his blood to make himself more powerful.

Lussit was awake now, all my movement disturbing her slumber. She placed a warm hand on my back. "Urgle?"

"I have to go for him," I said.

"What?"

I forced myself to my feet, nearly throwing up.

It was just like Blaze's baby.

Krepin would keep Cubby.

I had to stop him.

THIRTEEN

I took off into the trees, stumbling as best I could in the direction of the thundering falls.

Lussit's voice called after me. "Urgle!"

But I kept going. Krepin didn't want her. Krepin didn't want Serin. He wanted Cubby. He'd always wanted Cubby.

I crashed through the thick brush and mud, not caring about how loud I was being, not caring about the thorns and switches cutting my arms and legs and face. Every moment wasted was another moment Krepin was with Cubby.

"Urgle, please!" Lussit's voice wasn't far behind me, twigs and sticks crunching under her feet. "Please stop!"

But I didn't stop. I only went faster. He'd lied to me. And I'd let him! Blaze was right, I shouldn't have left Cubby there. But I did! And I'd run around the mountains on this—

I let out a scream, so loud and bloody I thought my throat might rip.

The mission! Why send me? Because I was useless! I should have died! I would have died if it hadn't been for

Lussit. And then who would come for Cubby? No one. There'd be no one to save him.

Krepin sent me to get rid of me!

And then another scream. But this one wasn't mine.

Lussit.

I stopped and listened. She was grunting and struggling somewhere not far behind me. "Urgle, please!"

I would have died if it hadn't been for Lussit.

I made my way back through the brush and there she was, waste deep in the mud. I stood at the edge of the sink-hole.

Her face lit up when she saw me.

"Why didn't you tell me?" I growled. Her head tilted to the side and she said nothing. "About the baby! About Rawley!"

Her eyes dropped and she shook her head. "I didn't think it mattered."

"It does matter! Krepin thinks he can use Cubby!"

Her mouth hung open, and her wide eyes watched me as her skin went pale. "What?"

"He thinks Cubby is like Belphoebe's baby! He thinks Cubby can complete his powers!" I broke a branch off a nearby tree and thrust it out towards her. She just stayed there, staring at me, her open mouth quivering.

"Take it!" I snapped.

She jumped at the force in my voice and carefully took hold of the stick.

With a violent yank I pulled her towards me until her waist was free.

"He doesn't want you," I told her as she lay there at my feet. "I'm going for Cubby on my own."

And with that, I stormed away back into the Baublenotts.

"Urgle, wait!" she called. She got to her feet, her beautiful robes stained a hideous Baublenott black, and followed. "I'll go with you."

"Go back to Av," I said, moving forward. "Let them know what's happening."

I felt bad for just leaving him, for not telling him what I was doing. But there wasn't any time. Cubby needed me now, and Krepin wasn't going to let him go. How could Av help? No, this was up to me.

"You can't just go to Krepin on your own," she said. "They won't even let you into the Temple. You need me!"

"I don't!" I shouted, and stepped up to her face. She stopped suddenly, gasping as I towered over her. She took a step back and I felt a sudden wave of shame. I'd come at her like she was Fiver making me angry. What was I going to do? Hit her? I wasn't mad at her. I was mad at myself. I should never have left that Temple without Cubby. I sighed and turned away, making my way towards the sound of the falls. "Just go back, Lussit. Av will be worried."

But she didn't go back.

She let me get a good distance ahead of her, and then she followed. She made no secret of being behind me, just gave me a lot of space and tried as hard as she could to keep up.

I should have told her to go back. I should have been mad that she didn't listen. But to tell the truth, I felt better knowing she was there.

The screams of the Tunrar were louder by the afternoon, and the rush of the water was a droning, ear-numbing thunder that told me we were near the falls. We'd made it back to the Temple.

I crouched on the banks of the river, hidden by the

undergrowth, while Lussit sat farther back, pretending she wasn't there at all. "Might as well come out," I called to her. "No sense hiding."

I didn't need to tell her twice, and she hurried out from her spot to join me on the bank.

Lussit lost her breath when she finally laid eyes on the giant colorful building standing tall in the middle of the violent current. She drank it in as though she'd been starving all her life for a sight like this. "It's so beautiful."

I didn't say anything. It had overwhelmed me too, the last time I was here. But now, it was just like the ugly, stagnant pools of the Baublenotts: dark and evil, full of nothing but filth and rot.

"How do we get to it?" she asked.

I shook my head. "*We* don't get to anything. I told you, Krepin won't want you."

"Yes, he will," she said. "I'm the leader of the Belpheban faith; he would love nothing more than to get his hands on me, I promise you."

"He just wants Cubby," I insisted.

"Fine!" she snapped. It was the first time I'd ever seen her react with anything but patience, kindness, and understanding. I was surprised. "So he wants Cubby. Do you really think he's going to be happy to let you in, just you by yourself? I'm telling you, he'll want me too. I'm your only way in those doors." She grabbed my hand and I suddenly found it hard to swallow. "So, how do *we* get to it?"

She waited for me to answer and I realized how much alike she and Av were. She was so ready to risk everything just to help someone else. She was selfless, just like her brother.

"No," I said. Seeing the water again and remembering

how we'd barely made it last time, I couldn't imagine Lussit making it across. "We don't have the boat. I can't ask you to swim that."

Lussit let go of my hand and she looked angry. She had the exact same frown as Av.

"It's too dangerous," I tried. "You don't know what that water is like."

"I'm not afraid of the water."

"You should be."

But what to do with her? She was here, with me. Av would be losing his mind with worry. He was probably already on his way, following the obnoxious trail of destruction we'd left. It wouldn't be long before he found us.

"Just wait here for Av," I told her. "He and Fiver will be here soon, they'll take care of you."

"Urgle," she said with that tone she'd used on Farka, that all-commanding, all-knowing tone. "I've told you I'm going."

A sound fell out of my mouth, a sound like *ugh*, and still crouched by the water, I rubbed my chin in my hand. That voice may have made her sound like some kind of holy authority to her sisters, but to me she just sounded foolish.

Then the splash.

I looked back to where she'd been standing and Lussit was gone, her blanket dangling on a low tree branch.

"Lussit!" I shouted.

The white water flew by and I followed it towards the falls, waiting for her head to pop up, my stomach heaving as I waited to watch her go over.

Then I saw her.

Lussit came up, sputtering and coughing until she was swallowed again.

Her head reappeared, but farther down the river this time. She was fighting the current, and she was losing.

I leaped in. I had to get to her.

The water was the same as it was the last time we'd battled—unfairly strong, undecided about my fate—and I thrashed with all my might as I tried to keep my eyes on Lussit.

"Lussit!" I screamed, before a gush of water strangled my voice.

Finally, my thrashing arms connected with hers and I grabbed hold of her with one hand. She coughed and gasped and her extra weight pulled me under, but I kept fighting. She kicked and punched too, wildly flailing her limbs against the raging torrent. It was no use. My arms were too weak to carry us both against the push of the water, Lussit's kicks too feeble against the pull. I kept on trying, every reach and pull burning, and I could hear the water laughing at me, only tickled by my effort. My eyes broke the surface and I could see splintered wood just ahead of me. We were cutting through, somehow. It was no thanks to me. I could feel it. Our muscles were no match for this. I became aware of something wrapped around the two of us, gently holding us against the current. I reached out in front of me and I felt the wood under my fingertips. We'd made it to the docks. I grabbed hold and Lussit and I sat there in the raging water, desperately trying to catch our breaths.

"What happened?" I coughed.

Lussit ignored me, greedily breathing the air. I don't think she knew what I meant. I wasn't sure I knew what I meant.

"The water," she shouted finally, raising her voice over the sound of the river, "it carried us!"

I felt the force of the current pushing against me, wanting to carry me away. The water didn't carry us because it couldn't. It was like Blaze's story, like the water at Krepin's feet. It carried us because it was asked to.

The wide grin on Lussit's face was infectious and I smiled even though I was afraid of what came next. If she had the power to ask the water to carry us, then I was grateful.

"Come on," Lussit told me. She lifted her leg over the railing of the jostling wooden walkway and stepped onto the marble steps of the Beginners' Temple.

"Wait!" I shouted, clambering over the railing to get to her.

She stood there, her soaked hair clinging to her neck and back, drops of water catching the sunlight on her face. My whole body was wet, but my throat was so dry with fear I could barely talk. "I don't—" I dropped my head, unable to look her in the eye. "I don't know how to protect you from him."

She smiled and bent down to find my eyes. She grabbed my hand. "Just don't let go."

FOURTEEN

Without ever having knocked, the giant gold doors swung open with a loud bang, and the melted face of Gorpok Juga stood before us, smiling and laughing. Behind her was a barrage of other Beginners, from old and withered to young Passages like Cubby. I scanned their faces for his toothless grin, but he wasn't there.

"Ikkuma! You have returned!" cried Gorpok Juga. "But where is you friends, ah?"

"I'm alone," I told her, my voice steady and aggressive. I heard Blaze in my head: *short answers.* I didn't listen to him the first time. This time, I wouldn't make the same mistake.

She laughed. "You lie already, Ikkuma. I see you have new friend."

I felt the warmth of Lussit's hand in mine and my heart began to pound in my chest. I had to be extremely careful. It wasn't just Cubby relying on me now—I had Lussit too.

"I want to see Krepin," I told the old woman. "We have to discuss Cubby."

"You have Belpheban Head?"

Lussit's grip on my hand tightened. She had her head

down and stood just behind me, struggling to keep her balance as the water spilled over our shins. She was sopping wet and breathing fast. She was nervous.

"I will only discuss that with Krepin."

"You speak to me first," she snapped.

"Fine," I told her, annoyed that she couldn't take me seriously. "Then we'll just be on our way and you can explain to Aju Krepin why you let the Sacred Innocent of the Belpheban faith return to her people."

Gorpok Juga's pink eyes widened and she looked at Lussit, who was sopping wet and shaking. I held my breath and thought about running, thought about yelling at her to leap in the water and swim with all her might. The truth was out, Juga knew who she was. I'd delivered Lussit right to them, which was the plan all along, Lussit's plan, but as Gorpok Juga looked her over, my stomach knotted and I knew we'd made a mistake.

Gorpok Juga descended the steps, the pounding water swamping her feet, and still the old hag maintained her balance. The power of the river was nothing to Gorpok Juga. Her amused smile was gone and she was pursing her lips as she looked Lussit over. Lussit reached up to wipe the hair from her eyes but Gorpok Juga stopped her, snapping her hand over Lussit's wrist with a sudden force that made a slapping sound. I nearly lunged at Gorpok Juga, but Lussit shot me a sideways glance that stopped me.

Juga held tightly to Lussit's wrist and then grabbed her delicate chin with her other hand.

"I am what he says," Lussit said, her voice calm and steady.

"I am judge of that," grunted Juga.

She inspected Lussit's neck, jawbone, face, and robes. Then she lifted Lussit's sleeves to inspect her milky arms, the

276

skin like soft eggshells next to the wrinkled mole-covered leather of Juga's. I wanted to tell her to stop, to take her ugly hands off Lussit, but Lussit, still holding on to me, gave my hand a reassuring squeeze. Juga turned Lussit around and pressed her fingers firmly along Lussit's spine. She grunted what I assumed was approval and then turned to her waiting entourage. She lifted her hands and yelled out something in a strange tongue that sent the group into a frenzy. They roared and cheered and several Tunrar rushed towards a terrified Lussit. I pulled her in behind me and prepared to fight the Tunrar, but the doorman from my last visit barked a command and the Tunrar stood down. The man came towards us, his spear at the ready, and I promised myself I wouldn't let him take Lussit. But he didn't want her. He grabbed me by the hair, his strong hand dragging me behind him.

I held tight to Lussit but the man wrenched my arm away and I couldn't hang on.

Gorpok Juga let out a laugh. "You Ikkuma boys! Very helpful boys! First you give us traitor Blaze, now holy girl is for Krepin too!"

Blaze. Because of me.

"Urgle!" Lussit screamed as I clawed and dug at the man's hand.

"Lussit, run!" I shouted to her, but it was too late. The crowd rushed her, and she was swallowed up. They were all grabbing at her, pulling her along behind Gorpok Juga, who waddled down the passage that I knew led to Aju Krepin.

I struggled and growled against the strength of the doorman's hand, and I managed to dig my nails in and rip at his flesh. He scoffed and threw me in front of him, and I stumbled and fell to my knees. I got up as quickly as I could and spun to face him. I wanted to rip his face off, tackle him to the ground, and pummel him with everything I had in me, but I knew I'd lose that fight. He was a monster of a man, twice my height with the wide build of a boulder. He stared right back at me, spear pointed at my chest, his face a blank, completely disinterested. This was his job, and he didn't care what happened to me. He wiggled the tip of his spear to tell me to keep going, and reluctantly I turned around and kept moving forward.

We veered down hallway after hallway, and walked up a series of tight, leaky staircases until I was so turned around that I doubted I'd ever find my way out, let alone find Lussit.

My nose burned as my eyes welled up. I'd let go of her.

When we came to the end of yet another narrow, dark hallway, it opened up into a giant chamber. The small open windows that lined the top of the room let in little natural light, so it was dark, and the mist from the water that spilled in through several openings made it foggy and even harder to see. I could make out the colors, though. The stone walls were a vibrant sky blue and adorned with pictures and detailed patterns made with gold. Vines spread themselves along the frescoes, stretching to the windows, weaving through as though threading a natural tapestry.

I stood staring up, my attention fixed on the twinkling specks that danced where the sunlight hit the walls in tiny patches. The man grabbed me by the hair again and dragged me to the right-hand side of the room, where a series of gold hoops lay strewn beneath the flowing water that trickled over the ornate red and gold tiled floor. With another strong shove he sent me to the floor and my hip slammed onto the hard stone. I waited there, soaking in the trickling water as he gathered up the metal hoops. He dragged me against the wall and I struggled and thrashed against his firm grip to no avail. In one swift motion he held me down and clamped one of the hoops tightly around my upper body, pinning my arms painfully to my sides. I struggled, but the hoop was so tight it kept my arms from moving much. Then he brought my hands together and clamped a tight gold hoop around them. Raising them just over my shoulder, he hooked them securely to the wall. It was an awkward position, and the hoops were so tight I could feel my arms starting to numb.

He clamped a hoop around my knees and another around my feet.

"I demand to speak to Aju Krepin!" I screamed, but the man just ignored me. He reached over my head for a round notch in the wall. He turned it and pulled and as soon as he did a spout of water gushed over my head and drenched me by surprise, water flooding my nose, eyes, and mouth. I spat and sputtered and screamed, "Aju Krepin!"

The man made one last tug at my bound hands to make sure they were firmly secured to the wall, then, without so much as a glance in my direction, left me alone in the giant chamber.

The water poured tirelessly over my face and it was cold; it wasn't long before I was shivering. It poured over my eyes and into my mouth. I shook my head and spat, but every time I did, the water just poured in again. It tasted sweeter than water should, than the Baublenotts should. I tugged and pulled at my hands and desperately tried to flex the metal bands into loosening but they were too strong.

I was stuck—trapped beneath a spout of water and

bruising from the tightness of my bindings. Lussit was gone, given up to Krepin and for what?

I spat.

I didn't have Cubby back. I didn't have a way out. I was completely helpless and trapped. But Krepin, I'd given him everything he wanted—and more. I screamed until I felt like my throat would bleed, the cool water flooding in and strangling the sound. I spat again and let out another scream. My whole body tensed and squirmed from the pressure that was finally being released.

When I was done, I let my head drop back against the wall, the water tickling my face like it hadn't noticed I was upset at all. I shouldn't have just taken off from Av and Fiver. I'd just left them and it turned out to be such a mistake. Av must have been sick with worry about Lussit. Or furious. And I didn't know if I'd ever get to apologize to him now. I swallowed hard and begged myself not to cry.

And the water kept on tickling, pouring down my face like it was searching for the tears. I closed my eyes and forced myself to breathe, a *fssshh fssshh* sound escaping me every time I let out a breath through the running water.

I wasn't resting long before I heard a shuffling noise, directly in front of me. I opened my eyes and moved my head just enough to keep the water out of them. I peered ahead through the murky shadows.

There against the opposite wall, bound in the same position as me, was a melted woman, her neck sporting the faded crossed-out blue mark much like Blaze's. The mark of a Beginner turned against them. Her dry, cracked mouth hung open, exposing empty gums, and her damp, sparse hair clung to her emaciated face. Her eyes were glazed over and she wasn't looking at anything, just focused on keeping her bobbing head from collapsing into her chest. She'd been here a long time.

I burst out screaming again, this time demanding attention, shrieking for the guard to return, for Krepin to keep his promise, for Av and Fiver to come find me. I didn't want to end up like that. Not like that.

The water poured its way back in, and I hacked and coughed, spitting it out and screaming some more.

"Ugh, just relax, Urgle," rasped a dry voice from somewhere to my distant right. The voice was nearly a whisper, a crackly shadow of something more familiar and clean.

I turned my head to see the owner of the voice, but still, the light from the high windows was minimal, and the figure was hard to make out in the shadows and mist and water running down my face. After a few seconds my eyes adjusted.

He was strung up in the corner about seven feet off the ground, his arms and legs spread out and bound with metal hoops attached to heavy hooks. Behind him the wall was marred by black flecks and smears, the shadows doing their best to conceal the color of his blood. His hair was wet and plastered to his face, but swollen, black bruises could still be seen on his eyes and his lips. His shirt was open and his entire body was carved up from a beating.

"Blaze?" I whispered.

He laughed maniacally, though I couldn't say what was funny given his miserable state. "They found me!"

Just like Juga said. *Because of me.*

I suppressed the bile threatening to spew out of me and tried to think of something to say. "How?" was the best I could manage.

"Ah, you know," he said. "I couldn't outrun them forever.

281

In the end there were about a dozen Tunrar coming at me at once. What can you do?"

He sounded funny, as though his head wasn't quite right. I wriggled in the hoops and felt my heart rate picking up. Blaze was trapped. He was beaten. What hope did I have?

"Blaze," I pleaded, shaking my head as though that might keep the water off me. "We have to get out of here. Krepin thinks that Cubby—"

"I know what he thinks."

"No you don't! He—" I stopped. *He knows?* My hand tickled. The Abish girl told him. "Why didn't you tell me?"

"Would you have understood me?" he snapped. "By Rawley, Urgle. You're like a newborn Sibble calf out here, blind and tripping over yourself. What would it have helped?"

I blinked tight, squeezing out some of the water that had made its way into my eyes. He was right about that. I'd been so helpless, so innocent of everything. "You should have told me," I said quietly.

I heard him heave a heavy sigh and then he mumbled, "I should have never agreed to help you. I should have never gone to the Pit."

"You're right," I said, the lump in my throat ready to explode. He helped me and now here he was, the great hero, hanging on Krepin's wall. "I know who you are, Blaze."

He said nothing.

"The Belphebans told me everything. About your wife. About your son. Norale Heights."

He still said nothing.

"How can you just stay like that when Krepin is out there, right outside those doors!"

"Stop it!" he yelled. "Krepin's won, all right? Just stop."

I was silent for a long time, listening to the rush of water flowing over my ears and racking my brain to think of something to make him snap out of it, something to entice him to help me escape, but I couldn't think of anything. There was nothing I had that he wanted.

"Please don't give up," I said with a shaky voice as the warm tears began to mix with the cool flow pouring over my head. "You got away from him before, you can do it again! We'll get Cubby and make a run for the Pit! Please!"

"There won't be any Pit."

Everything stopped—my breath, my heart, my brain. "What do you mean . . . ?"

Blaze began to laugh and a chill rippled up from my feet to my hair. "I only wanted to hide it for a little while. Just until I could get back to the Resistance. I couldn't let Krepin catch me with it."

"Hide what? What are you talking about?" I said, not understanding. Then all at once I saw it, the footprint of Tanuk's baby, the blue pendant around her neck. *Keeps secret things safe.*

"The flint box," I breathed.

Blaze let his head drop and said nothing.

"It's an Abish shroud, isn't it?"

Blaze didn't move.

"What's inside, Blaze?"

Silence.

"What's it hide!"

"Everything," he whispered. "All of Krepin's power."

"But . . . what is it?"

He stayed still for the longest time, and then, "Proof," he said finally, from somewhere under his limp hair. "The proof of what Ardigund really did. The Secret of the Ajus."

I swallowed hard, and Blaze went on, babbling to himself,

his voice on the edge of tears. "When my men came for me, when they let me go, I was here, right here. I thought if I could show his followers the truth . . . I'd been Krepin's favorite for so long, he told me exactly where he kept it. And there it was, the Secret of the Ajus, hidden in his chambers just like he said. With that one little thing . . . the war would have been over."

"That's why the Tunrar chased you," I said. "You stole it from Krepin. That's why you came to us, isn't it? To hide it from him."

Blaze hung his head. "I never meant to tell."

"Tell what?"

He winced and readjusted himself on the chains, his skin an angry landscape of bloody gashes and purple bruises. They'd tortured him.

"About the Pit?" I whispered.

I thought of the Brothers, playing Screamers, building fires, laughing and wrestling and feasting on Larmy. In my mind I saw him, Krepin, standing at the top of the East Wall, a swarm of Tunrar pouring down from the forest, descending on the Ikkuma Pit.

"He's coming for them."

Blaze nodded. "He needs something more than he did when he first tried to wage war, the war I thwarted. The Tunrar found the Pit when I came to you for help. Krepin just needed someone, like me, to tell them it's exact location."

My insides felt as if they'd withered and dried up, like everything I am, everything inside me, had been sucked out of my chest and handed over to Krepin. The Pit was ours, it was our home. *Untouched.* The Pit was everything this awful world wasn't, and it kept us safe because Belphoebe begged it to. But could its walls protect the Brothers from a man as powerful as Aju Krepin?

"We can't let him do this," I said. The lump in my throat felt like the size of my head.

"It's done."

"I won't abandon Cubby!" I shouted. "I won't abandon my Brothers!"

"Just stop it, Urgle!" he snapped. "He's won, so just stop."

The fight was out of him, all of it. He hung there like a lifeless carcass, drained completely. He had nothing left.

Getting out of here, getting to Cubby, getting to the Brothers was up to me.

Hours passed and the three of us ignored each other. Blaze didn't move the entire time. He just hung there, waiting to die. The old woman moved every so often, adjusting and shifting. She was so thin that the hoops hung loosely on her frame. If she hadn't been too weak to stand, she might have been able to escape. She didn't seem to have much of an interest in leaving. Unlike me. I'd pull and tug on my wrists, wriggling my feet and flexing my arms, grunting and stretching in an exhausting effort to escape. Nothing worked. I'd stop for a while and feel sorry for myself, feel the tickle of the cold water absorbing into my skin, chilling my blood. And then I'd think of Cubby and Lussit and the boys back home and begin my futile efforts to break the hoops all over again.

Blaze did his best not to notice, but I caught the old woman's interest every so often. She'd raise her weak head in my direction and watch me with black, disoriented eyes. Her gaze was more animal than human and I wondered if any part of the woman she had been once upon a time might still be inside her. Had she been like Blaze? Had she refused Krepin her only son? Or had she done something else? I wondered, just how many ways could a person make an enemy out of Krepin? I stared back, searching her face for any sign of life.

She'd always break the stare with a smack of her cracked lips.

I opened my mouth and let the water from the spout quench my thirst, but the sweetness always made it hard to swallow.

The light from the windows began to fade as the sun began to set, and I prepared for a long night under the gushing water spout, when the sound of a dozen approaching feet echoed from the hallway.

It was Gorpok Juga and the guard, a group of several Tunrar stalking in front of them. Behind them were two boys about my age sporting the braid that wrapped around their necks, the mark of the Beginning etched into their foreheads, and just behind them came Aju Krepin himself.

The guard stormed up to me and turned the knob above my head, ceasing the fall of water. I shook my hair and spat, relieved for the break.

The old, emaciated woman began shrieking—panicked animal wails from a toothless, wide-open mouth.

Gorpok Juga spoke to me, but I couldn't hear her over the noise. Krepin barked a command and the boy to his left calmly approached the old woman, backhanding her across the face. She was quiet after that.

"Where is Passage Linerk?" Gorpok Juga asked.

"What?"

Aju Krepin growled at me and then looked to Gorpok Juga, who nodded and translated his words.

"Linerk! You friends was seen stealing Passage Linerk from the north tower. Where they have him?"

"Cubby?" I said, my pulse thumping in my ears and my heart swelling with relief. "Av and Fiver!" I laughed. "They got him!"

The guard slapped me across the face and the force of it made me see stars.

"Where they have him?" Gorpok Juga tried again.

For the first time in hours, Blaze's voice filled the chamber, his deep laugh echoing off the walls. "So, Krepin, Ikkuma boys got the better of you again?"

Krepin looked to Gorpok Juga, who hesitated to translate, so Blaze did it for her. He shouted at Aju Krepin in Krepin's tongue and I heard Krepin take in a sharp breath through his nose. His body remained still, facing me, but his eyes looked over at Blaze and he said one word. Whatever it was, it set the Tunrar in motion, and the many that had arrived with them slinked over to Blaze.

Blaze laughed. What was one more beating to him? He'd already given up.

The Tunrar screamed and screeched as they leaped at him, clawing at his torso, biting his limbs. He tried not to scream but they were torturing him.

"Stop it!" I shouted. "Stop hurting him!"

Krepin scratched his nose nonchalantly and turned his attention back to me. He waited there, still expecting an answer.

"I don't know," I said. I didn't. I didn't even know how they did it, but they'd saved him. Cubby was free and Av and Fiver were all right.

Krepin murmured and Gorpok Juga translated. "And the woman? What woman was with them?"

"Woman?"

"Tall, strong. She kill four Tunrar before you friends disappear in the Baublenotts."

Farka.

"You lead Belphebans to Krepin?" Juga shouted.

"I don't know who she is," I lied. I was grinning defiantly, I couldn't help it. I was overjoyed. Sure, I was a prisoner of Aju Krepin, but Cubby was free and that was the only reason I came here at all.

Aju Krepin grinned right back, a sinister half smile that showed he wasn't overly bothered with one missing Passage. He spoke.

"No matter to Krepin," translated Gorpok Juga. "Soon he will have the Abish shroud and his pick of Ikkuma boys. Krepin's armies come for them soon."

I spat at Krepin's feet.

Without missing a beat, he slapped me in the face with his open palm and the sound echoed through the room. Stars danced in front of my eyes. My skin was so soggy that the impact split the flesh beside my eye and I could feel a warm stream of blood falling down my cheek. But even still, it had been worth it.

"The Beginning must receive our thanks," said Gorpok Juga. "To give thanks, Krepin will give you life to the Beginning."

I suddenly felt less bold.

Krepin grabbed my face in his hands, his expression calm and gentle, which had the unnerving appearance of caring. He spoke.

"Bet sah."

Gorpok Juga translated: "And hers."

Lussit.

"They're coming for her, you know? Belpheban warriors are on their way." I didn't know that for sure, but I knew they'd be looking for Lussit. And, based on his interest in Farka, I guessed Krepin didn't want them here.

Gorpok Juga translated for him and he nodded before he spoke.

"Then they will be right on time to view her die," said Gorpok Juga.

I struggled against the restraints, trying with everything in me to get at Krepin, to kill him before he had the chance to kill Lussit, to get to the Pit, but the gold hoops were too strong.

The guard slapped me in the face again, and I stopped squirming, biting through the pain that was throbbing in my cheek and seething.

Krepin bowed graciously to me, his face serene and calm. He called for his minions, and Gorpok Juga and the younger boys obeyed—even the Tunrar mercifully abandoned their exciting torture game to follow him out. The guard waited a moment, then reached for the knob above my head. The cold water poured over me and the guard left with the rest.

I could hear Blaze grunting and growling through the pain, his breathing labored. The old woman was whimpering, shaking her head back and forth over and over. I closed my eyes and focused on the water, letting the sound of it rushing over my ears drown out the sad noises around me. I tried not to think of Lussit, where they were keeping her, how they were treating her. I tried not to think of home, of what was about to invade the happy world of my Brothers. *Cubby is safe,* I thought. All I had to do now was save Lussit and warn the Brothers. I wouldn't let Krepin kill me first.

FIFTEEN

When night had come and darkness had swallowed the chamber, the chill from the falling water was seeping into my bones. My legs and my bottom had been sitting on the flooded floor for hours, and I could barely remember what dry hair felt like.

There was a calm to the darkness. Maybe it was the sound of the water, or the shadows that made it hard to see the ugliness around me, or maybe it was the knowledge that Cubby was safe. They'd come for me soon, and when they did, I'd be ready. With nothing but the quiet and hours of struggling against the restraints, I knew the only time I'd have a chance at escape was when they came. They'd drag me to my death, and I'd fight them the whole way. I had to. I had to get back to the Pit to warn them. But how? I could hear the crickets laughing at me, my plan suddenly ridiculous, even to me. They'd come, I'd fight, and if I was honest with myself, I'd die. I'd never fight another Tunrar. I'd never have to take any verbal abuse from Fiver. I felt a pang of sadness in my heart at the thought of never hearing him call me Useless again. There were a lot of things

I'd never get to see or do again. I'd never see Lussit again. Never see Cubby.

And Krepin would come to the Pit. What would happen to the Brothers? Would they fight? How? A bunch of boys against Krepin's legions of followers? They'd be slaughtered. Unless they fled. But where could they go? The world outside the Pit was not one they were ready for, not one I was ready for. Everything would change.

The lump in my throat came back, and this time I didn't fight it. I cried quietly, mourning all the things I wanted to do again and wouldn't.

And then I heard a noise, like a bird chirping from the open windows. I craned my neck upwards and saw the outline of a little head. Too small to be a Tunrar. It was a boy. He waved.

"All right," I whispered to myself, "all this water has driven you crazy."

Another head popped up beside the first.

"Useless!" It was Fiver's voice. Another head popped up beside his: Av's. "They manage to kill you yet or should we come back later?"

One, two, and three. Fiver, Av . . . and the little waver: Cubby.

Before I could smile, the withered old prisoner began to scream again. I was learning she startled easily.

"Shh!" I begged her.

She kept right on wailing, staring up at the three dark shadows of my friends.

"Shut her up!" whispered Av. "There's a thousand sleeping Tunrar up here!"

"Quiet, lady!" I begged.

She ignored me and kept right on crying.

Terrified and angry, I kicked my bound legs wildly, spraying water from the floor at her. The splash barely reached her, maybe only a drop or two made it all the way across the room, but it had got her attention. She looked at me with a frightened face.

"Be quiet!" I begged her.

She smacked her cracked lips and bobbed her head up and down, suddenly no longer afraid and more interested in an unattainable drink.

At the window, Cubby and Av were climbing their way in. Av moved carefully, clinging to the vines growing up the wall, Cubby slowly copying his every move.

When they made it down, I thought my heart would burst if I didn't get to hug Cubby in that instant.

He hopped off the vine and ran over to me, turning off the spout and flinging his arms around my neck.

"I knew you'd come back for me!" he whispered, barely able to contain his excitement. "I knew it, Urgle!"

I cried, overjoyed to see him, to feel his boney arms around my neck, to smell his fuzzy blond head. I wanted to hug him, to squeeze him as tight as I could, but my arms were held by the hoops.

Somewhere outside, the sound of a growling Tunrar broke the stillness of the night.

"Come on, you two," whispered Av. "We don't have a lot of time."

"Where's Fiver?" I asked as he and Cubby began working on freeing me from my golden shackles.

"Distracting Tunrar, hopefully. Where's Lussit?"

"Urgle?" Blaze was awake and groggy. Cubby and Av jumped at the sudden voice. "What's going on?"

"It's Blaze," I told Av.

Av stood rigid, unsure of what to do.

"Help him," I said. "It's our fault he's here, Av."

With nothing but a harrumph, Av hurried over to where Blaze hung, and using vines for support, he boosted himself up to undo his bindings.

There was the scream of Tunrar, more than one now, and I glanced up at the windows, worried I'd see them crawling in. Cubby wasn't bothered, and he kept trying to break open the hoop around my torso.

"Shh!" I told him.

Cubby stopped and stood up, staring at the windows. We watched and listened until the crouched, naked form of a Tunrar Goblin showed itself in the window. It sat there, trying to see into the dark with no success. It sniffed the air and growled. We were caught.

"I'll be right back," whispered Cubby.

"What? No! Be quiet."

"Don't worry, Urgs," Cubby giggled, and grabbed my face in his little hands. He was grinning and I noticed his adult tooth was replacing the empty space where his baby tooth used to be. "They can't catch me now!"

"What?"

Before I could stop him, Cubby yelled a big "Hello!" and waved his arms, jumping up and down.

The Tunrar sure saw that. It let out a scream, and a second popped its head in the window.

"Cub!" My heart was pounding, the Tunrar coming for him all over again. "Cubby, hurry. Get out of here!"

He ignored me and kept on waving his arms.

"Come and get me!" Cubby taunted.

The Tunrar didn't need an invitation. They barreled down the wall like spiders and Cubby squealed and ran off into the dark hallway.

"Cubby!" I yelled, but he didn't answer. All I could hear was the pitter-patter of his bare feet slapping the wet hallway as he ran.

I tore at the bindings, pulling and tugging even though I knew they wouldn't give.

"Av!" I shouted. "Av, go get Cubby!"

There was a loud clamoring of chains as Av let Blaze down.

"He's all right, Urgs," said Av, having difficulty supporting Blaze's weight. "He told us he does this all the time."

"Does what all the time?" I said. "Runs from the Tunrar? Are you insane!"

Av dropped Blaze and leaned him against the wall before hurrying over to work on my bindings. "He said he makes them mad for fun. They chase him but they never hurt him 'cause of the blue mark thing on his forehead."

I wasn't convinced. Today was different. Today Cubby was with the enemy. He was their target. I was squirming to run after him.

The tight hoop around my torso gave out when Av released the latch that kept them locked, and my arms were free. I frantically pulled and tugged to free my wrists, but Av was still working on them.

"Take it easy!" he ordered, but I couldn't. Cubby needed me and I couldn't let him down again.

My hands were free and I reached for my bound legs, tearing each hoop off with Av's help.

"Urgle, wait!" he said, grabbing me by the shoulders. "Lussit. Where did they take her?"

"I don't know," I admitted.

The sound of bare feet smacking wet tile echoed from the hallway and Cubby trotted in, out of breath and wheezing, sporting a proud grin that stretched from ear to ear. "See?" he said. "They're not that scary. And they're dumb too."

He ran over and grabbed my arm, pulling me towards the exit. "Now let's go, let's go! Take me home!"

My eyes were watering again and I kneeled down just to look at his face. Moments ago I was sure I'd never see it again, but it was here, right in front of me.

"Not yet, Cub," said Av. "We need to find our friend, remember?"

"But it's just a girl!" he whined. I had to smile. I would have told Av the same thing before this all started.

"Cubby," I said, squeezing his hands in mine, "she's our friend and she's in a lot of trouble."

"Do you know where Krepin would keep her?" said Av.

Cubby shrugged. "This is where he takes all the blasphemers. . . ." He trailed off and his brow knotted into his classic "thinking hard" face and I wanted to hug him again.

"But there's a room," he said, finally. "It's up near the north side of the Temple. That's where the devoted go to pray before . . . Aju Krepin sacrifices them."

"Take us there!" said Av.

Blaze stumbled into our huddle and waved his hands in our faces.

"No!" he said. "No way, Urgle. I am out of here."

"Will you go back?" I asked him.

Blaze scratched his neck and I knew he didn't want to. He only wanted to run. After everything, I couldn't blame him.

"Back where?" said Av.

"Home," sighed Blaze.

"The Pit?" Av was fuming. "You've already brought enough trouble there, don't you think?"

"No, Av. There's a problem."

He looked at me like I was crazy.

I sighed. "Krepin plans to invade the Pit."

The color drained from Av's face and I thought for a moment he'd faint.

"Without Cubby, he's going to be looking for another Brother."

Av swallowed, and I knew all that he could think about was Goobs.

"He'll take someone, and destroy the rest of the place until he finds his Abish shroud," I went on. "Blaze hid it there."

"Where?" said Av, doing his best to stay composed.

"In the Pit."

"No, I heard you. Where in the Pit?"

I looked at Blaze, who was wincing with pain as he held his arms close to himself. "In the Platform," he grunted. "There was a loose floorboard."

My hand flew up and hit my forehead.

"Third from the left, two up," the words came out of Av and me in sync. Everyone knew about that floorboard. It was not a good hiding spot. Not to the Brothers.

"Um . . ." Cubby was pulling on his thumb nervously, and his big green eyes looked at me the way they did when he'd done something wrong. "It's not there anymore."

"What?"

"I moved it."

"What?" Blaze stumbled, and I thought for a minute he'd wring Cubby's neck. "When? How?"

"I—I just wanted to play with it." He took a couple steps back from us, afraid he was about to be punished, but all I wanted to do was hug him, kiss his fuzzy head, and make that scared face go away. "I took it out to show Goobs, but Wasted saw me and wanted me to hand it over." His lip quivered and his eyes refused to look at us. "So we ran from him, but he chased us."

My stomach churned. "Cubby, are you saying you had the Abish shroud the night they took you?"

He nodded.

"Do they have it now?" said Blaze frantically.

"No! No!" he cried. "I hid it! So Wasted wouldn't take it, I hid it."

"Where!" Blaze demanded, his voice echoing off the walls.

Av dived onto Blaze and covered his mouth as a screech rang out overhead.

"My special place," Cubby said quietly. He looked at me quickly, then went back to pulling his thumb, waiting for me to yell. I'd told him not to go there, that I thought it was too dangerous. Cave-ins happened all the time on the slopes of the Fire Mountains. But right now, I didn't care about any of that. I just wanted to keep him safe.

The four of us watched the windows as several deformed shadows poked their heads in for a look.

We were running out of time.

So was Lussit.

"Cubby," I said quietly, "we have to get to our friend."

"This way," he whispered, heading for the corridor.

Av and I followed, and after a moment's hesitation, Blaze fell in behind. Just before we left, the withered old woman moved in the water and I could hear it splash as she propped herself up. She was dying, I knew that . . . but somehow, I couldn't bring myself to leave her there, all by herself, with no hope at all.

I rushed over to her, with Av growling at me to hurry up. I crouched down in front of her and she was shaking with fright, doing her best to shield herself from whatever horrible thing she expected me to do to her.

Her legs were so thin, I slid the gold hoops off them easily, the same with her torso. I unhooked her hands and she sat there, dumbfounded, slowly waving her arms back and forth, trying to remember how they worked. Then her glazed eyes wandered up to my face and I gave her a smile, a part of me certain that in this moment, I would see that glimpse into her old soul, the core of her that was still a human being. There was nothing. She just smacked her cracked lips and then slowly brought her head to the floor and slurped at the water.

Sad for her, I got to my feet and rejoined Cubby and Av. There was nothing else I could do.

"Through here," whispered Cubby. He was barely able to contain his excitement, thrilled to be the leader for the first time. I felt myself standing a little straighter. If only Fiver could see. Would a scroungee be able to outwit the Tunrar?

"How did you get him?" I asked Av, keeping my voice so low I could barely hear it over the trickling of water.

"Farka," said Av.

I knew she was with them, but the thought of her really helping us, of *saving* Cubby, made me nearly stop in my tracks.

Av grinned. "She helped us track you down. We got here just as Lussit was being dragged inside. We wanted to come after you but we weren't sure how to do it. It was her idea.

She watched the Tunrar on the rooftop and she pointed out how they were doing it."

"Doing what?"

"Getting on the roof. We figured it'd be our best bet for sneaking in."

"But it's crawling with Tunrar!"

"Yeah, well, that's where Farka came in handy. She said she'd distract them for us if we let her go so she could get back to her Sisters."

"You just let her go?"

Av shrugged. "She was kind of panicking about Lussit. She wanted to go back for help and I figured more help couldn't hurt." He was right about that. "Anyway," Av went on, "before we went for it, we were watching the place pretty closely, trying to figure out where Krepin might be keeping you. That was when Fiver spotted Cubby walking across some bridge towards one of the towers with a whole pack of little guys. There were only three windows on that tower, all opening to the same room, so we figured we might as well try and grab him while we knew where he was."

Cubby froze and threw out his arm to tell us to stop. We stood absolutely still, Blaze nearly bumping into us. There was nothing to hear, but I could see that the light from outside was getting brighter. Dawn was coming.

Finally, Cubby started moving again and we followed.

"How'd you avoid the Tunrar?" I asked.

"Like I said, Farka. She went ahead of us and just started screaming and hollering, working the Tunrar into a frenzy. They flew at her, ten at a time. I have to tell you I thought she was a goner, but she gave them a pounding. Anyway, when she made a run for the Baublenotts, most of them chased after her and it cleared the way for me and Fiver."

Ten at a time. I made a private wish that Farka would come back. Anyone who could fight off ten Tunrar alone would be a big help when we tried to get out of this place.

Cubby came to a narrow winding staircase, the walls barely wide enough for our shoulders to fit. "Up here," he whispered.

He scurried up the steps and out of view, and Av and I were ready to follow him when Blaze tapped my arm.

"This is it for me, Urgle," he said. "I'm getting out of here now."

"To go back?"

He shook his head. "To get help."

"Help? From who?" But I already knew who. "The Resistance?"

"They need to know what's happening," he said. "It's too important."

"But you don't know where the Abish shroud is," I reminded him.

He let his head drop and I knew he was losing his strength. He rubbed his shoulder and I wondered how far he would get on his own.

"You're hurt," I said.

"Krepin doesn't know where it is either," he told me. "But he's coming just the same. I won't abandon my Brothers."

He was right. Blaze had done enough for us. Now the rest of his Brothers needed him. He was Ikkuman, and I'd never forget that.

I nodded and he turned to leave.

"Hey, Blaze?" He stopped and looked back. "Don't mention my name."

A smile spread across his face. "For you, Urgle, I can't

make that promise." And with that he disappeared into the shadowed corridor, limping his way to freedom.

Av and I climbed after Cubby in the dark, but we nearly ran into him at the top of the stairs. Cubby was frozen, staring straight ahead. Two Tunrar stood just a couple of feet in front of him, snarling and waiting to pounce. Behind them were two men holding spears.

"Run!" shouted Av.

The three of us turned and threw ourselves down the steps as the Tunrar screamed and tore after us. The two men were shouting, alerting the entire Temple to our escape. I grabbed Cubby and pushed him in front of me, forcing him to run faster than I knew he could.

We flew out of the staircase and down a wide corridor. Torchlight glowed at the end where several more guards were waiting.

"Here!" screamed Cubby, ducking down a hallway to the right.

Av nearly missed the turn, grabbing the wall to stop himself and hurling around the corner.

Our feet thundered along the marble floor, water flying up in all directions. My foot slid out from under me on the wetness and I fell face-first onto the ground.

"Urgle!" screamed Cubby.

Behind us, the guards were closing in.

Av ran to me, grabbing my arm and dragging me back to my feet. I nearly slipped again, and every moment wasted to find my footing was a moment the guards used to draw closer.

They were nearly on top of us when the leader of the group came to an abrupt stop as something hit his nose. His friends stopped too, holding up his arms to try and block the string of stones smacking them on their heads, legs, and arms.

"Move it!" I heard Fiver roar overhead. I looked up and saw him perched in a high window, a fistful of stones gripped in his hand.

He didn't have to say it again. We ran after Cubby, careful not to fall, and he led us through small hallways and winding staircases. I had no idea where we were or where he was taking us. I doubted he knew.

Cubby stopped at the top of yet another staircase, grabbing his thumb and pulling on it over and over as he tried to decide which way to go. He was lost.

"Where are we going?" I yelled at him.

Cubby just kept pulling his thumb, and his eyes welled up with tears. "I don't know," he whimpered, doing his best not to cry.

I was so mad at him then, just like I would have been at home, just like the old me. I couldn't be like that to Cubby again. Not now, not ever.

I squeezed his shoulder gently. "Come on, Cub. You can do it."

He gulped in air to try and calm himself down, and Av was bouncing on his feet, ready to flee from the gang of guards that were clambering up the stairs towards us.

"There!" Cubby shouted, pointing to the left, and he darted off, followed by Av. I ran after them, and Cubby stopped abruptly at a door. He turned the knob and opened it. "Get in, get in!"

Av and I rushed inside and Cubby quickly closed the door.

The room was immense. Much bigger than the chamber

they'd held me in, and the space was filled with massive shelves, packed tightly with rectangular objects.

Cubby led us down the middle aisle and swerved in behind the last giant shelf and curled up in a dark corner. He held out his frightened hands to me and Av and we joined him on the floor.

"Where are we?" I asked him.

"The library," he whispered. "All their teachings and stories are written down in all of these books, and they keep them here for Krepin and the scholars to study."

Av didn't care, he was thinking like a hunter. "What do we do now?" he said. He didn't see the size of the shelves or that there were more writings and stories than a person could count. All he saw was a dead end. We were trapped.

Cubby didn't answer him and neither did I. We couldn't hide here forever, and the sun had begun to rise. We were running out of time to save Lussit.

A loud rumble split through the morning and Cubby screamed at the sudden surprise. Av was quick to cover the kid's mouth, but there wasn't really a need. The rumble was so loud it shook the entire Temple, Cubby's little squeal barely audible for the two of us sitting right beside him.

There was a sun ray across Av's left arm and I turned to see where it was coming from. A small window in the next aisle. I jumped up and ran round the shelf, Cubby begging me to come back.

When I peered out, there was a huge plume of smoke near the front of the Temple; I could see the tips of flames licking their way up the turrets as Tunrar screamed and fled, leaping off the roof and climbing in windows. For a moment I thought I was in the Pit, the Fire Mountains ready to explode.

"What is it?" asked Av.

Along the banks of the river I saw the cause of the explosion, and I wanted to laugh and throw up all at once. A group of four women were hurling flaming bundles at the Beginners' Temple. I watched as they released another and when it hit, explosion—the fireball shattered when it slammed into the marble steps, spraying fire in all directions.

"It's the Belphebans," I told him.

Av and Cubby ran to get a look and the three of us watched as still more Belphebans poured out of the Baublenotts and advanced on the Temple. I was relieved—our army of four had just increased by dozens. But Gorpok Juga's words repeated in my head: *They will be right on time to view her die.* We needed to find Lussit, and fast.

"This is about to get really bad," said Av.

I knew he was right as we heard the angry shouting of the Beginners, another explosion, and the battle cries of the Belphebans.

"Take Cubby and find Fiver," he told me. "Get back to the Pit. Quick. I've got to find my sister."

"Your what?" Cubby asked.

We both ignored him. "No, Av, I'll find her. I brought her here, it's my fault."

"Urgle, you can't possibly save Lussit on your own," he snapped. "You just can't. You're . . ." He bit back what he wanted to say, trying not to start a fight, but he was too late.

My cheeks went hot. "I'm what, Av? Useless? Is that what you were going to say?" After everything, he still thought of me as that bumbling, awkward underdog from the Pit.

"I didn't mean that!" he shouted as another explosion

rattled the Temple. "Would I have come all this way if I thought that? Would I have bothered if it was useless?"

I glared at him, not sure what to say. He was here. He'd been by me through everything.

"You have to get back to the Brothers, you can't waste time! You have to warn them about Krepin. By Rawley, Urgle! Some things aren't just about you!"

"Isn't that Fiver?" interrupted Cubby, his little arms pointing across the rooftop.

Av turned his attention from me to Cubby, but I wasn't done talking. I wanted to help him. He'd helped me, it was my turn.

"What's he doing?" said Av.

I looked out the window and sure enough, there was Fiver, lying on his belly and snaking his way towards the action.

"Fiver!" called Cubby, and I covered his mouth, afraid the Tunrar or guards might hear.

Fiver cocked his head in our direction and scurried over as soon as he saw us.

"It's getting a little rough out here, boys," he said. "Maybe it's time to call it a day?"

"I'm going back for Lussit," said Av.

"I'm going with you," I said.

"You'll slow me down! Just keep Cubby safe, Urgs. That's all you have to do."

And that was it. He wouldn't hear of me helping, and he ran out the door to find his sister.

SIXTEEN

As the door slammed shut I thought about ignoring what Av said. I thought about trying to find Lussit anyway. Then we could go back together, help our Brothers, together.

Suddenly I felt the wind knocked out of me as Cubby shoved me violently in the gut.

"You were going to leave me alone again?" he shouted, his lip quivering. "For some girl!"

I looked at his weepy eyes and hated myself. Av was right. My job was to keep Cubby safe.

"No, Cub," I said, hugging him tight. "I'm sorry, I'm so sorry. It's you and me, right?"

Cubby wiped his eyes and took a big long sniff as he brushed his nose with the back of his wrist. When he was done, he looked up at me and managed a weak smile. "Right," he said.

"And me too, right?"

I laughed when I looked at Fiver, his bottom lip jutting out in a fake frown.

"Come here, Cub," said Fiver, smiling. He helped Cubby hop out the window and onto the roof. "We'll head that way, the southeast side. There's a ton of Tunrar, but it's away from the fighting. The Tunrar seem too spooked from the explosions to care much about us anyhow."

I nodded, barely hearing him as I made sure Cubby was safely out the window and tried not to think of Lussit, the sound of her voice when she screamed my name, the feel of her hand on my wrist. I didn't want to leave her behind. I wanted to find her.

Suddenly, without warning, I was thrown and my ears were ringing. I sailed through the air for what felt like forever, sparks dancing in front of my eyes. I landed with a painful thud on stone floor, debris and dust raining down on top of me.

Everything hurt and my head was spinning. I stumbled to my feet and looked around. The Belphebans had hit the library, splitting it open and throwing me across the room.

On the other side of the roof, so far away from me, I could see Fiver and Cubby. Cubby was all right, helping a dazed Fiver to his feet. They were near the southeast corner, exactly where Fiver had wanted to go. . . . Cubby was as good as safe. And with that knowledge, all my brain could think about was Lussit.

"Fiver!" I shouted. "Get Cubby out of here! We'll meet you at Abish Village."

"What?" screeched Cubby.

His big green eyes were sparkling with tears and his little mouth hung open while he tried not to say whatever angry thing he wanted to. And he was right to be angry, he didn't understand. But he was safe now, he was free.

"I'll be right back, Cubby, just listen to Fiver!" Cubby made a step towards me but Fiver grabbed him by the shoulders. "Listen to Fiver! I'll see you soon!"

I turned and ran, my feet taking me to Lussit as fast as they would go. I heard Fiver call my name, and I heard Cubby screaming at me to come back, but I couldn't. I had to save Lussit. I brought her here, it was my fault. Saving her was my responsibility.

I leaped over the crumbled remains of fallen walls and tripped over books and trinkets strewn across the hallway. The north, Cub had said. That's where they kept the sacrifices.

I ran to the north end of the Temple, dodging crumbling pieces of fallen ceiling. There were Belphebans and Beginners everywhere, fighting and killing. The noise was deafening; I couldn't even hear the Tunrar coming before it threw me into the wall.

My shoulder was blasted with pain from the impact, and the Tunrar screeched and launched itself at me.

Pressing my back to the wall, I lifted my feet and slammed them into the beast's gut, and it squealed and fell back, hacking and coughing. I didn't wait for it to compose itself.

I ran, ducking and dodging as arrows pummeled the floor, blades swung barely missing me. They were dropping all around me: Beginners, Belphebans, Tunrar. Bodies littered the wet marble floors.

"Ikkuma!" growled someone from behind me. I whipped round to see the beast of a guard who'd apprehended me. He ran at me with his spear and I froze, unable to think as I watched him barrel towards me. There was a loud, familiar bang, and the man fell to the ground, dead.

I looked around for the pistol-wielder and I found him locked in battle with two other guards and a Tunrar Goblin. Blaze. He hadn't left. He didn't acknowledge me, he was too busy. A pair of Belphebans rushed to his side and the three of them took down the guards and the Tunrar with ease. I wanted to thank him, but now was not the time.

I ran. I ran fast and I ran hard with no more thought in my mind than north. I slipped more than once. The destruction to the Temple had let in more of the water from the Baublenotts. I was up to my ankles in the fast-moving current. The Beginners' Temple was falling. I couldn't get to the north end fast enough.

When I finally got there, it was practically a pile of stone. The Belphebans had torn the whole front apart and my heart sank. Did they move her somewhere safer? A different part of the Temple? Or did Krepin flee the Temple before the attack, taking Lussit with him? What if they hadn't moved her at all? What if she'd been right here, in one of these splintered rooms, when the attack started?

A wall to my left exploded into a million pieces and I fell. "Lussit!" I screamed, huddled on the floor. "Lussit, where are you?"

And then there she was, not Lussit, but the withered old prisoner, standing not five feet from me. She was standing, though her body was bent forward and her hands were wringing in front of her. Her eyes were different, not glazed like the last time I had seen her. They were alive and alert, like she knew something I didn't. Then she turned to me and reached out a spindly, long-fingered hand. She motioned for me to follow and she turned down one of the corridors that was still standing. I followed, not sure where she was leading me, but the explosions intensified around us, and getting out of here was the only thing to do. She stopped at the end of the corridor, which led to an outside courtyard, a staircase stretching to the upper levels of the Temple. She pointed to it while she smacked her gummy mouth together.

"Up there?" I asked her.

She nodded with that glazed-over expression that gave no indication she had any idea what was going on, and turned away, walking dumbly in no particular direction. But crazy old woman or not, her staircase was all I had to go on.

I climbed, having to cling to the stairs every time an explosion rattled the building. I could hear the battle now, the distinct cries of the Belphebans and the rumble of their weapons, the roars of men that fought for Krepin.

As I neared the top, the sounds of the battle died down, and I heard the voice of Aju Krepin booming over the Baublenotts, followed by the voice of Gorpok Juga.

"Aju Krepin urge all you blasphemers!" Gorpok Juga cried. "Expel this demon's lies from you heart. Let the Beginning keep you!"

When I reached the top, I saw them. I saw everything. They were facing their audience below, the Belphebans and Krepin's army, their battle paused to hear his words. A group of soldiers, priests, and Passages stood around Krepin and Gorpok Juga, praying and chanting.

"She is the wrong path!" Gorpok Juga preached, and there, in the center of the group, was Lussit, on her knees in front of Krepin, facing the horrified eyes of the Belphebans below, her hands bound in her lap. She wasn't crying and there was no sign of the fear she'd shown when she'd screamed my name. Her posture was defiant and noble.

The tall, spindly man who'd nearly killed Cubby, the one Krepin called Karlone, was there too, holding a jeweled dagger on a white cloth. Krepin lifted the dagger into the air, ready to bring it down on her at any moment.

"Krepin!" I barked.

Every head turned in my direction, and it was then that I realized I really should have thought a bit longer before I opened my mouth.

Krepin shouted words that I assumed meant something along the lines of "Get him!" because his guards and priests were quick to apprehend me. I flailed and kicked and wriggled with everything in me until I saw how close I was to Lussit. Shoving me beside her and forcing me to my knees in front of Krepin, his followers readied me for sacrifice.

"With they lives," announced Gorpok Juga, "the Beginning will be happy. They go home to the start. All you who are sinners, forget lies of this unholy daughter of evil."

Lussit kept her chin up, ignoring Gorpok Juga's words. She ignored me too. All her focus was on keeping a brave face. I admired her.

I suddenly found myself feeling light-headed. The height and the knowledge that my death was moments away were too much for my brain to process.

"Turn from—" Gorpok Juga's words were interrupted by my stomach juices spewing from my mouth. With a violent gag I vomited down the front of the Temple, my bile taking forever to fall to the crowd below.

Everyone was silent, good guys and bad guys, all of them shocked that I had done that. I was shocked myself, but mostly embarrassed. I didn't care about everyone else, just Lussit. I looked at her, but she was still facing forward with her chin held high. I watched the corners of her mouth twitch and I realized she was suppressing a laugh.

As my insides withered and I felt my cheeks blush, I saw out of the corner of my eye the naked skin of Krepin's ankle near my wrist. In that moment I had a choice: die humiliated or live a hero.

Seizing the distraction, and not thinking beyond that, I reached out and grabbed the Aju's ankle, yanking it towards me and sending him falling forward.

"Run!" I yelled, grabbing Lussit by the arm.

Krepin let out a shriek as he went head over feet over the front of the Temple. A roar of cheers from the Belphebans erupted below us.

Startled, Lussit scrambled to her feet, gripping me for support while Juga wailed and nearly threw herself after her leader. Guards and servants leaped to where Krepin had fallen, forgetting us entirely.

I could still hear him crying out, and when I peeked over the edge I could see him, his knuckles white from gripping to a decorative red stone protruding from the wall of the Temple. Juga nearly had her hands on him, still more of her followers reaching down to grab him.

Karlone stood dumbfounded, still holding out the cloth ceremoniously. His eyes, puffy bags drooping beneath them, locked onto mine and the corners of his lips gave a twitch, like a smile was hiding behind them.

"Urgle!" Lussit screamed.

Behind us, an army of Tunrar was crawling its way down the parapets, their angry faces trained on us.

A pair of guards, spears held at the ready, advanced on us and I felt Lussit frantically grabbing at my clothes as we backed closer to the edge.

Through them. That was the only way out of here.

With a roar, I threw my body onto the first guard, taking him by surprise, and the two of us went crashing to the ground with a thump.

I heard Lussit scream behind me, and I was seized from behind, the second guard trying to tear me off the first.

I flailed and kicked as wildly as I could, my left foot connecting with the jaw of the guard beneath me, knocking him out.

The second guard had his arm wrapped around my neck and I couldn't breathe as the Tunrar screamed and bounced with excitement, making their way closer to join the fight.

The guard let out a yelp and his grip loosened a moment, just enough for me to break free.

I turned to see Lussit on his back, digging her nails into his face as hard as she could while he did his best to shake her off.

I threw myself into his knees and the two of them went flying to the ground.

"Come on, come on!" I screamed, dragging her to her feet as the first wave of Tunrar began to surround us.

The second guard's arm shot out, grabbing Lussit by the ankle. She cried out, clinging to me for help. I pulled her away, but his grip was firm. She screamed at him, and with one shot from her leg, she kicked him in the face, and the man went limp.

"Ikkuma!" roared Juga.

She and the others were dragging a furious Krepin onto the roof, while Juga started screaming in her own tongue, pointing at me and Lussit. The Tunrar screamed back and tightened their circle around us. My heart was ready to break out of my chest but I gritted my teeth, prepared to fight them all if I had to.

"Run!" I heard Av yell from somewhere overhead.

Everyone looked up and there he was, his body half out one of the top windows of the Temple, Farka handing him a ball that she lit up in flames. He hurled it right at us, and

I knew what was about to happen. I grabbed Lussit by the arm and tried to pull her out of the way.

The ball exploded and threw us sideways, but I never let go of her hand.

Krepin, Juga, and their entire entourage were thrown too, and when I opened my eyes the doorway was only steps from us.

"Come on, Lussit!" I screamed, dragging her to her feet. She was dazed and disorientated, but we had to move.

The warriors below were frenzied and the battle continued as I ran as fast as I could down the steps, dragging Lussit behind me. The riverbank. We just had to make it there.

We rounded the corner in wild flight from the angry guards that had survived the blast, and my body slammed into another. Lussit let out a shriek, but it was Av. Farka was with him and her sword was drenched in red.

"This way! Follow me!" said Av, running off towards the south, taking us farther away from the riverbank.

Farka stayed behind, fending off the advancing soldiers with her skilled blade.

We kept running. We couldn't wait for the woman who had saved our lives.

Av made a sharp left into a giant space of nothing but rubble, the rushing water of the river barreling over the piles of debris.

Av didn't hesitate and he started climbing his way across the river, hopping from pile of rubble to pile of rubble.

We were closer to the falls back here; their thunder was deafening and the water was even more violent. There'd be no fighting this if you accidentally slipped and fell in.

"What about Farka?" cried Lussit.

"She'll be fine," said Av, trying to keep his balance as the pile of debris beneath his feet shifted. "I've watched her kill every guard and Tunrar that came our way—there were a lot, and I don't think any of them ever landed a blow!"

Av was gushing. Farka had impressed him.

I felt like a fool. I'd run after Lussit even though he told me not to, bumbled headfirst into a pathetic rescue attempt only to wind up throwing up in front of everyone.

The rubble beneath Av's left foot gave way, and his whole left leg plunged into the racing river.

I threw out my arms and gripped his shirt as he slipped farther in, the pull knocking me off balance. I fell and my hip slammed into the rubble. I dug my nails into the tattered stone to keep from going in with him. With my other hand on Av's shirt, I pulled as hard as I could.

He gave a strained grunt, and his hands managed to fly up from the water to grab the stone that supported me.

"Thank you," he said with a shaky breath as I pulled him up beside me.

I nodded, relieved that he wasn't mad at me anymore.

"Not just for that," he said, "but for what you did, back there."

I looked at him, surprised, and he was grinning.

"You saved her life," he said.

"I puked."

He laughed. "However you did it . . . you did it."

I nodded.

"I'd have probably puked too."

I grinned, knowing full well he would not have.

"Where are we going?" Lussit asked.

"To find Cubby," I told her.

SEVENTEEN

The three of us made our way through the Baublenotts and I was sorry I'd told Fiver to head to Abish Village. That was a long way off. It would take me forever to get back to Cubby, and I wanted to get back to him as soon as possible. I'd left him alone again; I shouldn't have done that. And for a girl. I knew Lussit wasn't just a girl, but explaining that to Cubby would be hard. I didn't think he'd understand at all.

I thought about how to make it up to him as we trudged through the thick vegetation. Maybe I'd get him one of those golden Abish cakes. He'd love the sweet taste of those spongy yellow bricks. Then I'd find the man with all the Abish shrouds. We'd pick one out together, me and Cubby, the most colorful one we could find so Cubby could have his very own. Or we could try and find the little fortune-teller, get her to read Cub's palm. It wasn't long ago that I never wanted to see her little face again, never wanted her to look into my soul through the lines on my hand. Whatever she said she'd seen had frightened me, and it had kept me nervous through everything we'd done. But here I was,

with Av, and on my way to Cubby. She'd been wrong about me. Completely wrong.

But Krepin wanted his Abish shroud. The Beginners were still coming.

My legs were aching from the effort of moving them through the muddy, swampy marsh, and Lussit was struggling to keep up, her white tunic soaked black from the journey.

"She's sort of nice-looking, huh?" said Av.

"What?" I blushed, terrified he'd seen my thoughts about Lussit.

"Farka, I mean. She's nice-looking."

I tried not to laugh and I saw Lussit bite back a grin. "Sure," I agreed, though she'd only ever seemed scary to me.

Av stopped. He was watching something in the distance, a lump sitting on a pink-speckled stone.

"That's Fiver," he said.

He was sitting there, hunched over, his knees up to his chest.

"Fiver!" Av called to him. Fiver's head turned to see us, but he didn't acknowledge us in any way.

"Where's Cubby?" I said to Av, a cold chill running up my spine. "Cubby!" I shouted, and ran to Fiver as fast as I could through the mud and water that tried to slow me down.

I scanned the landscape, hoping I'd see him bouncing up and down, waving excitedly, but there was nothing. Just Fiver, sitting alone in the middle of the marsh.

Not Cubby.

My stomach tied in knots as I got closer and still Fiver didn't acknowledge me.

"Where's Cubby?" I shouted, gulping in air and gripping

him by the arms. His eyes were swollen and red. He'd been crying. I felt myself getting sick again.

Not Cubby.

"We were on the roof," he said, refusing to look at me. "It all happened so fast. I don't remember letting go of his hand."

I heard Cubby's screams in my head, begging me to come back as I ran to find Lussit.

"What happened?" said Av as he and Lussit caught up to us.

My whole body was trembling and my turning stomach was sneaking its way up my throat. I looked at Lussit, her big dark eyes, her perfect lips. She was filthy and tired, but she still looked so beautiful. Her hair was still firmly tied back, her silver band sitting atop her head. I'd left Cubby alone . . . for a girl.

"A ball," said Fiver. "I saw a ball of fire. It flew over our heads and—and when it landed, there was so much smoke, I couldn't see."

"Cubby!" I yelled at him. "Where is Cubby?"

"I fell," he said, his voice wavering as tears overtook him. "I fell so far, the entire roof just collapsed, the whole south side of the building."

I thought of the pile of rubble we'd crossed over at the south side.

"When I landed, it hurt so bad, but I tried to ignore it. I could hear Cubby screaming, he was screaming and coughing and when I could see through the smoke I could see him. He was in the water—"

Not Cubby.

"And he was screaming, trying to fight the river but he couldn't. He's just so small."

"Where is he?" demanded Av, his hands gripping at the roots of his hair.

I thought I might fall down and I crouched to the ground, closing my eyes to keep the world from spinning.

"I tried to get to him," said Fiver, trying to gain his composure. "I moved as fast as I could but . . . I was too late. The water was just too strong for him."

I threw up.

"What . . . what do you mean?" said Av, but we all knew what Fiver meant.

"He's gone," said Fiver. "The falls swallowed him up. . . . I lost him."

Everything inside me radiated with grief and I screamed on my hands and knees in the mud. Every silly grin, every angry scowl face flooded my memory, and all I could see was him. I'd had him, I'd had my Cubby back, and I let him go.

I felt Lussit's hand on my back and I wrenched myself away.

"Don't touch me!" I screamed at her. How could I have done it? How could I have abandoned him for her? This girl, this Mother in the making. Cubby was my family. And now he was gone. After everything, I'd failed.

EIGHTEEN

None of us had spoken since Fiver finished his story. I led the way, walking ahead of all of them, running from their concerned faces.

My eyes were swollen and even after I'd finished sobbing for Cubby they still flowed with tears while the rest of me went numb to the pain. I felt dead, empty.

We reached Abish Village by sunset. It was the same way we'd left it, you'd never know the world had changed forever from the looks of the place. It was still as busy as ever, a hodgepodge of stands and strange people, a bustling marketplace that buzzed with life. It was the last place I wanted to be.

Serin and Farka were there, waiting for us, for Lussit.

"Well done, little Urgle," laughed Serin when she saw us. I ignored her, not wanting her praise, dropping back while Av, Lussit, and Fiver approached the women.

"I don't think any man has been able to strike that kind of fear into Krepin. I guess he underestimated the Ikkuma boys, huh?"

"I wish you'd come back with us, Brother," Lussit said to Av. "There are so many talents inside you that I can help you master."

"I can't," he told her. "My Little Brother is back at the Pit." Happy and safe.

For now.

"He needs me," said Av.

Lussit gave a sad nod of understanding and kissed Av on the cheek. She gripped Fiver's hand and he nodded, still too traumatized to say anything. Then her eyes fell on me.

I looked away. Lussit's very existence was the reason Cubby was gone. I could never look at her again.

She kept her distance, sensing I had nothing more to say, and joined Farka and Serin as they prepared to leave.

"The Beginners are preparing to move out," Farka told us.

"Yes," laughed Serin. "You've scared Krepin so thoroughly, you've got him on the run!"

"The Pit," Av said suddenly. "He's not running. He's planning to go to the Pit."

Fiver's head snapped in my direction. He didn't know. I turned away, unable to look at him.

"How?" said Serin, eyeing him skeptically.

"Krepin's Abish shroud." My voice was hoarse, they could barely hear me.

Farka moved closer to me. "What Abish shroud?"

The sun was a blazing orange and it burned my eyes as I stared. "It hides proof. About Ardigund."

"The Secret of the Ajus," Farka breathed.

"Impossible," said Serin.

"Blaze told Krepin," said Av, "how he hid it in the Pit. Krepin tortured him. He told Krepin everything."

"Blaze had the Secret of the Ajus?" she hissed incredulously.

Serin regarded Av a moment and looked to Farka. Something passed between the two women, and Serin held her face in her hands as though she had a headache.

"Someone must retrieve it," said Farka.

My voice was lodged in my throat; it was dry and hoarse but I felt like a flood of tears was ready to flow out of me. Cubby's green eyes, his little fingers carefully holding the stone treasure—Cubby's treasure.

"I will," I croaked.

Serin ignored me, nodding to Farka.

"Farka, you will go with the boys to the Ikkuma Pit. Urgle, you will give the Abish shroud to Farka and Farka will run it north to the mountains for safekeeping."

"Serin," Farka said, shaking her head vigorously, "I am a warrior, you will need my blade."

"I will do it," I said, raising my voice.

Serin put up her hand to stop me. "No, child, this is not a game."

"A game?" My cheeks flushed with anger.

"You will give it to Farka."

"I can't do that," I said. Cubby's green eyes hungering for the dagger I'd never give him were all I could see. "It's hidden, and you don't know where."

"Who does?" demanded Serin.

Cubby.

Av tried hard not to look at me as he bit his bottom lip and his eyes began to water.

"I do," I barely managed to say. I was the one now. I was the only person who knew where Cubby would have hidden it.

"Then, Farka, the boy will show you where to find it."

"Serin, this is not a task for me!" Farka stomped.

"It's a task for me," I insisted.

Serin held up her hand to me. "Quiet, boy, this is too important."

"No!" I shouted. "One of us 'boys' is the only reason that thing is safe right now!"

I thought of Tanuk's story about Blaze. He'd done so much and he was just a boy like me not that long ago. He'd been a part of something bigger than any Ikkuma could imagine. Cubby had been a part of something big.

"He beat him!" My voice was trembling, breaking, but I didn't care. "One of those little boys. My Brother beat him by keeping it safe."

I felt a heat creeping down my face, the salty taste of tears on my tongue as I tried to talk instead of cry. I wiped my nose with the back of my wrist and took a deep breath.

"I'll keep it safe for Cubby."

The two Belphebans stood in stunned silence, looking down at me, but I glowered at them defiantly. Krepin didn't know what Cubby knew, that the Abish shroud was not where Blaze had said it was. This was Cubby's secret treasure. And there was no way I was going to let Krepin have it.

Av was wiping his chin on his shoulder, getting rid of the tears he was pretending not to have. He cleared his throat and stepped in beside me to face the two women.

"Yes," he said, "we'll go to keep it safe."

Fiver didn't make a sound. He didn't even look at me. And he wouldn't, not after what had happened. Fiver would never forgive himself, I knew that. But it wasn't Fiver's fault. It was mine. With his head down, he pushed past Serin and Farka, and joined me and Av.

I thought of the ember glow of the Hotpots, the soothing rumble of the Fire Mountains, the warmth of the air. It was my home, my home with Cubby. I thought of all the Brothers who would be there to greet us, all the Brothers I'd have to tell that Cubby was gone, that the Beginning was coming. They'd never understand that their world was about to rip open. That nothing would ever be the same.

They wouldn't be ready, not for this. This was too big. And the three of us, we would die for our Brothers, I knew. But we were still only three.

Serin smiled, all of her protests dissolving when she saw the looks on our faces. "Very well. Look to the east in three days' time. We will come."

Farka grabbed me by the back of the neck, forcing me to look at her. "We will not forget you."

I said nothing and she tousled my hair before joining Serin and Lussit. We watched as the three women ventured into the village and Lussit turned to look at me one last time. I looked away, my stomach still stinging where Cubby had shoved me.

"What will we tell the Brothers?" Av sighed.

"Their Mothers are coming," I told him.

I turned and began the journey towards the Pit, Av following on my left, Fiver on my right. The sun hung high in the sky and I couldn't help but notice there was no ache in my head anymore. As Abish Village teemed with life around me, I was barely aware of the smells, the sounds. I'd grown so used to this world outside my childhood home, and with every step, I was bringing that world closer to my Brothers.

A GOODBYE BETWEEN BROTHERS

It all starts to look the same, the fire glass, when you've worked with it forever. Even your reflection looks the same, the way each piece catches you inside its shiny black surface.

Except this piece.

I caught my image in the blade, half my face obscured by the bright swish of blue running up the center. I looked different, thinner maybe, but not just that. My eyes looked smaller, probably because they were still swollen. And my jaw looked different too.

Well, it was all different now, wasn't it?

I put the blade aside. I didn't want to look at it anymore. I rested it beside a careful assortment of stones and bones—all of them interesting shapes and colors. All of them secret treasures, all of them special as far as one boy could've told you.

I could feel the heat from the tiny fire crackling at my back, the strain in my neck from ducking my head low below the tiny cave's ceiling. I was cramped in this little space, tucked away in the side of the tallest of the Fire

Mountains. But that was how it should be. This cave wasn't meant for me.

I flipped open my pack. My tools tumbled out, and I picked up the Cavy skin that kept my newest piece safe. I unwrapped it carefully and stared at the wood nestled safely inside. My nose began to burn and a lump formed in my throat.

Two rough faces had been carved into it. The top one grinning. A gap where his tooth was missing. The one on the bottom, tight-lipped, empty-looking. On both their foreheads were two curling lines, one big, one small, wrapped around each other.

Brothers.

Born of fire.

Tears stained my vision and I bit my lip, looking out the mouth of my tiny little cave. If I looked straight ahead, I could see the tree line of Nikpartok, below me the black ashen floor of the Ikkuma Pit. It was quiet, save for the deep rumbling of the Fire Mountains. Nothing moved outside the brown A-Frame, somehow smaller than it used to be.

My Brothers were all inside.

Waiting for what would come.

Carefully, I fitted the fire-glass blade to the handle and secured them together. It wasn't the longest I'd spent carving a handle for a dagger. It wasn't the most detailed I'd made either. But never had I tried so hard to make it perfect, tried so hard to make it my best. And now, I couldn't even be sure it was.

He was always here to tell me.

But there was still one thing it needed.

I felt around inside the Cavy skin for the piece I had been saving, the piece I put on all my daggers—a little piece of the A-Frame. I'd taken it from our nook. My fingers felt the little wooden circle and I fitted it to the empty space where the handle met the blade.

I held the dagger to my heart and tried my best to turn around, my knees cramping and my head scraping along the cave ceiling, so that I faced the tiny burning flames. Blaze's green flint box and the Abish shroud sat just in front of it, its shiny surface reflecting the glow.

I picked up the flint box and in its place, I laid the dagger.

So it would be there for him when Rawley came.

So Rawley would know, the fire burned for Cubby.

ABOUT THE AUTHOR

Meaghan McIsaac grew up in Canada. A sci-fi/fantasy nerd, she packed up all her movies and books and shipped off to the UK to complete an MA in Writing for Children. Meaghan eventually returned to Canada broke and worked at a series of unpaid internships at publishing houses, magazines, and gossip rags. Through it all, she was writing stories in the office, on the subway, and on her lunch breaks. *The Boys of Fire and Ash* is her debut novel.